JACK VANCE
MASKE: THAERY

JACK VANCE was born in 1916 and studied mining engineering, physics and journalism at the University California. During World War II he served in the merchant navy and was torpedoed twice. He started contributing stories to the pulp magazines in the mid-1940s; his first book, *The Dying Earth*, was published in 1950. Among his best-known books are *To Live Forever, The Dragon Masters*—for which he won his first Hugo—*The Blue World, Emphyrio, The Anome*, and the *Lyonesse* sequence.

THE JACK VANCE COLLECTION

published by ibooks, inc.:

The Dragon Masters • *Maske: Thaery*
The Gray Prince
[coming December 2003]

ABOUT THE MAKING OF THIS BOOK

ibooks, inc. wishes to express its gratitude to the VIE Project, for the assistance they provided in the making of this book.

The VIE Project is a virtual gathering of enthusiasts from all over the world, working together via Internet, and dedicated to the creation of a complete and correct Vance edition in 44 volumes; a permanent, physical archive of Vance's work, doubled by digital texts. Texts are restored to their pristine condition, reviewed and corrected under the aegis of the author, his wife Norma and his son John. The text that they supplied for the present edition is therefore the definitive, authorized version.

For more information about this unique, original group of people, the Reader can visit the VIE website at: www.vanceintegral.com.

MASKE: THAERY

JACK VANCE

ibooks

new york
www.ibooks.net

DISTRIBUTED BY SIMON & SCHUSTER, INC.

For Norma

A Publication of ibooks, inc.

Copyright © 1976 by Jack Vance;
renewed 1990 by Jack Vance

An ibooks, inc. Book

Distributed by Simon & Schuster, Inc.
1230 Avenue of the Americas, New York NY 10020

ibooks, inc.
24 West 25th Street
New York NY 10010

The ibooks World Wide Web Site Address is:
http://www.ibooks.net

ISBN 0-7434-7524-0
First ibooks, inc. printing November 2003
10 9 8 7 6 5 4 3 2 1

Printed in the U.S.A.

MASKE: THAERY

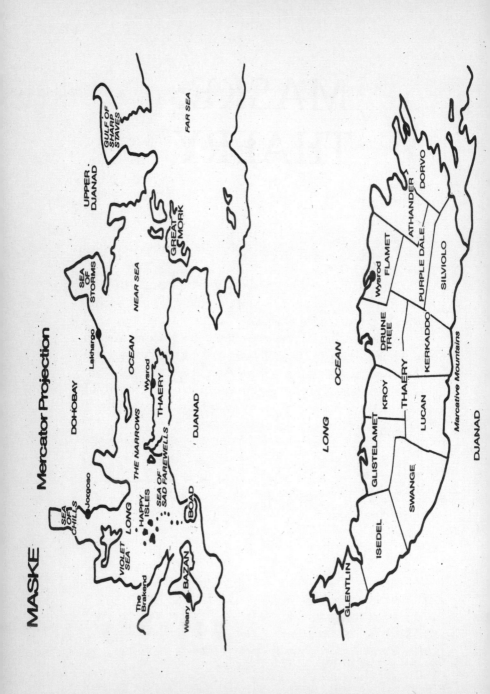

The eastern* fringe of the Gaean Reach is bounded by a remarkable pocket of emptiness: the Great Hole. The region is virtually untraveled: spacemen find no inducement to enter, while beyond hangs Zangwill Reef, a flowing band of stars with a baleful reputation. The Great Hole, therefore, is a lonely place.

At the very center of the Great Hole hangs the star Mora. Two of its attendant worlds, Maske and Skay, constitute that celestial oddity, a double planet; in tandem Maske and Skay orbit Mora, swinging around each other in ponderous epicycles.

Both Skay and Maske are inhabited. No one knows how many waves of human migration have crossed the Great Hole to Mora; perhaps no more than two. The most recent arrivals, a fourteen-ship contingent of Credential Renunciators from the world Diosophede, discovered upon Maske and Skay a population of great antiquity, human but considerably diverged from *homo gaea*: the Saidanese, of a species which became known as *homo mora*.

With Zangwill Reef barring the way beyond, the fourteen ships landed upon Maske. They expelled the Saidanese from a region to which they gave the name

---

The conventions of galactic direction are like those of a rotating planet. The direction of rotation is east, the opposite west. When the fingers of the right hand extend in the direction of rotation, the thumb points to the north and opposite is south. 'Inward' and 'outward' refer to motion toward or away from the center of the galaxy.

Thaery, after Eus Thario, Explicator of the True Credence.
The company of the thirteenth ship would not concede
the 'Triple Divinity' of Eus Thario and was banished to
Glentlin, a spare and stony peninsula west of Thaery.
The 'Irredemptibles' of the fourteenth ship refused to
acknowledge either the Credence or the sublimity of Eus
Thario; they were driven away from Thaery.

The 'Irredemptibles' of the fourteenth ship refused to
acknowledge either the Credence or the sublimity of Eus
Thario; they were driven away from Thaery. The ship
crashed into the mountains of Dohobay, apparently after
attack by a pair of Credential pinnaces, and so disappeared from history.

The Twelve Companies parceled Thaery into twelve
districts and organized a state in strict conformity to the
Credential Precepts. Diosophede, their world of origin,
became an exemplar of everything to be avoided. Diosophede was urbanized; Thaery would be bucolic. The
Diosofids controlled natural forces and preferred artificial
environments; the Thariots dedicated themselves to natural landscapes and natural substances. The Diosofids
were frivolous, cynical, disrespectful of authority,
addicted to novelty, artificial sensation and vicarious
emotion. The Thariots pledged themselves to duty, simplicity, respect for status.

In Glentlin the company of the thirteenth ship, adapt-
ing to their harsh environment, isolated themselves from
the Thariots, and became the Glints. Each saw the other
in terms of caricature. In Thaery, 'Glint' became synonym-
ous with 'boorish', 'crude', 'boisterous', while for a Glint
'Thariot' meant 'devious', 'secretive', 'oversubtle'.

Many Glints took to sailing the Long Ocean; gradually

these mariners evolved the concept of 'Sea Nationalism'. Other Glints, notably those ilks resident in the High Marcatives, became bandits, raiding the depots of Isedel, and even Swange and Glistelamet, for tools, fabric and wealth. The Thariots retaliated, using draughts of Saidanese warriors, the so-called 'perrupters', but only after three centuries were the Glints subdued, whereupon Glentlin in effect became the thirteenth district of Thaery.

Conditions elsewhere upon Maske took on new forms. Those Irredemptibles who had survived the wreck of the Fourteenth eventually reappeared as the Waels of Wellas and the various tribes of Dohobay. The Saidanese, confined to Upper and Lower Djanad, became known as the 'Djan' and persisted in their incomprehensible old customs. They evinced neither curiosity nor rancor toward those who had conquered them; the same was true with the Saidanese of Skay.

Centuries passed: eras of glassy somnolence. Credential stringencies relaxed; Thaery became a land of many textures and cultivated contrasts. Despite the ancient interdicts, certain of the towns became cities, of which the first was Wysrod by Duskerl Bay. During the same period the population of the countryside expanded, until presently the overflow was forced to seek employment elsewhere, sometimes in vain, and young folk coming into their maturity, in either town or country, found little scope for their energies. Imaginations turned outward, and the Mandate of Isolation began to seem a nuisance. A bitter-sweet malaise hung over the land like an autumn haze, and the folk were affected by contradictory emotions; love of the countryside, nostalgia, and the still-vital Credential doctrines disaccorded with a pervasive staleness and spiritual claustrophobia. A certain number of folk considered emigration; a small fraction of these put the tragic and irreversible process into effect; they were heard from no more.

Another influence troubled the public awareness: rumors of a secret organization known as the Pan-Djan Binadary, apparently dedicated to the expulsion of the Thariots from Maske. The Binadary mystified responsible officials, since neither Djan nor Saidanese were notably apt at intrigue. Who then had instigated the Binadary? Who formulated its programs and supplied the militancy? Such questions perturbed the Thariot intelligence agencies, since no meaningful information could be discovered.

Chapter 1

The Marcative Mountains between Thaery and Djanad, extending to the west, became Glentlin: a barren unproductive land of small population, but in proportion to its resources no less crowded than Thaery proper.

The northwest tip of Glentlin, extending from Cape Junchion to the Hacksnaw Hills, was Droad land, owned by Benruth, the Droad of Droad House and first of the ilk. His oldest son Trewe would eventually come into total possession, by the rigid entailment laws of Thaery. For Jubal, the second son, the future offered no such optimistic prospects.

Nevertheless, blessed with a strong body and a confident disposition, Jubal passed a pleasant childhood, enlivened by the weekly banquets at which Benruth entertained the Droad kindred and celebrated the sweet fugacity of existence. The banquets often became boisterous. On one occasion, what might have been a practical joke was carried too far. Benruth drank a flask of wine and fell to the floor in cramps. His brother Vaidro instantly forced sugar and oil down Benruth's throat, then pounded Benruth's belly until he vomited, unluckily upon a priceless Djan rug,[*] which ever after showed a yellow stain.

Vaidro tested a drop of Benruth's wine upon his tongue and spat it out. He made no comment; none was needed.

Benruth suffered pain for several weeks, and for a year his pallor persisted. All agreed that the event had transcended any reasonable definition of humor. Who had perpetrated the irresponsible deed?

The persons on hand included Benruth's immediate family: his wife Voira; Trewe, along with Trewe's young wife Zonne and daughters Merliew and Theodel; and Jubal. Also present were Vaidro; Cadmus off-Droad, Benruth's illegitimate son by a Thariot girl of the Cargus ilk who had spent her Yellow[†] at Cape Junction; and four others of the Droad kindred, including a certain Rax, notorious for blunders and immoderate conduct. Rax denied perpetration of a joke so outrageous, but his protestations were heard silently. Rax would return to Droad House on a single other occasion, to participate in events even more fateful.

Benruth's banquets were thereafter both less frequent and more subdued. He began to wither and lose his hair, and three years after the poisoning he died. Cadmus off-Droad appeared at the funeral in company with one Zochrey Cargus, a sharp-faced Thariot from the city

---

[*]*The Djans weave rugs of unexampled splendor and intricacy. Ten thousand knots per square inch is not unusual. The rugs are occasionally characterized as 'one-life', 'two-life', and so forth, to indicate the aggregate number of lifetimes invested in the creation of the rug.*

[†]*See Glossary #1.*

Wysrod, who declared himself a genealogist and arbiter of disputed inheritances. Even before Benruth's corpse had been set upon the pyre, Cadmus came forward to proclaim himself Droad of Droad House by right of primogeniture. Zochrey Cargus, stepping up on the funeral platform to achieve a more advantageous projection, endorsed the claim, and cited several precedents. Trewe and Jubal stood shocked and numb, but Vaidro, without excitement, signaled several of the kindred; Cadmus and Zochrey Cargus were seized and hustled away, Cadmus cursing and calling over his shoulder. Like Rax Droad he would return to Droad House on a single other occasion.

Trewe became the Droad of Droad House, and Jubal was forced seriously to ponder his future. The choices were not inspiring. Toil in the Thariot factories he rejected out of hand, though a diligent and punctual man might eventually do well for himself. As a Glint he would find no advancement in either the Air Patrol or the Militia. The Space Navy and the Beneficial Service[*] were reserved to scions of the high Thariot ilks and so completely closed to him. The skilled professions not only demanded years of preparatory discipline, but worked psychological distortions upon their practitioners. He could remain at Droad House in the capacity of bailiff or fisherman or handyman, a not-unpleasant life but quite at odds with his self-esteem. He might sail the Long

---

[*] *The Beneficial Service advises the Quadrates of the various Djan Territories and discreetly monitors Djan activities for signs of Pan-Djan agitation.*

Ocean on a National[*] felucca, or he might undertake the final and irrevocable step of emigration.[†] Each possibility led to equally barren destinations. Impatient and depressed, Jubal went forth into Yellow.

From Droad House he took the road which wound up Coldwater Glen, through the Hacksnaw Hills, across the Five Falls, and into County Isedel, then down the Gryph River Valley to Tissano on the coast. Here he helped repair the trestle which carried a plank walkway on spraddling fifty-foot piles across the tide-flats[††] to Black Rock Island. He continued east along Broad Beach, sifting sand, burning driftwood and dry sea-wrack; then, turning inland, he wandered County Kroy, trimming hedges and cleaning meadows of hariah weed. At Zaim he veered south to avoid the city Wysrod, then worked his way across Drune Tree and Famet. At Chilian he cut up fallen spice-wood trees and sold the logs to a timber merchant. Proceeding into Athander he worked a month in the forests, clearing the trees of saprophytes and pest-bug. For another month he mended roads in Purple Dale; then

---

[*]*The seafarers of the Long Ocean assert sovereignty over offshore waters; they describe themselves as Nationals of the Sea Nation.*

[†]*The Alien Influences Act forbids off-world traffic to and from Maske, and proscribes the return of emigrants.*

[††]*Long Ocean tides, controlled by the mass of Skay, average forty feet between high and low. Graband Claw, reaching across the Long Ocean, creates a mirror which deflects the tidal wave through the Happy Isles, where the cycle is dephased and confused. Around the world at the Throtto, the Morks perform a similar function. Except for these circumstances the tidal wave, sweeping around the world, might reach heights of two hundred feet.*

moving south into the Silviolo uplands, he came to the High Trail. Here he paused, to look long in both directions. To the east spread the vineyards of Dorvolo and further months of wandering. To the west the trail climbed into the High Marcatives and, paralleling the Djanad frontier, led back to Glentlin. Somberly, as if he were already entering the autumn of life, Jubal turned westward.

The trail took him into a land of white dolomite crags, flat lakes reflecting the violet sky, forests of thyrse, kil and diakapre. Jubal traveled slowly, mending the trail, cutting back stands of thistle, burning tangles of dead brush. At night, for fear of slanes and poisonous imps, he slept in mountain inns,* where often he was the single guest.

Across the southern edge of counties Kerkaddo and Lucan he worked his way, and into county Swaye. Only Isedel now separated him from Glentlin and he tramped ever more thoughtfully. Arriving at the village Ivo he went to the Wildberry Inn. The landlord worked in the common-room: a man elongated as if he had stepped from a comic mirror: an impression enhanced by his top-knot, which he wore contained in a cutwork cylinder.

Jubal stated his needs; the landlord indicated a corridor: "Bird-song Chamber is ready for occupation. We dine at the second gong; the tavern is at your convenience until middle evening." He appraised Jubal's dust-

---

*The inns of Thaery are, by force of law, situated no more than seven miles apart, for the convenience of those who walk the countryside. Their facilities are uniformly pleasant, clean and comfortable, partly through the diligence of the Bureau of Trade inspectors.

colored hair, cropped short for coolness. "You would seem to be a Glint, which is all very well, if only you will contain your contentiousness, and defy no one to trials of daring or capacity."

"You have an odd opinion of Glints," said Jubal.

"To the contrary!" declared the innkeeper. "Already you are mettlesome; is it not as I predicted?"

"I plan to issue no challenges," said Jubal. "I take no interest in politics. I drink moderately. I am tired and plan to retire immediately after I take my supper."

The innkeeper gave an approving nod. "Many would consider you a dull fellow; not I! The inspector has only just departed. He found a roach in the kitchen and I am bored with tirades." He drew a mug of ale which he set before Jubal, then drew another for himself. "To ease our nerves." Tilting his head, he turned the ale into his mouth. Jubal watched in fascination. The hollow cheeks remained hollow; the gaunt throat neither shuddered nor pulsed. The ale disappeared as if poured down a sump. The innkeeper put down the mug and gave Jubal a melancholy inspection. "You travel on Yallow, then?"

"I'm close to the end of it."

"I'd go out again tomorrow, if my legs would stand the tramping. Alas, we can't be young forever. What's the news from along the way?"

"Nothing of consequence. At Lurlock they complain of slow summer rains."

"There's the perversity of nature for you! Last week we took a cloudburst that broke all our drains! What else?"

"At Faneel a slane* killed two women with an axe. He escaped into Djanad, not half an hour before I came along the trail."

"Djanad is too near for comfort." He raised his arm and pointed a long finger. "Only seven miles to the border! Every day I hear a new rumor. Djanad is not the placid land we like to believe! Do you realize that they are twenty to our one? If they all went 'solitary' together, we'd be dog's-meat in hours. It's not lack of emotion which deters them; don't be deceived by their courtesy."

"They follow," said Jubal. "They never lead."

"Look up yonder!" The innkeeper pointed up through the casement to the monstrous bulk of Skay. "There are the leaders! They come down in space-ships; they land practically on our borders. I consider this arrant provocation."

"Space-ships?" asked Jubal. "Have you seen them?"

"My Djan bring me reports."

"The Djan will tell you anything."

"In certain respects. They are vague, agreed, and also frivolous, but not given to inventive fantasies."

"We can't control the Saldanese. If they choose to visit Djanad, how can we prevent them?"

"The Servants must make such decisions," said the innkeeper, "and they have not come to me for advice. Will you take more ale? Or are you ready for your supper?"

---

*The mild and placid Djan, if kept in solitude, is apt to erupt in berserk fury upon trivial provocation. If thereafter he escapes to the wilderness he becomes a cunning and sadistic beast—a 'slane'—committing atrocity after atrocity until he is destroyed.

13

Jubal took his supper, then, for lack of better entertainment, went to bed.

The morning was clear and bright. Departing the inn, Jubal walked out into a land of gleaming white crags and air fresh with the scent of damp thyrse and groundmint. Two miles west of Ivo, on the south slope of Mount Cardoon the trail came to an end, swept away by a rockslide.

Jubal surveyed the damage, then turned back to Ivo. At the location he recruited three Djan, borrowed tools from the factor and, returning to Mount Cardoon, set to work.

He had undertaken no trivial task. A retaining wall of rough-laid stone, seventy feet long, from five to ten feet high, had been carried three hundred feet down-hill and lay in a tumble of rough stone.

Jubal put the Djan to work preparing a new footing, then cut four straight thyrse, from which he constructed a rude derrick overhanging the gully. When the footing was dug, the four men hauled stones up the slope and started a new wall.

Seventeen days passed. Two thousand stones had been slung, lifted, fitted, and the soil tamped behind them. The eighteenth day dawned cool. A bank of heavy clouds lay in the east, where Skay floated: a great black ball on a scurf of foam. Djan cosmology was both supple and subtle; their portents derived as much from caprice as coherent systemology. On this morning Jubal's three Djan, by mysterious common consent, kept to their huts. After waiting ten minutes beside the inn Jubal walked down the hill to the location. He had hired Djan from three huts to minimize malingering and slowdowns,[*] and now walked from hut to hut beating on the roofs with a pole and calling out the names of his employees. Presently they crawled forth and followed him along the trail, grumbling that the day was unlucky and at the very least threatened rain and chill.

During the morning the clouds edged closer, striking at the mountains with claws of purple lightning; wind groaned through the high crevasses of Mount Cardoon. The three Djan worked nervously, accomplishing little and pausing every few seconds to appraise the sky. Jubal himself became ill at ease: it was never wise to ignore the intuitions of the Djan.

An hour before noon the wind stopped short; the mountains became unnaturally quiet. Again the Djan halted in their work to listen. Jubal heard nothing. He asked the nearest Djan: "What do you hear?"

"Nothing, master."

Jubal climbed down the slope to the rock-slide. He rolled a stone into the sling. The line remained slack. Jubal looked up the slope. The Djan were listening, graceful heads raised. Jubal also listened. From far away sounded a curious pulsing whine. Jubal looked around the sky but mist obscured the view. The sound dwindled to nothing.

The rope tightened; the Djan worked the winch with a sudden access of energy.

Midday arrived. Safalael, the youngest Djan, brewed tea and the four took lunch in the shelter of a great boulder. Mist blew up the moor, condensing to a fine drizzle. The Djan made finger-signals among themselves.

---

[*]*See Glossary #2.*

When Jubal returned to work, they hesitated, but, being three, could form no common purpose, and followed without zest.

Jubal returned down to the rock-slide. He threw the sling around a stone and gave the signal to lift. The line remained loose. Jubal looked up the slope to find the Djan once again poised in the act of listening. Jubal opened his mouth to bellow orders, but checked himself and also listened.

From the west came a jingle and a grunting chant: the march-measure by which a Djan troop coordinated its step when on the move.

Along the trail appeared a Thariot riding a single-wheeled ercycle; then a column of thirty-two per-rupters—warriors recruited from Djan 'solitaries'—trotting four abreast. The Thariot rode sternly erect: a man of striking appearance, with large prominent eyes, a proud mouth, a black ram's-horn mustache. He wore a black tunic over gray velvet trousers, a black hat with a wide slanting brim. He displayed no culbrass;* his appearance and posture nevertheless suggested high caste. He rode in evident haste, with no thought for his panting escort.

In puzzlement Jubal watched the approaching column: where had they come from? The trail led to Glentlin, making no connection with the Isedel lowlands.

Arriving at the break in the trail the ercycle-rider stopped short and made a gesture of petulant impatience. Then, suddenly becoming aware first of the three Djan workers, then Jubal, he drew back and tugged down the brim of his hat. Odd indeed! thought Jubal; the man

---

Culbrass: personal emblems, ornaments, tablets and other insignia of ilk or caste.

seemed furtive. Clearly he was in a hurry, and in a mood to attempt the precarious way across Jubal's construction.

Jubal called out a warning: "The trail can't be used! It will collapse under you! Go around the hill!"

The rider, from perversity, or arrogance, paid no heed. He rolled forward, down to the makeshift path. The perrupters plunged forward, four abreast. Jubal cried out in consternation: "Stop! You'll destroy the wall!"

The rider, with a sidelong glance down at Jubal, rolled on, wobbling and sliding. The front ranks of the troop, stubbornly four abreast, dislodged stones, which bounded down-slope. Jubal scrambled and dodged. "You cursed fool!" he screamed. "Go back! Or I'll have a warrant on you!"

The perrupters marched on, compressing their ranks where the path pinched them between mountainside and loosely stacked stones. The rider spoke something over his shoulder and accelerated his pace. The perrupters jogged forward, and the entire half-finished wall, collapsing, bursting apart, tumbled down the slope. Stones struck Jubal, knocking him down. Hugging his head with hands and arms he curled into a ball, and rolled down-slope with the rocks. He fell over a ledge and frantically sought shelter.

At the far side of the gap the rider halted his ercycle. Serenely he gazed down at the new rock-slide; then, giving his hat a twitch, he turned, and proceeded eastward. The perrupters followed at a trot. The entire column disappeared around a bend in the trail.

The three Djan, convinced that work was finished for the day, returned to their location. An hour later Jubal, bruised and bleeding, with a broken arm, broken ribs, and cracked collarbone, crawled up to the trail. He rested

several minutes, then heaving himself erect he staggered
away toward Ivo.

Chapter 2

In due course, Jubal again set out westward along the High Trail. At Mount Cardoon he spent ten minutes in contemplation of the new revetment, then continued toward Glentlin. After an afternoon's detour south into Djanad he reached the village Murgen, and the next day crossed into Glentlin.

At Droad House he found an affectionate welcome. Trewe urged him to remain upon the land, as bailiff and overseer. "We will build a new mole at Ballas Cove and a fine house on Junchion Meadow! Where is there a better prospect?"

"I know of none," said Jubal. "Still, I am restless; in all my life I have achieved nothing."

"Work and fatigue are well-known cures for restlessness! And what is achievement after all? Another name for vanity!"

"I agree to all you say. I am vain and brash. I consider myself equal to the best, but I'd like to prove this belief, if only to myself."

"All very well," argued Trewe, "but how and where? You know the difficulties, with twenty hands reaching for every plum. Also, never forget that you are a Glint among Thariots, hardly an advantage."

"True, all true. But I refuse to surrender before I am

defeated, in fact before I have even tested my weapons. Would you deny me this exercise? And there is also another business which presses on my mind."

"The mysterious ercycle rider? A madman! Let someone else punish him!"

Jubal snorted and shook his head. "When I think of him my blood boils, and I grind my teeth. He is no madman, and I will never rest until I touch him with a warrant."

"A serious risk. Suppose he wins the arbitration?"

"Small chance. I can bring forward three witnesses, and other evidence even more damning. He will not escape."

"It is foolish to waste so much emotion! Think of Junchion Meadow, with its cliff and waterfall and forest: the land of the Droads. This should be the goal of your ambitions, not intrigues and warrants and stealthy dangers in Wysrod."

"Give me time! Let me work out my rage, then we shall see."

Trewe threw up his arms and would have spoken more, but a visitor was announced. "He gives his name as Zochrey Cargus."

"Cargus? Zochrey Cargus?" mused Trewe. "Where have I heard that name?"

"Cadmus off-Droad's mother was Cargus ilk."

"Well, bring him in; we'll find what he wants."

Zochrey Cargus appeared: the Thariot litigator who a year before had pressed Cadmus off-Droad's claims. On this occasion he declared himself not an adversary but a negotiator. He said to Trewe, with a look askance toward Jubal: "Our discussion might better be conducted in private, if you have no objection."

"This is my brother," said Trewe. "There is no need for privacy."

"As you wish," said Zochrey Cargus. "I will go immediately to the gist of my business. Perhaps you recall that I attempted negotiations on behalf of your unfortunate half-brother."

"I remember the circumstances, and I am surprised to see you again."

Zochrey Cargus spoke on, his voice suave and mild. "At the time I familiarized myself with the Droad lands, and on this basis was able to advise a person of exalted ilk—needless to say, not Cadmus off-Droad. My client wishes to secure a parcel of scenic land. I suggested that neck, or peninsula, at the far north of your property: Cape Junchion. My principal has authorized me to explore the possibility of negotiations."

Trewe's voice was puzzled. "You are asking me to sell Cape Junchion?"

"That is the general effect of my proposals."

"To whom?"

"My principal prefers to remain anonymous."

Trewe laughed rather impolitely. "I would not sell an old shoe to someone I did not know."

Zochrey Cargus took no offense at the remark. "This is a not unreasonable point of view, and I must beg your tolerant understanding. My principal—I can tell you this much—is born to one of the noble ilks. You will be honored to deal with him."

"Does he not have estates of his own?" demanded Jubal. "Why does he want Cape Junchion?"

"Solitude appeals to him. Cape Junchion in my opinion fits his needs."

Trewe rose to his feet. "Had you telephoned, I could

21

JACK VANCE

have saved you an inconvenient journey. I will not sell
Cape Junchion or any other Droad land."

Cargus remained seated. "I carry a substantial sum in
toldecks. And I can make you a generous part-payment."

"Cape Junchion is not for sale," said Trewe gruffly.
"Now or ever."

Cargus rather reluctantly rose to his feet. "I am sorry
to hear you say this. I hope you will reconsider."

Trewe merely shook his head and Cargus departed.

An hour later Cargus telephoned Droad House. "I have
conferred with my principal," he told Trewe. "He prefers
outright sale, but will agree to a lease, upon terms to be
discussed."

"The answer remains the same," said Trewe. "I suggest
that your client look elsewhere."

"He is absolutely determined upon Cape Junchion."
And Cargus added thoughtfully: "It might be a mistake
not to cooperate with him. He is an influential man—a
valuable friend, a dangerous enemy."

Trewe digested the remarks in silence, then said coldly:
"I want him for neither. The subject is closed."

Cargus spoke on, as if he had not heard. "A lease perhaps is to your best advantage. You retain title while
gaining income. And, importantly, you will please, rather
than offend, my client."

Trewe could no longer restrain his anger. "Do you dare
to threaten me? You wisely chose to use the telephone."

"A prediction is not a threat."

"Do you care to name your client? I would like to hear
these threats from his own mouth."

There was no response; the connection was dead.

Days passed, and a week. Trewe made a few acrid ref-
erences to Zochrey Cargus and his client, and again dis-

22

cussed with Jubal a new tide-mole and locks across Ballas Cove. Jubal almost agreed to join him in the project, but was deterred by an emotion he could not quite define. He had undertaken Yellow; his wanderlust should be allayed; in fact, he wanted no more aimless wandering. At the top of his mind rankled the recollection of Mount Cardoon; a matter which cried out for resolution, and so it would be. Then what?

Perhaps Vaidro, his somewhat mysterious uncle, might offer a hint. Vaidro had traveled the length and breadth of Maske, and now lived like a minor magnate in an ancient hunting lodge, once the property of the Cimbar of the now-extinct Cimbar ilk. If Vaidro could not provide constructive advice, no one could.

Jubal borrowed Trewe's old ercycle and rode thirty miles up the side of Eirse Mountain, through forests of stunted ebane and tall thin thyrse, across stony glades and dark dells, and finally arrived at Vaidro's antique house: a rambling tall-roofed structure of dark wood. Vaidro, a somber man, compact and economical of movement, came out to meet Jubal and conducted him to a shaded terrace. They sat in wicker easy-chairs, and a Djan maid brought a silver tray with a carafe of wine and a dish of biscuits. Vaidro leaned back in his chair with a goblet of wine and studied Jubal through half-closed eyes. "Yellow has changed you, more than I might have expected."

"I have aged a year, certainly."

"How did you find Thaery?"

"Soft and lovely. The wines are sweet and the girls are charming. I visited every county except Dorvo. I avoided Wysrod. I destroyed thousands of thistles; I sifted acres of beach; I built a stone wall along the front of Mount Cardoon."

"So now, after Yallow, what do you propose for yourself?"

"This is a hard question to answer." Jubal tilted his goblet back and forth, to watch the silken oscillations. "I saw enough of Thaery to discover what I do not want to do. I find that certain careers are earmarked for a few high-caste Thariots, and these, as luck would have it, are the careers which appeal to me."

Vaidro nodded, with a faint smile. "What is the advantage of caste, after all, if it does not entail privilege?"

"I understand this," said Jubal, "but I am not reconciled to it. I have only a single life. I want to use it as best I can."

"The forces of society work against you," said Vaidro. "To displace a Varest, or an Ymph, or a Lamfery, simple resolve is not enough. You must present unique capacities. Can you do so?"

"If nothing else I can offer energy, forthrightness and candor."

Vaidro grimaced. "Why these? Certainly no one insists upon them."

"They could be the more valuable for their novelty."

"Perhaps they have already been tried and found wanting. Energy? Forthrightness? Both embarrassing. The only folk who can afford candor are those so securely powerful that they fear nothing."

Jubal managed a strained smile. "So, I may seem secure and powerful."

"And candor thereby becomes the greatest duplicity of all. Drink more wine. I congratulate you."

24

"I am more than half-serious," said Jubal. "At Wysrod everyone asserts his privileges and demands accommodation from everyone else. I am a Glint; how can I succeed unless I assert and demand with the best of them?"

"In theory the idea has merit," said Vaidro. "Practically—well, who knows? When do you go to Wysrod?"

"Something else lies on my mind. I would value your advice."

Vaidro refilled the goblets. "For whatever it is worth."

"You have traveled the High Trail; you must know the village Ivo. Two miles west the trail curves around Mount Cardoon..."

As Vaidro listened, his manner altered from detachment to concentrated attention. He said in an earnest voice: "You are a lucky man."

"Lucky? I escaped with my life; true enough."

"You are anxious for a career. It lies within your grasp, if you can stifle your candor."

"Please explain."

"Tomorrow you must go to Wysrod. You will fly by Blue Disk; I will supply a letter to a most important magnate: Nai the Hever. Deliver the letter only into his hands and at the earliest possible moment. I will write: 'This is my nephew, who wants employment. He brings information of great interest.' But you must relinquish your information only after Nai the Hever makes a definite commitment."

Jubal inspected Vaidro in awe. "How is it that you know the Wysrod magnates?"

"An accidental circumstance; please keep it confidential. In regard to candor and forthrightness: use them sparingly; don't give away advantages! Drive a hard bargain! You are a Glint and you must compensate by one means or another. About Nai the Hever: he is neither kind nor generous; he is neither candid nor forthright, unless you are of no use to him, when he becomes extremely direct. Unless you can control him, he will control you. He'll show no gratitude; on the other hand he bears no grudges. Trust him for nothing! If you manage correctly, your fortune is made."

"I'll do my best," said Jubal.

Chapter 3

Wysrod occupied the shores of Duskerl Bay: a sober city of irregular narrow-fronted buildings, each different from all the others. The Marine Parade skirted Duskerl Bay; all the other main boulevards, planted heavily with ebanes, moirs and deodars, converged upon Travan Square, the principal node of Thariot government. The Cham, a wooded finger of land, hooked around Duskerl Bay and was joined to Point Sul on the mainland by a massive mole, with two tide-locks.

With Mora two hours high, the Blue Disk landed at Wysrod Station. Jubal alighted, checked his two valises into a locker and left the depot. A dozen hacks awaited patronage, the hackmen in stiff black carapace-like uniforms, pinched, flared, scalloped like the back of a violin, with brass knobs fixed to the epaulettes.

Jubal approached the nearest of the hacks. The hackman saluted without punctilio. "Where to, sir?"

"Hever House, if you please."

"Hever House?" The hackman considered Jubal's clothes. "As you will. Climb aboard."

Somewhat nettled, Jubal seated himself. In due course he would dress to the Wysrod modes; until that time his present clothes, which were at least clean and durable, must suffice.

The hack moved along Sul Road to the Incline, and all Wysrod revealed itself through the crisp morning air: a million lines and angles, defining shapes of gray, black, pale lavender, white, each in turn showing smoke-colored tracings of further detail. Around Travan Square clustered the offices of government, windows glittering back sun-reflections. Out on the bay floated a dozen National feluccas.

Descending to the Marine Parade, the hack drove east beside Duskerl Bay, past shoreside inns and restaurants. The Marine Parade ended; the hack swung up the Baunder, turned left and proceeded along the ridge of the Cham to a stone arch, on which was displayed a two-headed flying snake of black iron: the emblem of the Hevers.

The driveway wound among deodars and rhodopods, past banks of purple daisies, white chanterbells, scarlet trangles. Hever House appeared: a tall gray structure with vast windows of a hundred panes and a roof of a dozen glass-bayed gables.

The hack halted; Jubal alighted and stood a moment appraising the structure. The hackman pointed. "Yonder is the main entrance, but you'll no doubt want the path around to the side. You'll find it among those bushes."

Jubal turned a cold glare upon the man. "Your remarks are insolent!"

"Take them as you like. Just pay me my quarter-toldeck and I'll be away."

The hack departed. Jubal resumed his inspection of Hever House. A stately mansion indeed. Ignoring the path to the side, he mounted broad steps, crossed a verandah and approached a pair of narrow twelve-foot-high doors, studded with iron rondels bearing flying snake motifs. They parted to reveal a footman in dark green livery, who stepped quickly forward. "Yes? What is your errand?"

"I wish to speak with Nai the Hever."

"The Nobilissimus* is not available for casual interviews."

Jubal brushed him aside and entered a grand six-sided foyer. It was clear that Nai the Hever lived in circumstances of elegance and comfort. The floor displayed a Djan rug of two or three lifetimes: a confection of astounding intricacy, each colour glowing with rich and subtle fervor. Archways opened into adjacent chambers; a staircase swept down from a balcony.

The major-domo appeared. He spoke in a coldly polite voice: "Yes sir?"

"I wish a word with His Excellency Nai the Hever. You may announce the Honorable Jubal Droad."

"Impossible. May I deliver a message?"

"Please inform His Excellency that I carry an urgent letter, which must be delivered into his hand alone."

A cool-faced young woman descended the stairs. She was slender, an inch taller than ordinary, and beautiful beyond anything of Jubal's experience. Glistening pale blonde hair with dark golden glints under the surface flowed smooth as water to her jaw-line, then flared to the sides. She wore tight white trousers and a loose gray blouse; a fashionable wisp of white cloak dangled down

---

*Honorifics are impossible to translate succinctly. The text provides what are at best more or less awkward approximations.

her back. She seemed not to see Jubal at all. "What is the difficulty, Flanish?"

"No difficulty whatever, Lady Mieltrude. This person carries a message for His Excellency."

"Take the message and place it on the library desk. Then have the conveyance brought around."

"The message, so I am informed, is urgent," said Flanish, "and apparently must be delivered to His Excellency's hand alone."

Mieltrude inspected Jubal; he thought he had never seen a gaze so devoid of expression. "His Excellency has gone to the Parloury. Is the message instantly urgent?"

Jubal responded in a voice as calm and chill as her own. "Nai the Hever will be able to judge this for himself."

Mieltrude gave her head a jerk of mild annoyance; her hair rippled and gleamed and showed its various colours. "You had better come with me; I am going to the Parloury and I will arrange an occasion for you."

Jubal performed a crisp bow. "As you suggest." But he addressed her already retreating back, so he discovered when he raised his head. Summoning his dignity, he followed her out upon the terrace, across the drive to a small black power-carriage. She stepped up into the compartment; Jubal entered and sat beside her. She stiffened, then gave a shrug of resignation. Jubal saw that she had intended him to ride with the chauffeur. Jubal managed a wintry smile. Ambition had suddenly crystallized into resolution. He would pursue a career; by sheer personal force he would excel, and command the attention of whomever he chose: perhaps even this stunning creature who now rode beside him.

The carriage proceeded by a complicated route through

the wooded hills, beside mossy walls and tall hedges of
fairy-spangle. The air carried an odor of dank growth:
moir, tree violet, heliotrope: a redolence somehow to be
associated with ancient wealth and long habitation. At
a tall old mansion overgrown with vines, the carriage
halted; the portal opened; a brown-haired girl ran out.
She approached the carriage and started to enter. At the
sight of Jubal she paused. "Oh, do we have company?
Who is this?"

Mieltrude looked at Jubal as if seeing him for the first
time. "A courier of some kind, I would think. He carries
a message to my father." She said to Jubal: "You might
more properly ride with the chauffeur."

"Quite wrong," said Jubal. "It is proper that I ride
where I am."

The brown-haired girl climbed into the carriage. "Tush,
it's not important."

Mieltrude said fretfully: "This is a formal occasion,
and I think he's a Glint."

"I am a Glint and of high caste," said Jubal. "Your
concern has absolutely no basis." He called to the
chauffeur: "Proceed!"

The two girls turned him wondering glances, then both
shrugged and thereafter ignored him. The carriage rolled
away, down-slope, toward the center of the city. The
girls made inconsequential conversation reflecting upon
events and persons remote from Jubal's knowledge. The
brown-haired girl's name was Sune; she was remarkably
pretty, thought Jubal, with a personality much warmer
and more volatile than Mieltrude's. He found her face
fascinating, with curls low over her forehead, long eyes,
wide cheekbones, flat cheeks slanting to a pointed chin.
A susceptible man, reflected Jubal, might find this face

maddening, with all its mutable expressions. She could not ignore Jubal quite as ostentatiously as did Mieltrude, and gave him an occasional quick sidelong glance which seemed to imply that, Glint or not, he was not offending her by his presence.

They spoke of a certain 'Ramus' with whom both were acquainted, and of a fête they planned to attend. Mieltrude showed little interest in the event and laughed when Sune reproached her. "After all," said Mieltrude, "there may be no celebration whatever. We can't be certain of these things."

"Of course there will be a celebration!" declared Sune. "Ramus has made the arrangements himself!"

"But he might not be urged. The process is not automatic."

In disquietude Sune peered into Mieltrude's face. "Do you know definitely how events will go?"

"I have heard my father speak. Quorce and Mneiodes will not certify."

Jubal became aware that frivolity had vanished. Mieltrude seemed to be playing a cat-and-mouse game with Sune.

"Angeluke and your father remain; we need only a single acclamation."

"Yes, that is true."

"Then why do you cast doubts? Surely your father will acclaim?"

"So I would suppose. Why else would he put me in such a peculiar situation?"

"Then we need not fear," said Sune confidently.

Mieltrude looked out the window, her glance passing Jubal as if he were air.

Sune presently spoke in a low voice: "There are many hateful things abroad...You know that, don't you?"

"Our world is as we have made it."

"It is cramped and dull," said Sune positively. "It needs remaking. Ramus speaks often to this effect."

"Maske is far from perfect: agreed."

"So Ramus must be acclaimed!"

The carriage, entering Travan Square, was forced to halt by reason of a multitude of folk streaming toward the Parloury.* The driver spoke through the voice-pass: "Shall I press on, Lady Mieltrude? There may be delay."

Mieltrude uttered a quiet expletive and looked across Travan Square. "We'd better walk," she told Sune, "if we're to meet my father."

Jubal jumped to the ground and gallantly prepared to assist Mieltrude and Sune. They looked at him with raised eyebrows, as if he had performed an odd antic, then, descending from the carriage by the opposite door, the two set off across Travan Square toward the Parloury. The crowd impeded progress; Mieltrude and Sune moved this way and that, trying to make haste. Jubal followed, a half-smile frozen on his face.

Arriving at the Parloury, the two girls went to a side entrance marked with the five iron emblems of the Servants: a squat fer, a Dohobay slange, a gryphon, a four-finned fish, a winged two-headed snake: tokens respectively of the Mneiodes, Ymph, Quorce, Angeluke, and Hever ilks. Two guards in black and purple uniforms saluted Mieltrude and Sune, but stepping forward crossed ceremonial maces to bar Jubal. "Let him through," said Mieltrude. "He's a courier with a message for my father."

---

*See Glossary #4.

The guards drew back their maces; Jubal was admitted. Mieltrude and Sune hurried along a passage, with Jubal trotting behind in what he felt must be a ridiculous fashion. They entered a salon illuminated by a green glass cupola and carpeted in dark green plush. A dozen men and women in formal robes stood by a white marble sideboard taking refreshment. Mieltrude scanned the group then spoke to an elderly man, who responded with an inclination of the head and a gesture. Mieltrude signaled to Jubal. "Give me the letter; I will take it to him. He has gone to our private box."

"Impossible," said Jubal. "You may or may not be reliable."

Sune laughed; Mieltrude looked at her with a careful absence of expression and Sune stopped laughing. Mieltrude said to Jubal: "Come along, then. We still may catch him."

She hurried off along a passage, halted at a door, urged Jubal to haste with an imperious jerk of the head that set her pale hair flying. She touched a lock; the door slid back and all three passed through, into a wood-paneled booth at the front of a vast chamber, now crowded to capacity with the magnates of Thaery. Conversations, muffled laughs, subdued ejaculations created a musical murmur. Scents enriched the air: attars from Wellas, polished wood, cloth and leather, the exhalations of three thousand magnates and their ladies; their snuffs and pastes and pastilles and sachets.

A pale slender man in robes of black and white stood on the rostrum, not fifty feet away. Mieltrude signaled but he failed to notice. Mieltrude beckoned to Jubal. "There stands His Excellency. If the matter is critically urgent, take your message to him yonder. Otherwise you must wait until after the ceremony."

Jubal found himself in a delicate position. Vaidro had counseled him to crafty maneuvers; Nai the Hever was now preoccupied and certainly unable to discuss Jubal's future in that mood of relaxed and constructive concentration which would produce optimum results. Jubal said thoughtfully: "I will wait." He looked around the box and seated himself on a long couch of purple cushions.

Mieltrude spoke to Sune in a mutter of hushed amazement. Both turned to look at Jubal, and Sune's barely suppressed amusement exasperated Mieltrude; she flung herself down upon the couch and sat in tight-lipped silence.

From a gong high in the cupola came a shimmering mellow reverberation. Four men came out upon the rostrum and seated themselves at four ebony desks, identified by iron emblems: a gryphon, a fer, a fish, and a flying two-headed snake. The animate murmur of the chamber became an almost palpable hush.

The Parloury Nunciant stepped upon the rostrum and flinging wide his arms rendered a declamation: "Magnates of Thaery! We have suffered a loss! One of our great leaders is gone. His wisdom guided us across the years; his generosity was a balm and a blessing; he is sorely mourned by all the folk of Thaery. The Grand Unctator of the Natural Rite will conduct the eulogy and guide his monic spire toward the Lambent Nescience. Revered Unctator, we hear you!"

The Grand Unctator stepped out on a balcony above the rostrum. In one hand he carried a crystal orb to represent the cosmos, in the other a lavender lulade blossom signalizing the fragility of life.

35

The ritual proceeded the stipulated twenty-three minutes, the Unctator calling out the challenges and the audience singing the rebuttals and finally uttering that aspirate ascending call signifying the lift of the deceased into the Diffusion.[*]

The Unctator, doffing his white and black mitre, then spoke the Seven Words. With orb and lulade blossom he departed the balcony.

The Nunciant returned to the rostrum and continued his declamation. "I speak again of the Ymph ilk! The lulade blossoms are fresh on the grave; the mourning knots are not yet unbound; still they will not renounce their famous program of Servantry. Again they dedicate their noblest and best! Who is this nominee? He is a man of caste and substance. He understands the lot of a Servant: the lonely burdens, the unrequited toil, the hours of soul-searching, prayer and creative vision; he does not shrink back.

"I refer of course to Ramus Ymph. He now comes to state his aspirations to the four surviving Servants; they are obliged to weigh his fortitude, zeal and vision." The Nunciant paused in his declamation. Stepping forward, he held up a solemn finger. "We rightly reserve infallibility to the Tendrils of the Ineffable Mist! A single act of urging therefore is sufficient to seat Ramus Ymph upon the seat of the Fifth Servant. Should the four Servants agree that Ramus Ymph somehow falls short, perhaps in

---

[*]*This rite and its implications originally differentiated the Twelve Regular ships from the Irregular Thirteenth. The Unspeakable Fourteenth—the so-called Irredemptibles—differed even more fundamentally. The descendants of the Fourteenth, mingled through some freakish process with homo mora, comprise the Waels of Wellas.*

trivial degree, then Ramus Ymph may not be seated, and the Four must urge another Ymph whom they deem more suitable.

"The Servants sit at their deliberations. At this very instant they weigh and ponder. Shall Ramus Ymph become the Fifth Servant? Or will they sadly insist upon another even more excellent? Approach, Ramus Ymph! Present yourself, make known your concepts and hear the decision!"

From the central adit under the boxes came three men in traditional vestments. They paced forward, using the interrupted *half-step step, half-step step* of immemorial custom. At the rostrum the gentlemen to right and left halted to stand in rigid postures of awe and respect. The third, Ramus Ymph, strode deliberately up on the rostrum. He turned and for a hushed minute gazed across the auditorium: a striking figure, tall, resolute, magnificently handsome. His garments were impeccable, tending perhaps toward fashion rather than tradition. Dark yellow pantaloons fitted without a crease into black boots encased in silver filigree. To his plum red waistcoat was affixed the iron slange of the Ymphs; he wore no other culbrass. The black cutaway cape, tightly molded to his shoulders, flared loose at the hips. A tall black dath* enhanced his already noble stature. Under the brim a fringe of dark curls framed a broad forehead; proud

---

*Dath: a tall hat, in the shape of a truncated cone, from six inches to as much as twenty-four inches in height. The article, when worn by women, is often enlivened by flowers nested in the crown, or a spray of dyed eph-plumes, or a flurry of ribbons. The male dath is ordinarily unadorned, except, occasionally, for a trifle of silver culbrass.

nostrils accented a high-bridged nose. The black eyes were wide and glossy; the full mouth drooped at the corners. He stood less than fifty feet from Jubal, who studied him in fascination. Remarkable circumstance!

The chamber was still; no sound, scuffle of foot, cough or murmur disturbed the silence. Jubal leaned back into the cushions of the couch. Mieltrude and Sune stared raptly at Ramus Ymph, though with different expressions. The Servants sat behind their desks blank as stones: eyes unfocused, emotions indeterminate.

Ramus Ymph turned to face the Servants. His two sponsors spoke in unison: "We are Ymph ilk; our caste is high. Here is Ramus Ymph, our first and best. We require that he be urged into Servantry."

"The request is noted," said Nai the Hever, now the Senior Servant. "Ramus Ymph, we recognize your presence!"

The sponsors spoke on in unison: "He will now state his doctrines. Let the examination proceed." Turning smartly on their heels, they marched to places left and right of the podium.

Nai the Hever, slender and silver-haired with silver-gray eyes and a thin ironic mouth, spoke: "We thank the Ymph ilk for their sacrifices—first Rohad tragically dead, now the notable Ramus. Let it be known that our examination may not be easy or casual. The problems of Thaery weigh on our minds; they must be solved correctly. I therefore invite the nominee to submit his views."

"Venerable Servants!" spoke Ramus Ymph. "I am anxious to apply my energies to these problems. Admittedly they are real and urgent. I hereby dedicate myself to their dissolution! The weal of Thaery hangs in the balance!"

Ambish the Quorce, newest of the Servants, a large grave man, ponderous of jowl and abdomen, made the response. "We are Servants; we are likewise nobles of Wysrod and not figments of pedantic abstraction. We are aware of each other; we know how each other's lives have gone, what causes we have advocated, what deeds we have done. Certain folk have suggested bold and unprecedented methods—I might substitute the words 'brash' and 'irresponsible'—to alter the conditions of today. What is your opinion of this?"

Mieltrude sighed and made a quick fluttering gesture. "What a hateful despot is Ambish! Always he reminds me of a shoad sitting on a glacier."

Sune spoke more fervently: "Lynaica has described his personal habits: he is incredible! Each day follows an unalterable routine, to the second. He enforces impossible schedules upon Lynaica, all in the name of Regularity!"

"I doubt if he will endorse Ramus," said Mieltrude in a wry voice.

"I find him altogether unpleasant," Sune declared. "Still what does it matter? Your father will endorse."

"If he intends the marriage, and why should he not?"

Sune gave her mouth a queer crooked twist. "Listen: Ramus speaks!"

"The future is an enigma," said Ramus Ymph. "The road across the future is strewn with obstacles; there are many dangerous detours. How shall we avoid them? We must use the best techniques at hand. Let me explain myself in this manner: if a person is coping with Problem A, and he finds that Solution B produces no effect, then he must consider Solutions C, D and E."

"What if Solutions C, D and E, in dissolving Problem

A, produce Problems F, G and H, to an even sharper detriment?" asked Ambish.

"It becomes our duty," said Ramus Ymph, "to consider possibilities and to calculate their risks."

"I will be blunt," said Ambish the Quorce. "You are not considered a patient man. The next Servant must not be automatically attracted by unconventional concepts simply because of their novelty. Our foremost problem, as I see it, is the continuity of tradition. Suppose we accept into our group a man who favors transformation and quick change? He has great power. He can be expected to survive the rest of us. With his power of single endorsement he might change the philosophical posture of the Five. For this reason I prefer a man older than yourself, of demonstrable discretion. I cannot urge your service, though you must not construe this as personal antipathy."

Ramus Ymph bowed rigidly. Mieltrude said with a faint smile: "For a fact Ramus has a volatile temperament. Ambish is not citing imaginary bugbears."

Sune said breathlessly: "Now, if ever, he must be calm. Oh Ramus, behave yourself!"

Ramus Ymph was calmness personified. "I regret that you fail to discern in me that prudence to which you attach so much weight. Naturally, I disagree with your assessment."

Mieltrude chuckled. "He won't win endorsement by claiming prudence; who will believe him?"

Sune leaned back into the couch. "Ramus is sometimes not altogether realistic."

Ramus Ymph, turning away from Ambish the Quorce, addressed himself to the remaining three Servants. "I had hoped for unanimous urging; I am sorry that this is not to be. The fact remains that these are strange times. We all know that change is on the way: the pressure hangs in the air and dampens our spirits, the more so because everyone resolutely ignores the matter. I say, let us bring the subject into the open, where it can be discussed and reckoned with. Is the prospect really so frightening? Not when sensitive, judicious, and high-caste men accept responsibility. I am willing to dedicate my abilities, such as they are—" Ramus Ymph made a gesture of deprecation "—to the weal."

"He is wrong to talk like that," Mieltrude observed. "He is really tactless and brash. Aren't those the words Ambish used?"

"Bombastic old Ambish! The others are not so obdurate."

Jubal at last felt impelled to speak. "Ramus Ymph will never be a Servant. I can assure you of this."

The two girls glanced at him, dark brown curls and smooth blonde silk swinging around in unison. Sune could not restrain a scornful snort; Mieltrude smiled stonily and turned her gaze back to the rostrum. She made a gesture of dismissal. "Expect no urging of an Ymph by a Mneiodes. They are good haters."

Myrus the Mneiodes, an old man, thin and small, withered and sallow, was third in precedence. He spoke in a husky voice. "The idea of 'change' has occurred to many people; therefore we must be ready to accept 'change' as an accomplished fact. This seems to be your position: sheer nonsense, of course. Lust and envy obsess many of us; do we therefore legitimize these impulses? Our ancient creed is correct. Rather than submitting to change we must divert the influences which conduce in such a direction."

Ramus Ymph listened with patient good humor. "The remarks of the sagacious Servant are persuasive, even though they fail to correspond with reality. The change to which I refer is not merely a whim or a fad, and its causes are not fanciful. I refer to our excessive population. The countryside is overworked; its beauty is becoming spoiled and stale. Change is upon us; who knows where it will take us if not controlled? Here is the key-word: 'control'! We must ride 'change' rough-shod and control it to our own advantage."

The sallow complexion of Myrus the Mneiodes had become darker as Ramus Ymph spoke, and eventually achieved the color of damp clay. "We must control 'change', to be sure! We must curb the indecent fecundity of the lower orders. What is intrinsically glorious about change? Nothing. You ask us to veer from our dear old avenues to go bumping and lurching across the wilderness. Why? Your purposes are over-intricate and too subtle for my comprehension. I will not compel you to Service."

Sune leaned toward Mieltrude. "Myrus is a cynical old harpy. Why won't he simply admit that the Mneiodes want to demean the Ymphs?"

Mieltrude shrugged. "Nothing anyone says can be taken at face value. Not excepting the remarks of Ramus Ymph."

"And your own?" murmured Sune.

"Sometimes I don't know myself."

Ramus Ymph had performed a gracious salute toward Myrus the Mneiodes. "I am sorry not to have persuaded the noble Myrus of my Regularity. The misunderstanding, I hope, does not originate in me."

Myrus the Mneiodes deigned no reply.

Mieltrude muttered to Sune: "My father discounted Quorce and Mneiodes. Angeluke is the uncertain vote."

"And if Angeluke won't urge?"

"I don't know my father's intent. He is not predictable."

"Not even to his daughter?"

"I never trouble to speculate; I obey without question."

Ramus Ymph again addressed the Servants. "I used the word 'misunderstanding' with design. After all, 'change' is not necessarily equivalent to unwholesome innovation. Subtleties are the curse of our old civilization. If change there must be, I would wish a renascence of simplicity, a re-dedication to Regularity."

Mieltrude shook her head in admiration and disparagement together. "Have I heard right? He who is most devious of all!"

"Poor Ramus has gone too far; he is fantasizing. Look at that odious Ambish; how he gloats!"

"Forget Ambish; he has already declared. Save your concern for Neuptras the Angeluke."

Neuptras the Angeluke, a man tall and fair, with eyes never fixing directly on their object, had listened to the proceedings with a moony smile of bewilderment. He spoke with careful attention to pitch and accent, as if intoning a strophe. "The third opinion is of course the most crucial. However, my quite definite ideas are not realized either by endorsement or rejection...Hm. It is necessary that I reflect and reflect again, deeply...I tend to feel that we, as Guardians Mandator of our delightful realm, must be all things at once. Each of us must, so to speak, play a dozen instruments together, in this magnificent concert which is our contemporary life...So that, while preparing for all eventualities with flexible vision, we also stand, like doughty warriors, ready to repugn the enemy...I admire and applaud the style of Ramus Ymph! The Ymph ilk has given of its best! But—" A pensive pause.

Mieltrude gave a quiet scornful laugh; Sune slumped desolately back in her seat. "He means 'no'," said Mieltrude.

"I will not attend his masque," declared Sune.

"—in so responsible a post, I wonder if a dynamic man is not at a definite disadvantage? Here is where intricacy and long slow deliberation, with ideas drifting, forming, dissolving, is most essential. Ramus Ymph is, naturally, anxious to serve Thaery. Perhaps he can serve us best where his magnificent abilities find their fullest scope: not here in this swirling pool of ambiguities and abstractions, but—let us say—as an important Equalizer*...I hasten to remark that I do not deplore intricacy or elaboration as evils in themselves; to the contrary. Are not these qualities our first line of defense against low-caste parvenus? With my effusive compliments and most glorious best wishes to Ramus Ymph, I will somewhat indecisively refrain from calling him to Service."

Ramus Ymph lowered his head and seemed to be studying the rug. He looked up, but before he could speak a gong sounded and the Nunciant called out: "It is the time of recess. The nominee chooses to retire to his chamber and the Four Servants must continue their reflections."

Ramus Ymph turned on his heel and strode to the waiting room followed by his two somber sponsors.

Ambish the Quorce and Myrus the Mneiodes rose to

The Marine Equalizer is that functionary who monitors National activity and in case of transgression commands the punitive measures.

their feet and spoke to each other quietly. Neuptras the Angeluke went to pay his respects to a group of magnates in a box to the left of the rostrum. Nai the Hever remained in his chair.

Mieltrude mused in bitter amusement: "Our delicate Neuptras passes the bouquet to Father."

"He is loathsome! But now; what of your father?"

"He will urge Ramus; how can he do otherwise? After all, he has created my predicament."

"Not truly a predicament!"

"I am unconvinced."

Jubal again stated his opinions. "Ramus Ymph falls far short. He is first of all a flamboyant bluff, and secondly a scoundrel."

Sune gave vent to a peal of laughter. "How perceptive! But these are the qualities which endear him to us!"

Mieltrude smiled grimly. "I'd forgotten you. One moment, I'll summon Nai the Hever and you may deliver your message."

Jubal scowled. "Don't trouble now. The message can wait until after—" But Mieltrude had called to her father, who rose to his feet and approached the box, a slender man of imperturbable dignity, with silver hair and bright silver-gray eyes. He touched fingertips with Mieltrude and Sune and glanced speculatively toward Jubal. "Are you enjoying the spectacle of Ymph discomfiture?"

"Not at all," cried Sune. "Poor Ramus! You will stop it, won't you?"

Nai the Hever's mouth trembled in a thin smile. "I am under pressure. Neuptras should have urged; instead he chose to appease the Mneiodes; he wants a favor from Myrus. Well, it all makes no great difference."

"To anyone but Ramus," said Mieltrude. "And perhaps myself—if you insist upon your scheme."

"We shall see," said Nai the Hever lightly. "Events move at great speeds; some are quite beyond comprehension. As for Ramus, if we make him a Servant, we keep him out of mischief, so to speak. Who is this person?"

"He is a courier; he came to the house with a most urgent message. I decided to bring him here."

Nai the Hever inspected Jubal with mild astonishment. "I am expecting no courier. Where is the message?"

Jubal reluctantly came forward. "Perhaps after the ceremony—"

"The message, if you please."

Jubal produced a beige envelope.

Eyebrows raised fastidiously, Nai the Hever broke the seal, unfolded the paper, and read aloud:

> *To Whom It May Concern:*
> *The bearer, my nephew Jubal Droad, seeks employment...*

Nai the Hever read no further. Raising his eyes he fixed Jubal with a baleful stare. "Why do you bring this here?"

"My uncle said to deliver it into your hands."

Sune put her hand to her mouth to smother a laugh. She failed; merriment spurted past her carnelian knucklebands. Mieltrude raked Jubal with a sparkling gaze, then turned a glance toward Sune, who stifled her mirth. Mieltrude spoke to her father. "He is a Glint."

Nai the Hever spoke in a carefully light voice: "Glint or not, you should know that one does not bring such messages to one's home as if it were a social occasion." He returned the letter to Jubal. "Deliver this to the Bureau of Public Employments at the Parloury offices and they will advise you as to what opportunities exist."

Jubal managed a jerky bow. "My instructions were to place this letter into your hands, which I have accomplished. It was evidently a mistake; I will destroy the letter. There is, however, another matter possibly more urgent than my personal concerns, and I feel I should advise you. The endorsement of Ramus Ymph is out of the question."

"Indeed?" Nai the Hever spoke in his flattest voice.

Mieltrude said with great boredom, "Send him away, Father; I want to discuss the fête."

"Just two words," said Jubal, "for your ears alone. Step over here, if you will."

Nai the Hever weighed the situation, then followed Jubal to the side of the box. The girls watched, Mieltrude in disgust, Sune in slack-jawed wonder. Jubal spoke a few quiet words; Nai's shoulders stiffened and his face became suddenly still.

"Oh what can the man be saying?" cried Sune softly. "Is he a *strochane**? Look how his eyes glow!"

"He is undoubtedly a peculiar person."

A gong-sound reverberated down from the cupola. Nai the Hever uttered a final few words and somewhat reluctantly turned away from Jubal Droad. Ignoring Mieltrude's signal, he went back to his place on the rostrum.

Mieltrude and Sune sat staring fixedly ahead, ignoring Jubal as if he were a noxious odor.

The Nunciant uttered a set of ritual exclamations, and

**Strochane: a mythical being with supernormal powers, whose commands no mortal men can disobey.*

again Ramus Ymph stepped forward. The Nunciant addressed him: "Three Servants, by their benevolent restraint, have spared you the arduous exertions of the Servantry. Nai the Hever remains to be consulted. From his special knowledge of your strengths he will form his decision. You may now address to him whatever remarks you deem proper."

Ramus Ymph, after a perfunctory salute to the audience, turned toward Nai the Hever, his manner still airily confident. "I need not enlarge upon the attributes of the perfect Servant. Certain of our Servants exemplify one virtue or another: Ambish is cautious as a rock; Myrus is noted for frugal economy; Neuptras for his sensitivity and discrimination; but only in Nai the Hever do all these elements attain a full development. If I am urged, I hope to emulate this noble gentleman's method, in order to provide continuity for what I consider inspired Servantry. Either I am of the proper mettle or I am not; Nai the Hever, who has honored me with his acquaintance, knows. His integrity warrants a correct decision. I expect and deserve no more than this." Ramus Ymph, so saying, threw back his head and stood waiting.

In a thin clear voice Nai the Hever said: "I can only hope, at best, to approach Ramus Ymph's exalted version of myself. He himself is of course a gentleman of remarkable attributes: and we cannot afford to waste his talents. I have deliberated long and painfully, and I now feel that we should urge Ramus Ymph into a new and special category, that of extraordinary counsel, where he can operate with flexible scope. If I urged Ramus Ymph into the Servantry I would limit his efficacy, and I will not do so. He can function far more usefully as our advisor, our eyes and ears. Speaking for the Servantry,

I offer him our great gratitude for deigning to appear before us."

Ramus Ymph's jaw slackened. He stood a long instant after Nai had finished speaking, then he made a formal gesture, turned on his heel and departed the rostrum with a sweep and swing of his black cutaway cape. The Nunciant came forth to utter a valediction; from the balcony the Unctator called down a blessing.

Mieltrude and Sune sat stunned and limp. Sune turned a lambent glance toward Jubal. "What could he have said?"

Mieltrude suggested tersely: "Why don't you ask him?"

Sune hesitated, then turned to Jubal: "Well then, what did you tell Nai the Hever?"

"I explained my opinion of Ramus Ymph; he saw fit to take my advice." Jubal bowed politely. "My excuses; I will now depart."

The girls glumly watched him leave the booth. Nai the Hever presently joined them. Looking around the box, he asked, "Where is the Glint?"

"He departed. Has he not done enough harm? If nothing else, he has spoiled our fête."

"He left no word, no message? Why did you not keep him here? But no matter. I will find him tomorrow. A warning now, to both of you!" He fixed each in turn with a glittering silver-gray glance. "Discuss these matters with no one, specifically those of your friends who are directly concerned in the day's events."

Sune's mouth drooped; she seemed subdued and crestfallen. Mieltrude gave a glacial shrug and looked away. "I am bewildered by what I have seen and heard. I seldom discuss what I do not understand."

"In that case," said Nai the Hever, "I will not trouble to elucidate."

Chapter 4

Jubal Droad fled the Parloury as if it were a pest-house. He crossed the square, jaw set, eyes glaring, and plunged into a district of twisting lanes, shadowed under overhanging roofs and balconies. Half-Skay, at the zenith, loomed through the crevice of sky. Jubal walked with long lunging strides, blind, deaf, heedless of direction. Other folk moved aside and looked back over their shoulders as he passed. A jog in the street took him abruptly into a small tree-bordered square. He stopped short, then went to a bench and seated himself...Nai the Hever was a man devious, obscure, repellent as a Marcative imp. If Jubal's disclosures had caused him discomfiture, so much the better! Unfortunately, there might have been no great discomfiture. Nai the Hever's manner had been ambiguous. The two girls? Jubal produced a sharp whistling suspiration through his teeth. Pale gold silk and brown curls! Both beautiful beyond reason! Mieltrude distant and chilly, Sune: soft, slight, subtle, warm. Odd that both, with apparently equal fervor, favored the advancement of Ramus Ymph. He could hardly be lover to both of them, or so it would seem. Perhaps they practiced one of those faddish erotic novelties which, so rumor had it, were endemic to Wysrod. Jubal considered Ramus Ymph. The score was not yet settled. Far from it! Jubal's grin became wolfish. A decent mid-caste matron on the bench opposite rose quickly to her feet and walked away. Jubal scowled after her. Were Glints considered inhuman here in Wysrod?...Wysrod, bah! Jubal growled in disgust.

Wysrod: where he had come with such naïve hopes to shape his future! He brought out Vaidro's letter. Nai the Hever had not even read it. Jubal threw the letter to the ground. Then hastily, so that he should not be apprehended for littering, he retrieved it and thrust it in his pocket. So much for his fine dreams. What now? The Bureau of Public Employment? Back to Glentlin and Ballas Cove? Jubal stirred restlessly on the bench. Life suddenly seemed stale and flat. He looked around the square, feeling strange as a wild beast among these sedate shops, each jealously guarding a small monopoly. He morosely studied the narrow store-fronts. A three-story structure offered jellies, candied fruit, dried pickle, conserves of a hundred flavors. Another sold Djan lace; the next sound-enhancers; the next drafting implements; the next cutlery; the next mythical bestiaries, globes of Old Earth, manuals of dream interpretation. Small enterprises, few less than three or four hundred years old, some so old as to be public institutions. Wysrod! a small town in the center of the Great Hole—but for the Thariots the focus of sentient life...Jubal rose slowly to his feet. Orienting himself by the angle between Mora and Skay, he set off toward Duskerl Bay.

Wysrod, a secret and complicated city, frustrated Jubal still another time. He walked back and forth, along angled ways and dog-leg lanes, in and out of sequestered squares, down a grand avenue flanked by tall townhouses which abruptly ended at the Palace of Memorials. At last

Jubal signaled a hack and required that he be conveyed to the Marine Parade. "It lies a hundred paces yonder," said the driver, after looking Jubal up and down. "Why not walk?"

"I trust nothing of this weird maze. Take me to the Marine Parade and a decent inn, where one can get a breath of air from off the sea."

"For someone like yourself the Sea-Wrack should serve."

"Very well," said Jubal sadly. "Take me to the Sea-Wrack."

The hack drove along the Marine Parade to a comfortably shabby building, shaded under three daldank trees, with a long verandah overlooking the water and a tavern to provide ale, wine, clam toddy, and fried fish to those desirous: the Sea-Wrack Inn.

Jubal was assigned a chamber halfway along the verandah. In the tavern he consumed a plate of fish-cakes and a jug of beer, then morosely went out upon the verandah.

Near his room waited a tall young man who twirled a bit of chain culbrass around his finger. He was spare, languid and superbly elegant; his demeanor suggested recondite knowledge and world-weariness.

Jubal halted to assess the situation. An assassin? Unlikely. There had been no time for the necessary formalities.

The man watched Jubal indifferently. Jubal went to his door, and the man spoke: "You are Jubal Droad?"

"What of it?"

"His Excellency Nai the Hever wishes you to appear at his Parloury offices tomorrow morning at the fourth hour."

A bubble of cold fury exploded in Jubal's mind. "What does he want?"

"As to that I can't inform you."

"If he wishes conversation, he may meet me here. I have nothing to say to him."

The young man inspected Jubal with dispassionate interest. But he only said: "You have heard the message." Then he turned to depart.

"You do not appear to understand me," said Jubal. "The situation is at equilibrium. I am not obliged to him, nor he to me. If he wants something he comes here. If I want something I go there. Please clarify this procedure to Nai the Hever."

The man merely smiled a dry smile. "The time is the fourth hour; the place is the Parloury." He departed.

Chapter 5

D escribe the circumstances in exact detail," said Nai the Hever. Leaning back, he fixed his transparent gaze upon Jubal Droad, who returned the inspection with as much dignity as he could command. Expostulation, irony, any sort of vehemence: all were equally pointless. Jubal responded to the instruction in a passionless voice. "There is little to add to what I have already told you."

"Nevertheless, I wish to hear the detailed account."

Jubal reflected a moment. "I lay in the Ivo infirmary for three weeks. During this time I studied maps of the region. Why had the man, whom I now know to be Ramus Ymph, traveled this remote region in such a peculiar style? I examined the maps. The trail after leaving Ivo proceeds toward Glentlin through a wilderness. Six miles from Ivo is the Skyshaw Inn. I telephoned from the infirmary: they had not seen Ramus Ymph, his ercycle or his perrupters. Ramus Ymph, therefore, had entered the trail between Mount Cardoon and the Skyshaw. On the Isedel side the ground drops away in steep gullies. There are no roads. From Djanad there is easy access by several of the plateaus. I decided that my deed-

debtor* had joined the High Trail out of Djanad. What would a man of this sort hope to accomplish in this region? I could come to no conclusion.

"When I left the infirmary I went west along the trail. At Mount Cardoon the broken wall was repaired and the trail was open. Thereafter I carefully studied the ground, hoping to discover where Ramus Ymph had joined the trail. I found the place after only two miles, on the other side of Mount Cardoon. The marks were not apparent; Ramus Ymph had tried to conceal them but nevertheless I found them. They bore to the left into Djanad, only a half-mile off the trail. Strange affairs were afoot.

"I followed the tracks, south across a moor and down-slope into a valley. The land was quite deserted: a wilderness. I could not know how far the tracks led, and I was afraid to travel alone into Djanad, since I carried only my Glint blade. I decided to proceed two hours, so that I could return to Skyshaw Inn before sunset. The wheel-marks were plain enough. They led down-slope around a forest, then disappeared on a meadow of gaddle-stem. I skirted the meadow but found no more tracks. A puzzle! How could tracks leave a meadow without entering? I crossed the meadow, and at the center I discovered several areas where the gaddle-stem had been crushed by great pressure. Between these marks the growth was discolored and wilted. I wondered if a space-ship had

---

*Loose translation of smaidair—i.e.: a person who has gained mana at the expense of another person, thus establishing a psychic disequilibrium. The imbalance is often mutually recognized and a voluntary reparation made. In other cases the balance is forcibly restored, and is barely distinguishable from 'revenge', though the distinction is very real.

not come down upon this meadow. I remembered the sounds I had heard during the morning, and I was quite certain: Ramus Ymph had alighted from a space-ship. He had gone off-world and returned."

"He might have come to meet the ship," observed Nai the Hever.

"The wheel-track left the meadow. No wheel-track entered."

"What of the perrupters? Did they wear a uniform?"

"Brown tunics on black breeches. I looked in the reference but found nothing similar."

"Please continue."

"I examined the place. I was certain that a space-ship had landed to discharge the man I now know as Ramus Ymph."

"So much is reasonable," agreed Nai the Hever.

"I then reflected that the perrupters could not know the exact time of Ramus Ymph's arrival, and that they must have awaited him for a certain period. I went to the woods and came upon a place where the troop had camped. I found a pit where they had buried garbage. The time was late. I returned along the wheel-tracks to the High Trail and Skyshaw Inn."

Nai the Hever looked off through a window, across Travan Square. Studying the placid face, something like that of a hyper-intelligent fox, Jubal wondered as to the chances of success for his ploy.

Nai the Hever turned back to Jubal. "The situation is as it stands."

"What of Ramus Ymph? Will you prosecute under the Alien Influence Act?"

"This would ordinarily be the case. On the other hand, when we wonder as to a person's peculiar activities, we pretend not to notice small delinquencies, in order to understand the whole affair. There is always time to reel in the slack, so to speak. But all this is of no conceivable interest to you."

"On the contrary. Ramus Ymph still owes me blood."

"He would not agree to this. He is savagely angry."

"That is not my concern. He broke my body; I have only denied him a trivial honor."

"You would find that Ramus Ymph rates each of his honors at the worth of one hundred bodies such as yours."

"I balance the scale differently."

Nai the Hever made a purposeful movement. The interview was ended. He thrust an envelope toward Jubal. "An honorarium for your services. There are no opportunities at Wysrod. Return to Glentlin and find useful work. I wish you every success."

Jubal rose to his feet. "Are you interested in Ramus Ymph's off-world business?"

Nai the Hever's voice became suddenly sharp. "Why do you ask?"

"Simple curiosity. I can easily discover where he spent his time."

"Indeed. How?"

"I must reserve this information until certain conditions are met."

Nai the Hever leaned back in his seat. "What are these conditions?"

"They are quite personal. But you are uninterested in such things. After all, we are not close friends."

"True," sighed Nai the Hever. "Nevertheless I see that I must hear you out." He gestured to the chair. "Please be expeditious."

Jubal seated himself once more. "Perhaps I am over-sensitive, but it seems that our relationship has not flowed as gracefully as I had hoped. I brought you a letter which you refused to read."

"Ah well, let us not mar the occasion with either recriminations or vain regrets."

"I cannot enforce amity upon you, but I can rightfully demand the respect to which I am entitled."

"My dear fellow," said Nai the Hever, "so far as I am concerned, you have exactly that."

"You might well display this regard rather more openly."

"It is really a matter of personal style."

"Very well, I will take your regard for granted. May I pay my addresses to your daughter?"

Nai the Hever's eyebrows rose. "They would be most unwelcome, especially since she has been planning to espouse Ramus Ymph."

"'Has been'?"

Nai the Hever shrugged. "Circumstances are altered. Who knows what will happen? But we make progress. I hold you in appropriate esteem. You may not pay your addresses to the Lady Mieltrude. Do you have other conditions?"

"Yes indeed. I came to Wysrod hoping for suitable employment. To this end I brought you a letter of intro-duction which I will ask you to reexamine."

"Very well." Nai the Hever languidly held out his hand; Jubal tendered him the letter.

Nai the Hever read, looked up slowly. "It is signed by Vaidro. The Iron Ghost. Why did you not tell me so to begin with? No matter." He sighed. "I see that I must do something for you, regardless of complaints elsewhere.

Do you realize that a dozen times a day I am asked to provide someone a fine career? Well then, I will place you—suitably."

"At what salary, and with what prospects?"

"Sufficient salary; and you must make your own prospects. I can only give you a start. Are there any further conditions? Then let us discuss Ramus Ymph."

"With pleasure. You wish to learn where he went. May I ask why?"

Nai the Hever straightened in his seat. He spoke crisply. "I have agreed to offer you employment, necessarily in one of the departments under my supervision. As a private citizen I tolerated your rather offensive latitude of manner. I am now your superior officer, and you must display conventional respect. Henceforth you will obey my instructions, curb your tongue and try to learn the rudiments of civilized behavior. Now, without further circumlocution, tell me what you know."

"After I examined the site where the ship landed," said Jubal, "I went to investigate the forest, where, as I informed you, I found evidence of a camp, with a filled-over garbage pit. Let us refer to this fact as Idea One.

"When Ramus Ymph attempted my death he was dressed as a Thariot nobleman. I asked myself, had he worn these garments during his trip into space, or had the perrupters brought them along with the ercycle? If the latter, where were his off-world clothes? This was Idea Two.

"Combining the two concepts, I dug up the garbage pit and found a parcel of clothes, of unusual style, and I carried them back with me into Thaery."

Nai the Hever made a slight sibilant sound, which, so

Jubal would learn, constituted his only signal of approval. "Where are these garments now?"

"I have them secreted nearby."

Nai the Hever spoke toward a mesh. "Send in Eyvant. Your classification is Junior Assistant Inspector in Department Three of the Sanitary and Hygiene Office. Eyvant Dasduke will be your superior. He will instruct you in your duties. Conceivably you will make a successful career; if so you will have Eyvant to thank."

Long after, when recalling those words, Jubal would smile wearily at the recollection.

Into the office came the tall young man who only the evening before had summoned Jubal to the office of Nai the Hever.

"Jubal Droad has accepted a post with Department Three," said Nai the Hever. "You will instruct him in his duties. Now, however, I wish you to accompany him to a place nearby, where he will place a parcel into your custody. Bring this parcel here immediately."

Eyvant wordlessly walked from the room. Jubal hesitated.

Nai the Hever had turned away and was inspecting a pamphlet.

Jubal followed Eyvant Dasduke.

Chapter 6

The Wysrod hacks were famous across Thaery. The gaunt silhouettes, the tall coffin-like compartments on disproportionately short and squat undercarriages, were ubiquitous; lurching and swaying around corners, swarming the boulevards like grotesque insects, flitting through the night unseen except for dangerously dim side-lamps. In such a hack Jubal and Eyvant Dasduke proceeded to the airport. They rode in silence, by Dasduke's preference. Jubal could not help but envy his lofty assurance, as if all his opinions were naturally and inherently right; as if nothing conceivable could provoke him to an incorrect reaction.

At a convenient way-place in his musings, Eyvant Dasduke turned Jubal a side-glance. "What's to be your grade?"

"I am Junior Assistant Inspector."

Eyvant gave his head a sour and wondering shake. "We're top-heavy now. I can't imagine how you got aboard." And he added thoughtfully, "We dance to nervous music around D3."

Jubal ventured a polite question: "What are to be my duties?"

"I'll have to look over the work-sheets." Eyvant's tone became brisk and brassy. "Our principal job is inspection of the inns—checking cleanliness, cuisine, courtesy. You'll take an orientation course, then go out and train in the field. Promotions come slow, I warn you."

Jubal heaved a sad sigh. This was not the career he had in mind. Better than nothing? Perhaps.

Eyvant asked idly: "What is this parcel we are about to secure?"

Jubal's hesitation was imperceptibly brief. Nai the Hever had not specifically enjoined silence, but by the very nature of things discretion was surely in order. On the other hand, he was not anxious to antagonize his immediate superior. "I think it contains fabric—perhaps a garment." So much Eyvant Dasduke would notice for himself.

"A garment? Whose garment?"

"This, I believe, is what Nai the Hever wishes to determine. You yourself are a Full Inspector?"

"Yes, quite." And he grudgingly went on to say: "It is not a prestigious occupation, but Dasdukes have no great influence in Wysrod. We are Drune Tree folk."

"How do Departments D1 and D2 occupy themselves?"

"D1 maintains industrial safety. D2 controls price and quality standards. D4 regulates weights and measures. D5 makes property evaluations. D6 of course is the Thariot Internal Police Force. D3 is the most inglorious of the lot."

"Why then did you select D3 for your career?"

"I might ask the same of you."

Jubal gave a starkly honest response. "It was the best I could get."

Eyvant looked out the window of the hack. In an even voice he said: "The work has certain compensations. As an inspector you will travel everywhere across Thaery and meet a multitude of people."

"And my salary?"

"You will start at seventeen toldecks a week, with travel expenses in the field."

"Seventeen toldecks! That is not a large sum!"

"Our budget is low; we meet it by paying poor salaries to the juniors."

Jubal sat limply back in the seat. Nai the Hever had used the word 'sufficient' rather than 'generous'; at Wysrod an ear for such distinctions was clearly indispensable. "How much do I earn as a Full Assistant Inspector?"

"Your rate is then twenty-nine toldecks."

"Then, finally, when I achieve Inspectorship?"

"You might earn forty or fifty toldecks a week. Much depends upon the man."

They arrived at the Point Sul depot. Jubal secured the parcel and placed it in the custody of Eyvant Dasduke; the two returned down-hill and out upon the Marine Parade. At the Sea-Wrack Inn Jubal chose to alight. Eyvant Dasduke gave him instructions: "Report to Chamber 95 tomorrow morning at the first hour. A Sub-Inspector will supervise your training."

The hack rattled down the Marine Parade. Jubal went to the balustrade and looked out over Duskerl Bay, where the locks were admitting a beautiful purple-hulled felucca* of two orange kites...Seventeen toldecks a week. Instruction in the lore of bathroom drains and soiled linen. Junior Assistant Inspector Jubal Droad, alert and keen to pay his respects to Lady Mieltrude of Hever...

---

*See Glossary #3.

Eyvant Dasduke entered the office of Nai the Hever by a disguised door. Nai the Hever unsealed the parcel and spread the contents across a table.

There were four articles. First: a brick-red jacket cut to an odd loose-shouldered, pinch-waisted pattern. Second: trousers, vertically striped yellow and silver, loose about the hips and knees. Third: shoes of glossy dark green leather with rakish ankle-flaps, a long pointed toe, a sole of twin resilient disks under the heel and ball of the foot. Fourth: a hat of dark red velvet, cocked and creased into a complicated shape, with a rosette of yellow ribbons at the side.

"Do you recognize these?" asked Nai the Hever.

"I have seen similar in the files. I recall no exact correspondence."

"Ramus Ymph wore them down from off-world."

"How do you know this?"

"From the Glint. It would appear quite definite."

Eyvant surveyed the garments with distaste. "Surely not Skay?"

Nai the Hever smiled thinly. "I can't imagine Ramus Ymph as a Binadary. No. He's been farther than Skay."

"Odd."

"Very odd. The usual motives seem not to fit. Well, it's all one. Let him lead; we will follow."

"As you say."

Nai the Hever indicated the clothes. "The technicians may be able to learn something. We are sadly provincial here in Thaery, probably to our great advantage. By the same token we are ignorant of the universe. Perhaps the time has come to repair the deficiency."

"We'll need considerably more funding than we have at present."

"True. Money is tight. How would I explain such a need to Myrus? I must give the matter thought. How do you find your new inspector?"

"The Glint? He seems reasonably intelligent, and quite discreet. But I doubt if you'll find your 'passionless precision' here." Eyvant alluded to one of Nai the Hever's more vivid pronouncements: "Department D3 is my tool; I require that the human components function with passionless precision!"

Nai the Hever said, "Handle him carefully. He will be employed where emotional motivation is a positive factor."

Jubal Droad loitered along the Marine Parade. The time was early evening; the sky showed a plum-violet afterglow. Low in the west Skay was an enormous thin silver hook. Others strolled the Marine Parade: dark shapes, musing upon their private affairs.

Jubal leaned on the balustrade and looked off across Duskerl Bay. Seventeen toldecks a week: an inspector of fleas and complaint books. The advantages were real but modest: an easy life roaming the counties of Thaery, good food and good wine, compliments from the innkeepers—but he must bid his dreams goodby...The same held true if he became a National. Suppose he emigrated off-world? Jubal studied the sky with brooding fascination. Little was visible except a wavering panel of the Zangwill Reef, hanging slantwise behind Skay.

Jubal straightened up from the balustrade. "Already I feel an old man." He slouched along the Marine Parade to the Sea-Wrack Inn and stepped into the tavern. He seated himself on a bench to the side and presently was served a goblet of soft fruit wine. At seventeen toldecks a week, he must satisfy himself with less than the best. Conditional, of course, upon his accepting the post offered by that prince of generosity, Nai the Hever. With a somber eye Jubal inspected the other patrons of the tavern and speculated as to their occupations. The two middle-aged men, both short with soft little bodies, were tradesmen, or clerks of advanced skill. They chatted and giggled and prodded each other's arm like schoolgirls. One of these men, meeting Jubal's mordant gaze, stopped short as if startled. He muttered to his friend; both turned surreptitious glances toward Jubal. Hunching in their seats, they continued their conversation in a manner more subdued. Jubal turned away. Nearby stood a man of different quality, a tall dark-visaged man wearing tight black trousers and a tall black dath. His face, pale, gaunt, and melancholy, seemed somehow haunted, or obsessed by secret thoughts. His shoulders and arms were knotted with muscle; his legs, under tight cloth, showed hard knobs and cords. A manual laborer, hazarded Jubal, or more likely an artisan: a man skilled with hands and strength, who had known recent tragedy. At a nearby table a man in a faded gray blouse supped upon a platter of goulash, bread and leeks. A National, thought Jubal, and no doubt a hard lot. His hair, a dun harsh stubble, showed thin spots, as if the growth had been impeded by blows or scrapes; his nose splayed to the side. The man's movements, however, were slow and easy, and his eyes showed no more than a placid interest in the surroundings.

Jubal waited until the man had wiped his platter with the bread, then took his own flask and goblet to the table. "May I intrude upon your company?"

"As long as you like."

"I assume you to be a National."

"This observation, which surely you do not intend offensively—"

"By no means."

"—is correct. I am master of the *Clanche*, whose mast swings yonder; my name is Shrack."

"I am Jubal Droad, a gentleman of Glentlin. I would like to ask your advice."

Shrack made an expansive gesture. "A National's advice is generally reckoned no more and no less profound than the cry of the kakaru-bird. Nonetheless, ask away."

Jubal signaled to the waitress for wine. "My dilemma is this. I am a Glint of irreproachable caste; however this serves no purpose at Wysrod. I have been offered the post of sewer inspector at a salary of seventeen toldecks a week. Needless to say, my ambitions reach beyond a career of this sort."

Shrack accepted a goblet of wine from the waitress. "Seventeen toldecks would seem an inadequate stipend for a gallant gentleman. I, a mere sea-farer, average almost half this amount."

"I see three choices for myself," said Jubal. "I can become a National; I can emigrate; or I can submit to expediency and become an inspector."

The sea-farer drank from the goblet. Leaning back, he turned his mild gaze up to the ceiling. "Each of these courses, it is safe to say, entails a characteristic set of consequences which a stranger to the situation can only imagine. His projections will be inaccurate; how can anyone create real worlds from will-o'-the-wisps? Experience is the only source of wisdom: by which I mean, the competent conduct of life. In short, I can advise you only in regard to sea-faring. To complete your survey you should confer with an inspector and then an emigrant."

"By coincidence I know one of each," said Jubal, "but I can rely on neither for information, especially the emigrant. Will you drink more wine?"

"With pleasure! But allow me to arrange this phase of our discussion." Shrack the sea-farer acquainted the waitress with his needs, then resumed his easy posture. "Like yourself, I was at one time forced to make a hard choice. By and large, I have not regretted it. I have seen strange sights; I have known startling experiences of which no city-dweller could be aware, no matter how agile his intellect. The *Clanche* is my home. I love each splinter of her fabric, but I agree that a boat is different from a parcel of land, with a cottage, a stream, a meadow and an orchard of fruit. Better? Or worse? I have known both and I cannot decide."

"Please continue," said Jubal. "Your remarks bear directly on my problem."

"I have taken the *Clanche* fourteen times around the Long Ocean. I have visited the Happy Isles, the Morks, and the Apparitions. I have bartered honey for musk with Wolvishmen of Dohobay. I have sailed up the Swal River of far Djanad to the town Rountze; on the Rountze mud-flats, during the dark of Skay,* nineteen Binadaries attacked me with sharp staves. I have traded at Weary

---

*When Skay eclipses Mora, the Djans become disturbed and sometimes perform unconventional or even irrational acts. The Binadaries—i.e., those Djans of Maske and Saidanese of Skay who intend the expulsion of the Thariots—often perform aggressive acts during the dark of Skay.

on Bazan; at Thopold on the Sea of Storms; at Erdstone Pool on Wellas. In exchange for a good adze, a half-witted Wael dryad took me to a talking tree, and was subsequently planted—"

"Planted?"

"That is the Wael punishment. I consider them the strangest folk of Maske, perhaps of the whole Gaean Reach; they are said to derive from a union between the Vile Fourteenth and a band of rogue Djans."

"I have heard a similar theory, but I am not convinced."

Shrack nodded. "The coupling of Gaean with Djan produces no issue, as we all can attest. Still special potions might have been used; who knows the truth? I hope to visit Erdstone Pool soon, if only to drink rum punch at Tanglefoot Tavern."

"Might you need an inexperienced assistant?"

"You have applied to the wrong ship," said Shrack. "I am as land-bound as you; I cannot sail till I clear myself of certain writs. Rather than shipping as a deck-hand, which pays nothing but hard work, save your seventeen toldecks until you own a boat of your own."

"What would be the price for a decent vessel?"

"Five thousand toldecks, or more."

"At seventeen toldecks a week? This is a long-range goal."

"Somehow you must augment your income."

"Easier said than done."

"Not at all. The secret is to seize upon the opportunity and wring it dry."

"No such opportunity has ever been offered to me."

"That is the common complaint." Shrack rose to his feet. "I must return to my vessel. Certain rogues noticing the dark portholes might think to recognize one of these precise opportunities of which we spoke. Goodnight and good luck."

"Goodnight to you."

Shrack departed the tavern. Jubal sat brooding. The two fat businessmen were dining upon an enormous poached buttle-fish. The man with the knotted muscles and gaunt visage conversed with a burly man wearing a maroon quat.* Other folk had entered the tavern: a party of three young bravos in pretentious garments; a pair of old ladies who now sat blowing into pewter mugs of hot spiced beer.

Jubal saw nothing to interest him. He paid his score and left the tavern.

For a moment he stood on the verandah. Waves lapped quietly along the beach. Skay had set; deep darkness had come to the sky; a single filament of Zangwill Reef yet showed above the Cham.

Jubal went slowly along the verandah. Wan light shone briefly on his back as the tavern door opened and closed; behind him came firm measured steps. Against the street glow appeared a pair of silhouettes: one tall and gaunt, the other squat and burly....Jubal lengthened his step and reached his chamber; when he tried to open the door a plug in the keyhole blocked his key. He jerked it loose, inserted his key, but the two men stood at his shoulder.

The tall man spoke in a precise voice. "I address Jubal Droad the Glint?"

---

*Quat: a flat four-cornered hat, sometimes no more than a square of heavy fabric, occasionally weighted at the corners with small globes of pyrite, chalcedony, cinnabar or silver.

"I do not care to acknowledge my identity, whatever it may be, to strangers. I suggest that you transact your business at a more conventional time."

The tall man's voice did not seem to change; nevertheless Jubal detected a rasp of amusement. "Sir, we proceed along conventional lines. I am known as 'Scales'. My colleague may be addressed as 'Balance'. We are officers of the Faithful Retribution Company. We carry a proper warrant, signed and officially stamped, for a 'Well-Merited Extreme', to be applied to your person,* at this moment."

Jubal spoke in a voice he tried to hold firm. "Let me see the warrant."

Balance produced a sheet of parchment; Jubal took it into his room. Scales attempted to follow; Jubal roughly shoved him back. Balance, however, inserted his foot in the door.

Jubal read the document. His offense was defined as 'wanton, unreasonable, cruel, and unverifiable slander, rendered against the reputation of the Excellent Ramus Ymph.' The complainant signed herself 'Mieltrude Hever, affianced bride of the said Ramus Ymph.'

"And what is this 'Extreme Penalty'?" asked Jubal through the door-opening.

"We must infuse you with hyperas," explained Scales. "This is a hyperaesthesic agent and a glottal inhibitor. Then we bathe you for twenty minutes in lukewarm herndyche, a dermal irritant; then we make thirteen applications of the bone-breaker upon your limbs. Your penalty thereupon is fulfilled."

"I contest and appeal the penalty," declared Jubal.

---

*See Glossary #5

73

"The arbitrator will strike down this warrant; so take your foot from the door."

"All formalities have already been accomplished in your name. Notice, at the bottom of the page, where the arbitrator has rendered his findings."

Jubal saw a stamp and a red seal. The subscription read:

> *Appeal indignantly denied. Let justice be done.*

A signature was appended:

> *Delglas Ymph,*
> *High Arbitrator to Wysrod.*

"The Arbitrator is an Ymph! He is related to Ramus Ymph!" croaked Jubal.

"That matter lies beyond our instructions. Now, Sir Droad, allow us to enter your room."

"Never. Stand back or I'll kill you."

Scales spoke in a hoarse rasping monotone: "Most unwise, even to talk so, Sir Droad. We are simple men, bent only on our duty."

As he spoke Jubal noticed a soft hiss; near the floor he observed a large nozzle from which exuded a wisp of condensation.

Jubal turned and sprinted for the window across the room, only to find that a wooden panel had been fitted from the outside, blocking his escape.

Scales laid a hand on his shoulder. "Sir, we are experienced; please come with us now."

Jubal drove his fist into Scales' stomach; it was like striking a tree. Balance caught his arms and pinned them. Jubal was frog-walked out the door, across the verandah, and down upon the dark beach. He lurched and kicked;

Scales adjusted a preventer over his head with prongs entering his mouth; Jubal could no longer struggle without breaking his teeth.

The three moved fifty yards, to halt where a copse of water-holly screened the beach from the Marine Parade. Balance caused a blue-lamp to glow; Jubal saw a tank seven feet long, half full of an iridescent liquid. Thrust in the sand was the bone-breaker—an iron club four feet long.

Scales told Jubal: "You may disrobe or not, as you wish; our warrant does not specify. We have learned that entering the bath fully dressed is distinctly more uncomfortable; one notes the chafe of fabric. But first we must administer the hyperas. Just relax, sir..." Jubal felt the pang of a bladder-sting and a wave of sensitivity expanding across his skin.

Balance approached. "These shackles, sir, prevent you from flailing your arms and legs; we find them indispensable. But first, do you wish to disrobe?"

Jubal wrenched himself from Scales' grip; he thrust against Balance, and driving his feet into the sand, pushed. Balance, lurching backwards, tripped against the tank and fell back full length, with a sluggish sucking splash. His outcry, first hoarse in horror and anger, became swiftly shrill.

Scales had seized Jubal. "That was a very unfair act. You have injured my colleague in pursuit of his lawful duties. I will not be surprised if he solicits a warrant against you."

For a moment the two stood immobile, Scales clamping Jubal's arms, both watching Balance as he tried to scramble from the tank, only to trip and fall back, but finally to heave himself over the lip and writhe upon the sand.

"The herndyche is a particularly pungent formulation," observed Scales. "Poor Balance mixed it himself. He works no good for himself rolling about on the sand. Balance! Oh, I say, Balance! Remove your clothes, then make for the water! This is my best advice."

Balance, whether he heard or heeded, crawled for the water, howling high-pitched curses.

"Poor Balance," said Scales. "He has been seriously injured. It is the risks of the trade; nevertheless I deplore your action. Be so good as either to disrobe or enter the tank as you stand."

Jubal squirmed, heaved, kicked. His skin ached and crawled in response to the hyperas; the hair felt heavy on his head. He could not break Scales' clutch; the hands gripped with numbing force. Jubal's head began to spin; his mouth felt dry; he, a Glint and a gentleman, to be dipped into a tank like a baby? He heard a thud, a voice; the hand-grips loosened. Jubal fell to the sand and lay flat on his face. Thuds, gasps, a bleat of rage. Jubal leadenly raised himself to his hands and knees. With stately composure and smiling dignity Scales fought the man who had attacked him.

Jubal tottered erect. He seized the bone-crusher, raised it high, swept it down at Scales' head, but struck only the shoulder. Scales moaned. Jubal swung again, and Scales fell. Jubal struck again and again, with all his force.

Hands drew him back. Shrack spoke. "Enough. You may have killed him already. The bar has broken his bones."

Jubal let the implement fall to the ground. He stood

gasping. "For speaking simple truth must a person be tortured and killed?" Even to his own ears his voice sounded high-pitched and hysterical.

"Truth offends worse than falsehood." Shrack gazed in awe along the prone shape of Scales. "He is a prodigy. No man has dealt with me so easily."

Jubal looked to sea, where Balance thrashed fitfully somewhere out in the dark. He gave a crazy laugh. "Scales' bones are broken; Balance took the bath; I am dosed with hyperas...My thanks to you. I am in your debt, to whatever extent you name."

Shrack grunted. "If I stood quiet to watch two men harm another I would doubt my manhood. Sometime do as much for another man, and the debt shall be justified."

Jubal reached to the ground, seized the warrant. "Notice this warrant. They laid it for arbitration even before I knew it existed! Imagine the insolence!"

By the glow of the blue-lamp Shrack read the warrant. "You have strong enemies."

"Tomorrow I will learn whether I have friends as well. If not, please hold open a berth for me aboard the *Clanche*."

A horrid blood-stained face rose into the illumination; Scales tried to grasp Jubal's ankle but his right arm seemed to articulate on four joints instead of two and he could not control the motion.

"Vermin!" spat Jubal, stepping back. "Shall I break more of your bones?"

Scales' voice was guttural and profound. "I must execute the warrant."

"An illegal warrant, you ditch-skulker?"

"The warrant was in legal form."

"As to that, we shall see tomorrow. I too have connections." The hyperas had inflamed Jubal's brain; words poured forth in a spate. "If you fail to die here on the beach as I hope, you will be disbarred from your trade, and that wallowing Balance as well. Lie here and suffer."

Jubal tottered away, the soles of his feet tingling and tender from the drug. Shrack gave Scales a civil nod and followed. They walked along the beach to where Shrack had drawn up his dinghy; ahead the lights of the inn glimmered through the daldank trees.

Shrack hesitated a moment, then said in a pensive voice: "A thought has entered my mind which you may wish to consider."

"Speak; I can only profit."

"Tonight we discussed opportunities and how they must be grasped. Need I say more?"

"Your idea throws a new light upon the incident," said Jubal. "I will certainly consider it."

"A restful night to you."

"And you as well." Jubal limped to his chamber, which now reeked with decomposing narcogen. Wearily he considered the barred window, but lacked the strength to go around to the back and pry it loose.

Gingerly he removed his clothes: a sensation like ripping away adhesive bandages. The linen prickled like stubble when he lay upon the pallet. Presently he fell into an uneasy doze and the night passed without further incident.

Chapter 7

Midmorning: two and a half hours after that time stipulated by Eyvant Dasduke. Mora, a crackling violet-white ball inside a magenta coruscation, hung halfway up the sky. Skoy was nowhere to be seen; the sky, to use the Thariot terminology, was 'free'.

Jubal Droad, departing the Hall of Chancery, crossed the plaza to the ancient black hulk of the Parloury. The parcel of off-world clothes had earned him a mere seventeen toldecks a week; he had failed to extract maximum advantage from Nai the Hever. On this occasion he would take a firm line.

Jubal entered the Parloury foyer, an enormous hall painted a dingy and depressing yellow-brown. At a number of counters the citizens of Wysrod conferred with functionaries, both in tranquil accord and rancorous debate. Along the walls hung a row of placards, designating the location of the various departments; Jubal learned that Department Three of the Bureau of Trade occupied the north wing of the third floor.

An escalator carried him aloft and discharged him into an octagonal chamber. Behind a semi-circular desk sat a stern old man wearing an official black quat. He thrust his head forward, scrutinized Jubal from head to foot, and seemed to arrive at no favorable opinion. "Your business, sir?"

"I am Jubal Droad, an employee of this department. I wish to—"

The functionary incisively interrupted him. "Your name is not on our lists; your person is not familiar to me. You have made a mistake. Return below and consult the proper index."

Jubal said coldly: "Notify the Eminent Eyvant Dasduke that I am being kept waiting by an underling."

The functionary reappraised Jubal. "You work for D3?"

"I do indeed."

"What is your rating?"

"I am a Junior Assistant Inspector."

The old man gave a hoarse chuckle. "Your time is of the least possible value. You will be kept waiting for hours on end; you might as well learn patience now!"

Jubal raised his eyes to the ceiling; he must learn to ignore petty provocations. In an even voice he said: "Your opinions are not as absorbing as you may believe. Announce me, if you will, to Eyvant Dasduke."

The functionary spoke into a communicator. "Yes, sir...A fellow here to see you...What is your name?"

"Have I not told you? Jubal Droad!"

"He is called Jubal Droad, and looks to be a Glint...Admit him?"—a quaver of surprise. Then, in resignation: "Just as you say." He turned to Jubal. "Enter by the blue door, follow the hall to the junction, turn left, proceed to the end and announce yourself."

Jubal marched to the blue door, which slid back at his approach. He passed through, into a high-ceilinged hall, painted a fusty green and broken at regular intervals by doors peculiarly tall and narrow through the caprice of some long-dead architect. The floor creaked underfoot; the air carried the bitter-acrid reek of decaying varnish.

The hall angled, then joined another hall. Jubal turned left and presently was brought to a halt by a door even taller and more dilapidated than the others. The placard read: *Bureau of Sanitary Inspection. Use the Admittance Signal.*

Jubal found a toggle, which he twitched without apparent effect. He rapped on the panels and rattled the latch, and presently the door opened. An old woman wearing a brown turban peered forth. "Yes sir: what are your needs?"

"I am Jubal Droad, attached to this department. I wish to see Eyvant Dasduke."

"Enter, then."

Jubal stepped through the door. "This is a place most difficult of access."

"True. Too many folk with grievances bring them here to lay at our feet, like faithful hunting dogs. They are most difficult, and refuse to be consoled by a word or two, so we keep them away, and our lives are the easier for it. Come along; this is our waiting room." She led Jubal into a chamber furnished with only a pair of benches and her own desk. She spoke into a mesh: "Jubal Droad awaits your convenience."

The response, which Jubal could not distinguish, satisfied her; she beckoned, and wheezing from the exertion trotted ahead to a door marked: *Assistant Supervisor.* Thrusting her head through, she remarked: "Here is the Glint."

Eyvant's office was rather more pleasant than the waiting room. A Chrystosoram rug, in blocks of faded greens and blues, covered the floor. The furnishings were an eclectic set of antiques: a desk of carved black *ing*, a pale green velveteen settee, a table with a tea urn, a pair of Mork chieftain-chairs. Eyvant Dasduke, standing by the far wall, inspected Jubal with a supercilious expression. "You are confused, as well as very late," he said in an even voice. "I ordered you to report to Chamber 95 at the first hour of the morning."

"I remember your instructions," said Jubal. "I disregarded them for very good reason."

"Personal concerns?"

"Yes, naturally."

"I emphasize that your official duties take absolute precedence over personal considerations."

"The 'personal concerns' in this case supersede my official duties. Please give me credit for at least a primitive level of judgment."

Eyvant raised his eyebrows. "You do not respond amiably to censure."

"Censure should be based upon understanding of the facts, not an automatic outcry."

"My tingling ears!" murmured Eyvant, "and what have we here?" He went to lean against his desk. "What then are the facts?"

"The matter most directly concerns Nai the Hever. By his orders I must approach him through you, which is why I am here."

Eyvant allowed himself to display a flicker of interest. "You may safely explain to me." He held up his hand. "Yes, yes, I know. I am a paltry subordinate; you are a genuine Glint from the highest crag of Junchion, and intend to deal only at the most important levels. Nevertheless, in Wysrod, Nai the Hever is inaccessible until I request his attention. By this same token I do not casually put through every hole-in-trouser vagabond. So please explain yourself."

Jubal seated himself on the velvet settee. "You are Nai the Hever's personal confidant?"

"In certain matters."

"My business concerns Nai the Hever in an intimate sense; when I finally confer with him, he will have to learn that you insisted upon inquiring into his private affairs."

For an instant Eyvant looked blank. Then he smiled grimly, and seating himself thrust his long elegant legs across the carpet. "Your conduct is bizarre—even for a Glint. Instead of the propitiation typical of a new appointee, you prefer to hector that superior who will control every stage of your career. The tactics are novel; I ask myself, will they prove successful? I admit that I am starting to take an interest in your future."

"I am here today in a private capacity," said Jubal, "not as an employee of the Bureau."

Eyvant tilted his head back and laughed, and for an instant seemed someone far different from his usual self. "I will explain an elemental fact. When you become an employee of D3, you are altogether in D3: morning, day, night, asleep, awake. So now, with this understood, explain your business."

Jubal made no further protest. "The substance of the matter is this: last night the daughter of Nai the Hever, and I refer to the Lady Mieltrude, committed a serious crime. She procured a warrant against me on factitious grounds, then immediately, without my knowledge, obtained a totally illegal validation from an arbiter. She then sent forth two thugs to torture and kill me. Since I am Jubal Droad and a Glint, the thugs may or may not survive. Still, I am far from pleased. The offense cries out for justice."

Eyvant heaved a weary sigh. "First, remember this: a sanitary inspector never becomes agitated. Secondly, this: girls will be girls. You demolished her favorite; in her pique she proposed the same for you."

"Did I thrust Ramus Ymph into a tank of algesic fluid? Did I break his arms and legs in thirteen places? Is this a lover's solicitude, or vicious irresponsibility?"

"Calm yourself. The matter can be adjusted. I will quit the warrant; give it here."

Jubal produced a document. Eyvant read with austere indifference. "This isn't—" He read on, and his complacence disappeared. He stared at Jubal. "You are mad."

Jubal seemed bewildered. "I cannot understand your subtleties."

"I mean that your conduct borders upon the inconceivable."

Jubal slowly shook his head. "You disapprove of this document?"

"Yes."

"By Thariot law, a crime must be properly requited; this is common knowledge. I therefore secured this warrant against Mieltrude Hever. I now notify her father, to learn if he wishes arbitration."

"You are either insane or a fool."

"I am a sanitary inspector. You have forced me to reveal Nai the Hever's private affairs; now what do you propose to do?"

"Consult Nai the Hever. What else?" With exaggerated politeness Eyvant inquired, "Would you care to take a cup of tea while you wait?"

"It is kind of you."

"Not at all." Eyvant touched a toggle; a door across the room slid open and a young woman considerably more comely than the crone in the outer office looked through. "Sir?"

"A cup of tea for this gentleman. He has had a taxing experience and needs refreshment."

"Immediately."

Eyvant left the chamber. A moment later the young woman brought tea and a dish of small cakes. "Will these suffice?"

"Very well," said Jubal, and the young woman withdrew.

Five minutes passed. Eyvant returned, his usually placid brow creased with a frown. "Nai the Hever wishes to consult with you."

"So I would suppose."

"What are your exact intentions in this matter?"

"Does not the warrant state them in explicit language? I intend to see the vixen punished."

"It has occurred to you that Nai the Hever is one of the most influential men of Thaery?"

"What has that to do with the case? If he is honest, he will be anxious to assist me."

"Well, we shall see. Come along."

They walked along creaking halls and dismal corridors, up an escalator to a passage illuminated by groined skylights. At a door enameled glossy vermilion, Eyvant halted and knocked. Nai the Hever himself slid the door aside. Passing through, Jubal found himself standing on a blue, white and black star-dazzle carpet under a skylight of a hundred facets. At a signal Eyvant went back the way he had come.

Nai the Hever took Jubal to a couch, motioned him to

sit, and deliberately settled himself in a nearby chair. "Tell me precisely what occurred."

Now was not the time for expansiveness or passionate imprecations. Jubal recounted the events as tersely as possible.

Nai the Hever's quicksilver eyes never left his face. "And why did you procure your own warrant? What were your motives?"

"Resentment and a desire for justice, respectively."

"I notice that you carefully displayed the warrant to Eyvant Dasduke."

"I had no choice. He insisted upon learning why I wanted to see you."

"Well then—exactly why do you wish to consult with me?"

"So that you may, if you choose, put this warrant to the arbitrator."

"Has it occurred to you that I might easily channel this warrant to Delglas Ymph?"

"You would be ill-advised to do so."

"And why?"

"When your daughter used his connivance to validate her warrant against me?"

"I would show very poorly. Of course, I could have you quietly killed."

"Not quietly. My uncle Vaidro has been apprised of the entire affair."

Nai the Hever looked over the warrant. "You specify 'penal servitude for two years, with a stroke of the rat-whisk each midafternoon, at the discretion of the jailer.'" He frowned. "Under the circumstances, a relatively mild demand."

"It is sufficient. She is witless, irresponsible and over-civilized. Also, why should I unreasonably offend you?"

"Why, in fact, should you offend me at all?" Nai the Hever paused, then said reflectively: "So far, we have not listened to Mieltrude. In all candor, I am astounded by her act...Yes, most curious. Now as to this warrant: do you intend to implement it?"

"If your daughter has procured a warrant, as it seems, why should I not?"

"I might well resent your conduct, and your career would suffer."

"What career? Junior Assistant Inspector, at seventeen toldecks a week? My 'career' hardly weighs in the balance. Still, I am not unreasonable. I can see circumstances—"

Nai the Hever interposed a thoughtful remark: "You used the word 'justice'. I would not demean you by suggesting a promotion with an increase in salary; we must seek elsewhere for resolution."

Jubal frowned. After a moment he asked: "Do you intend to arbitrate this warrant?"

"Naturally not." Nai the Hever, looking across the room, tapped his pale fingers on the arm of the chair. "I will inquire into the matter; in the meantime, please delay the service of your warrant."

"You do not understand my problems! The warrant against me, no matter how illegal, still operates."

Nai the Hever touched a toggle on the wall. "Connect me to the Faithful Retribution Company."

Several musical chords in crescendo announced that the connection had been made. A grave bass voice spoke: "Who calls on Faithful Retribution?"

"This is the Nobilissimus Nai the Hever. Yesterday you

accepted a spurious warrant, purportedly signed by my daughter, the Lady Mieltrude. Do you admit as much?"

The grave voice raised a half-tone in pitch. "We did indeed accept such a warrant, Nobilissimus. With such a complainant, would we suspect duplicity?"

"The warrant was obviously fraudulent. An innocent man has been victimized."

"Innocent man? Who crippled my operatives? He is a menace to law and order and must be reprimanded. I have assigned four keen operatives to the task."

"On whose warrant?"

There was silence. "The warrant is invalid, Nobilissimus?"

"Naturally, as you well know. If your operatives process Jubal Droad, I will personally swear an executive warrant against you, at triple damages."

The grave bass voice became baritone. "I am convinced of my error, Nobilissimus. I will cancel the emergency."

"Make absolutely certain. I hold you responsible, and you still have not heard the last of this."

"Be tolerant, Nobilissimus! I acted on the strength of your name!"

"You insult me," said Nai the Hever. "Disconnect." He turned to Jubal, a sardonic twist to his lips. "You are safe from official justice."

"What of the magistrate Delglas Ymph?"

"His case will be considered by the proper agency. You may consider the case closed."

To his annoyance Jubal found that he had nothing more to say. In some perplexing fashion advantage had again eluded his grasp. He rose to his feet. "In that case I had best be pursuing my 'career'. In the meantime, I am to restrain this warrant until you have made inquiries and clarified the matter to me."

"That is the essence of the matter," said Nai the Hever in his driest voice. He touched the toggle. "Eyvant Dasduke."

Eyvant entered the room. Nai the Hever said: "We have come to an understanding. Take Jubal Droad to the orientation officer, that he may begin his training. Let us hope that there are no more interruptions, since already his pay has been diminished by the value of one half day."

"What!" roared Jubal. "My miserable seventeen toldecks?"

Eyvant said smoothly: "The Department holds itself rigidly separate from its operatives' private lives. Your pay starts when you report for duty."

"So be it," sighed Jubal. "Please conduct me to my work before I fall in debt to the Department."

Chapter 8

I n a musty hall deep in the Parloury basements Jubal received instruction from a pair of middle-aged men, of castes not immediately identifiable. Clary was the older and more sedate of the two; Vergaz, a wiry nervous man with a restless gaze, affected the 'Windy Mountain' hairstyle, close-cropped on top with side-tufts drawn through a series of gold beads.

Clary explained the theory of inspectorship. "Basically, the work is simple. You study the Complaint Ledger; you look; you measure; you smell. When in doubt, consult the Code. From time to time, say: 'This will not do.' If the innkeeper is sufficiently deferential; if his offenses are trivial, and not the same offenses of which he was previously warned; if his beer is sound and his beds soft: then you endorse his certificate. Otherwise, you plaster a great yellow seal across his door, and—ignoring bribes, threats and outcries—you roll smartly off on your ercycle."

"All this seems well within my compass," said Jubal. "Where do I obtain the ercycle?"

"It will be supplied, along with a valise, a day and night uniform, and a copy of the Regulatory Code. I touched upon the subject of bribes, and I do not recommend them, as they are a poisonous solace. Your pay, a meager twenty-four toldecks though it may be—"

"Seventeen toldecks."

"—is far more comfortable money. A bribe is usually discovered; you are rebuked and humiliated. If not, the innkeeper takes a high hand and serves you bramble wine and the dry end of the joint."

"No innkeeper would dare suborn a Glint."

"Perhaps you are right," said Clary. "Still, innkeepers are a mettlesome lot. Here is your Code; assimilate as much as necessary, and keep it at the ready, like a warrior with his weapon. And that is the sum of it! You are now a Junior Assistant Inspector, except for a few incidental techniques which Vergaz will demonstrate."

Jubal heaved a grateful sigh. "I had feared that the course might be tedious."

"Not at all! Now, in regard to these incidental techniques, we might as well commence with calisthenics."

On the following day Vergaz told Jubal: "We must prepare you for every phase of your work. Innkeepers, as a group, are unpredictable. Often, when an inspector condemns an innkeeper's drains, or faults his cuisine, or perhaps only speaks a cordial word to his daughter, the innkeeper reacts with paranoid excitement, and the inspector must know a few simple tricks of both defense and retaliation. Over the centuries we have evolved a secret system which is never revealed to the general public. For example, aim a blow at my face. Come now, in earnest!"

Three weeks later Jubal protested: "I had no idea so much agility and unprincipled cunning was demanded of an inspector."

BORDERS

BORDERS
BOOKS AND MUSIC
151 ANDOVER STREET
PEABODY MA 01960
(978) 538-3003

ORE: 0059   REG: 03/63   TRAN#: 1095
LE   07/09/2004   EMP: 00124

SKE
    7257708   QP T   11.95

        Subtotal   11.95
        MASSACHUSETTS 5%   .60
  Item Total   12.55
        MASTERCARD   12.55
CT # /S XXXXXXXXXXXX8273
        AUTH: 644230
ME: ZAMBELLO/JAMES R

CUSTOMER COPY

07/09/2004 04:20PM

Check our store inventory online
at www.bordersstores.com

Shop online at www.borders.com

purchased by check may be returned for cash after 10 business days.

Merchandise unaccompanied by the original Borders store receipt, presented for return beyond 30 days from date of purchase, must be carried by Borders at the time of the return. The lowest price offered the item during the 12 month period prior to the return will be refund via a gift card.

Opened videos, discs, and cassettes may only be exchanged replacement copies of the original item.
Periodicals, newspapers, out-of-print, collectible and pre-owned ite. may not be returned.
Returned merchandise must be in saleable condition.

BORDERS

Merchandise presented for return, including sale or marked-down ite must be accompanied by the original Borders store receipt. Returns m be completed within 30 days of purchase. The purchase price will refunded in the medium of purchase (cash, credit card or gift card). Ite purchased by check may be returned for cash after 10 business days

Merchandise unaccompanied by the original Borders store receipt, presented for return beyond 30 days from date of purchase, must carried by Borders at the time of the return. The lowest price offered the item during the 12 month period prior to the return will be refun via a gift card.

Opened videos, discs, and cassettes may only be exchanged replacement copies of the original item.
Periodicals, newspapers, out-of-print, collectible and pre-owned ite may not be returned.
Returned merchandise must be in saleable condition.

BORDERS

Merchandise presented for return, including sale or marked-down ite must be accompanied by the original Borders store receipt. Returns n be completed within 30 days of purchase. The purchase price will refunded in the medium of purchase (cash, credit card or gift card). It purchased by check may be returned for cash after 10 business days

Merchandise unaccompanied by the original Borders store receipt presented for return beyond 30 days from date of purchase, mus carried by Borders at the time of the return. The lowest price offered the item during the 12 month period prior to the return will be refur via a gift card.

Opened videos, discs, and cassettes may only be exchanged replacement copies of the original item.
Periodicals, newspapers, out-of-print, collectible and pre-owned it may not be returned.
Returned merchandise must be in saleable condition.

"You have learned the merest rudiments," said Vergaz. "For instance—" his eyes shifted across the room; his expression changed. "Ah, Nobilissimus!"

Jubal looked around, only to receive a kick in the backside.

"Just so," said Vergaz. "An inspector should never allow his attention to be distracted. A favorite trick of the innkeeper is to keep the inspector chatting over a bottle of spirits while scullions scour the kitchen, and empty pots of illicit offal."

"I will hold this in mind."

Clary said: "It is also necessary to develop your mental powers. The brain is a remarkable organ which junior and assistant grades never use to best capacity. We will subdivide our exercises into categories. First, acuity and awareness. Second, mnemonics. Third, precognition, intuition, telepathy and the like. Fourth, simulation and dissimulation. Fifth, the techniques of persuasion and suggestion. Sixth, induction and deduction. So much is adequate to the seventeen-toldeck level. What time is it? Middle afternoon? We might as well begin at once." He looked across the room and his expression changed. "Nobilissimus!"

Jubal was not to be tricked the same way twice. "Ignore the old buffoon. Let him wait until we are finished for the day."

"When you can spare the time," said Nai the Hever, "I wish a few words with you."

"Certainly," said Jubal after a pause. "At your convenience."

They departed the orientation chamber and entered an elevator which conveyed them to the fifth floor. Nai the Hever led Jubal on a detour through a white-tiled corridor banded with dull metal strips. A light over the exit flashed blue. Nai the Hever nodded in satisfaction. "A signal that no eavesdrops, microphones, or beacons are concealed upon our persons."

Jubal was more amused than impressed. "Who would eavesdrop upon us?"

"You ask a most profound question," said Nai the Hever. "I can answer only this: strange events are occurring upon this world. Do you think Thaery a haven of placidity, a bucolic paradise? You are wrong."

Leaving the white-tiled passage, he led the way to his office. "Please be seated."

Jubal settled himself into a chair and waited politely while Nai the Hever looked over the messages which had been placed on his desk. He found nothing urgent and turned his attention upon Jubal. "Now—to business."

"I take it," said Jubal, "that you have fully analyzed the whole affair?"

Nai the Hever looked at him blankly. "What affair is this?"

"The illicit warrant solicited by your daughter against my person; what else?"

Nai the Hever considered. "Yes. That matter. It is not yet resolved. I made an inquiry or two, but elicited ambiguous information. In all candor I have been preoccupied with matters of large scope." He raised his hand as Jubal started to make an indignant comment. "Quite so. We will talk of it another time."

"It has already been three weeks!"

Nai the Hever's voice took on an edge. "All will be arranged to your satisfaction. Now listen closely. As you may have divined, D3 is a complex organization. Occasionally we undertake inspections which might be considered unusual. These inspections are always secret, and our present conversation is confidential; you must never repeat it, in gist or otherwise. Is that clear?"

"Certainly."

"One of these special inspections has now become necessary. I need a man of resource, tact and self-assurance. You are possessed, at least, of the latter. Are you willing to undertake this task?"

"For seventeen toldecks a week? No."

"The compensation will be adequate."

"In that case I will be glad to listen."

"It is a job which should gratify your savage Glint vindictiveness. I take it that you are not reconciled to Ramus Ymph?"

"A man who twice has attempted my life? Why have you not tracked down the responsibility for this warrant, so that I might act?"

"This is not presently consequential. Listen." Nai the Hever leaned his elbows on the desk and knit his pale fingers. "Your information warned us of Ramus Ymph's off-planet activities. My misgivings were instantly aroused and I placed Ramus Ymph under close surveillance.

"One week ago Ramus Ymph covertly departed Wysrod. He flew to Tissano, then rode ercycle south through Isedel, making continual efforts at stealth. Near Ivo, during the dead of night, he slipped across the border into Djanad, and we were unable to track him further, but radar reported the passage of an object into space.

"In short, Ramus Ymph has once more departed Maske: presumably to the place he visited before. The clothes you supplied have been exhaustively studied and our experts trace them to a certain world of the Gaean Reach. So now—what next?"

"I would not presume to advise you."

"We might ask Ramus Ymph for the facts," said Nai the Hever. "Two objections mar the elegant simplicity of this plan. First, the Ymphs are a powerful ilk, whom I do not care to antagonize. In fact, I struggle constantly to appease them. Secondly, putting questions to Ramus Ymph might well bar us from a much larger knowledge. Therefore I have decided that inquiries should be made on the scene. It is a task which falls within your competence, and you shall make this inquiry."

For all his speculations Jubal had expected nothing so remarkable. After a moment he asked: "Why do you select me for this job?"

Nai the Hever made an urbane gesture. "You are strongly motivated; you know something of the background; you show a marked investigative talent. These facts compensate to some extent for your inexperience. Also, we are reluctant to use other inspectors, whose loss, let us say, might cause us inconvenience."

"I do not care for suicide any more than these other inspectors," said Jubal.

"Quite possibly there will be no risk whatever," said Nai the Hever. "You will of course be thoroughly briefed and transportation will be provided. Additionally—yes, yes! Do not anticipate! You will receive a suitable compensation."

"Just what do you have in mind? A raise to twenty toldecks?"

"Of course not. Promotions do not come so easily. I propose a lump sum payment of, let us say, five hundred toldecks upon the successful completion of your mission."

Jubal showed a grin of derision. "If I were a fool enough to take your proposition seriously, I would insist upon altering the terms. The word 'successful' would be omitted and 'five hundred' changed to 'ten thousand'. You would pay me five thousand toldecks before I left Wysrod and another five thousand upon my return, before I so much as made my report."

Nai the Hever leaned back, his face pale and brooding. "Ten thousand toldecks? For a journey most folk would pay to enjoy? Your avarice is really grandiose!"

"What is ten thousand toldecks to you? I will be paid from public funds. There is clearly dire risk to this mission. My life is precious to me, if not to you. Send Eyvant Dasduke; he'll go for five hundred toldecks, and I'll take over his job."

"The figure," intoned Nai the Hever, "will be based upon two thousand toldecks, plus a bonus of two thousand toldecks if you produce valuable results. That is a generous, definite and final offer. Accept or return to your sewer inspecting."

"I might more readily accept," said Jubal, "if you had resolved that other affair. I have suffered the capricious cruelty of your daughter—"

"Your terms are probably not accurate."

"'Probably'! Why haven't you discovered the truth?"

"I have been busy with other matters. If you are so interested, ask her yourself."

Jubal snorted. "When? How? Where? She would refuse to see me, much less answer my questions."

"We will clarify this matter once and for all," said Nai the Hever. "Come to Hever House this evening, at sundown. Present yourself at the side entrance. I assure you that the Lady Mieltrude will respond to your questions."

At a wineshop Jubal considered the extraordinary proposal made by Nai the Hever... A concept took shape in his mind, so obvious, so natural, so monstrous, that he sat back stunned.

An hour passed, and another; Mora sank down the sky. Jubal returned to his lodgings, in one of the crooked lanes behind the Parloury. Somberly he arrayed himself in his none-too-splendid best. From the commode he took the gray steel blade given him at his boyhood rite, wet with three bloods. The blade had a secret name: *Saerq*—'Mountain Wind'; it was an unusually heavy weapon, of crystallized steel strengthened by a lattice of iron threads, balanced evenly for throwing. Jubal hefted the blade on his palm, then fixing the sheath to the inside of his waist-band, hung the comforting weight of Saerq along his thigh.

The time still lacked an hour to sunset. Seating himself at the table, Jubal carefully composed a document, which he folded and tucked into his pocket.

Mora now hung low in the west. Jubal went down to the street and hailed a hack. "To Hever House, along the Cham."

Along crooked lanes, overhung by tall crabbed gables, up one of the boulevards into the hills, around to the Cham and so to Hever House. Jubal walked under the entrance arch, sauntered up the steps to the stately main portal. The twin doors slid aside; Flanish the major-domo hurried forward. He recognized Jubal. "Please, sir, what is it this time?"

Jubal stepped into the foyer and Flanish was forced to give ground. "Announce me, if you please, to the Nobilissimus," said Jubal. "I am expected."

Flanish hesitated. "What name shall I announce?"

"I am the Honorable Jubal Droad; where is your memory?"

Flanish signaled a footman and whispered a word in his ear. With a resentful glance from the corner of his eye toward Jubal he marched from the room. The footman stood by the wall, unobtrusively keeping Jubal under surveillance.

Five minutes passed. Nai the Hever appeared, in casual gray evening dress. He surveyed Jubal with barely concealed annoyance. "I believe that I asked you to use the side entrance."

"As you know, I am a Glint," said Jubal. "I use no man's side entrance."

"This is Wysrod, not Glentlin, and we must make concessions to local propriety."

"If you recall," said Jubal, "I am here to discuss a matter of propriety: a criminal act committed by your daughter. She is the one who should use the side door, not I."

Nai the Hever made a small crisp gesture. "Come, let us make an end to this sorry affair. Flanish, ask Lady Mieltrude to join us in the small salon." And to Jubal: "This way, please." He led Jubal into a room hung with a pair of magnificent Djan tapestries: jungle landscapes woven of violet, green and dark red filaments. A white carpet muffled the floor; a pair of ancient Djan pots rested on an ivorywood table. Nai the Hever remained standing, nor did he invite Jubal to sit. A minute passed. Nai the Hever spoke casually: "I am accustomed to informality; in my position I deal with persons of every caste. The Lady Mieltrude, on the other hand, is quite conventional; she allows considerations of decorum to influence her conduct, so be guided."

Jubal's jaw dropped in astonishment. "Can you not understand that your daughter has committed a vicious crime? Do you consider this decorous conduct?"

"We shortly will hear the Lady Mieltrude's views on the matter. I emphasize that she will respond only to correct behavior."

"Perhaps then you would prefer to question her."

"Not at all," said Nai the Hever. "You are anxious to learn certain facts. This is a reasonable request; I acquiesce. But I am not here to assist your inquisition."

"As you wish."

"Please do not lean on that table," said Nai the Hever. "It is extremely old and has never been dealt with roughly."

"I only laid my hand on the piece!" retorted Jubal in indignation. "What do you take me for?"

Nai the Hever gave an uninterested shrug. He turned as Mieltrude entered the room. She wore an informal white gown; under a quat of limp pale blue leather her pale hair hung smooth to the turn of her jaw. Ignoring Jubal, she looked with an almost demure expression to her father. "You asked me to join you?"

"Yes, my dear, a matter to be clarified. This is Jubal Droad, whom you brought to the Parloury."

"I remember distinctly."

"He claims to have suffered inconvenience; he begs to place one or two perplexities before you, that you may elucidate the facts to his understanding."

"I will resolve his problems as best I may, but I hope he will be expeditious, as I am expecting a telephone call."

"Thank you, my dear. Jubal Droad, you may explain your difficulties."

Jubal had listened with amazement, looking from one to the other. He addressed Nai the Hever. "Do I hear aright? Are these the terms in which we discussed this matter?"

"Please explain the areas of your uncertainty."

Jubal struggled with words, then brought out the bogus warrant: "Did you or did you not take out this warrant against my life?"

Mieltrude inspected the document with minimal interest. "I recall something of the sort."

"The warrant is illegal. You have committed a crime."

Mieltrude let the warrant slip from her fingers to the floor. "The events have run their course." She turned to her father. "I do not think we need take them any further."

Jubal persisted. "You admit that you elicited this warrant?"

"The topic has no present application; my best advice is that you dismiss the entire matter...Will you be at home this evening, Father? We must make a start at reworking our guest-list."

Jubal turned to Nai the Hever. "Sir, will you be good enough to explain to your daughter that this is not one of her usual frivolities. Please point out that a warrant has been issued against her and that she is liable for punishment."

Nai the Hever reflected a moment. "Allow me a conjecture. Perhaps a paper was placed before the Lady Mieltrude, with a suggestion that traditional stabilities should always be supported, and the Lady Mieltrude signed the paper with no more deliberation than she thought the subject merited."

Jubal's voice cracked in outrage. "And an innocent

man barely escapes a scalded skin and broken bones? And that innocent man is me, a Glint nobleman of the highest caste? This transcends girlish fun."

"I will be in the music room with Sune," Mieltrude told her father. "As soon as you are free, we shall discuss the placings."

"In due course, my dear."

Mieltrude sauntered from the room. Jubal thoughtfully retrieved the warrant from the floor.

"So there you have it," said Nai the Hever. "Let us consider the matter closed. Come this way, into my library, which has been proofed against eavesdrop; we have other affairs to discuss."

In the library Nai the Hever waved Jubal to a straight-backed chair and went to lean against a long table covered with documents and journals.

Jubal seated himself with deliberation. "I understand then that you are waiving arbitration of this warrant? If so, there will be no difficulty in having it processed."

"My dear fellow, you are a positive monomaniac! Can you not leave off a subject when clearly all are bored with it? I cannot spend the entire evening with you, and we must discuss your mission."

"This remarkable mission," sneered Jubal. "It is not flattering to be taken for a lackwit!"

Nai the Hever seated himself in an easy-chair. Leaning back he contemplated Jubal with clinical dispassion. "You have been offered a challenging assignment and a chance to earn a handsome wage. I am puzzled by your attitude. Surely you are not trying to jockey for more money?"

"I am trying to tell you that your plot is transparent."

"Indeed. Which plot is this?"

"You intend to ship me off-planet forever to dissolve the embarrassment of your daughter's crime. What good are six thousand toldecks if they are here and I am there?"

Nai the Hever smiled in wry amusement. "I see that you will make a competent inspector after all. You have a natural bent for subterfuge and deceit. Compared to you, I am an innocent. But in this case you are wrong. No such plot exists."

"I would like you to prove this."

Nai the Hever's amusement swiftly became scorn. "As you yourself pointed out, it is not flattering to be taken for a lackwit. Would I waste such elaborate machinations upon so trivial a problem? You live in a world of distorted reality."

Jubal was unmoved. "This is precisely the indignant bluster you would use if in fact you were working a plot against me."

Nai the Hever reached into a drawer and brought forth a sheaf of notes. "There is proof that you can understand. Two thousand toldecks." He tossed them to Jubal. "Four thousand will be your total wages, not six thousand. Let us have no misunderstanding on this account, at least."

Jubal sheafed through the notes. A sizeable sum. With another two thousand, almost enough to buy a boat like the *Clanche*. "Two thousand toldecks carry conviction," Jubal agreed. "Fetch out paper and ink, if you please, and write as I dictate."

Nai the Hever made no move. "And what will you dictate?"

"Write, and you will learn."

"Dictate and I will record. Then I will learn. So what is this statement of yours?"

Jubal brought out his paper. "First the place and date...Then: 'Know all men by this document that I, Nai the Hever, in my official capacity as Servant of the Thariot Servantry, hereby request and contract with the Honorable Jubal Droad that he undertake a task at his inconvenience and peril in furtherance of the public weal. It is stipulated that this task, by my explicit instructions, shall take Jubal Droad on a voyage away from the planet Maske, that this voyage shall not, by my executive decree, be considered a contravention of the laws of Thaery, and that Jubal Droad may publicly and freely resume his full former caste and privileges as a Thariot and a high-born Glint upon completion of the work. I guarantee to furnish safe and comfortable transport to Jubal Droad, from Wysrod to the stipulated destination and back. I agree to pay him the sum of six thousand toldecks—'"

"Four thousand toldecks."

"'—four thousand toldecks, said payment to be made immediately upon Jubal Droad's return to Thaery, or as soon after as is convenient to him. I acknowledge Jubal Droad to be both my personal agent and the agent of the state, and I solemnly undertake to hold him guiltless and defend him with all the power of my office against any accusation which may be brought against him in connection with the above-named task, specifically contravention of the Alien Influence Act.'" Jubal leaned back. "Then you must sign, and affix your seal, your thumb and your secret Hever oath, and the document must be witnessed."

Nai the Hever stopped the recorder. "You make unreal demands. Such a document, if publicized, might conceivably be used to my disadvantage by the Ymphs. You must rely upon our unwritten compact."

"I must trust you, in short?"

"Exactly."

Jubal tossed the two thousand toldecks to the table. He rose to his feet. "Good night Nai the Hever."

"One moment." Nai the Hever tugged at his pale pointed chin. Presently he said: "If I provided you such a document, where would you keep it?"

"In a safe place, naturally."

"Where?"

"That is my private affair."

Nai the Hever reflected further, the metal lights dancing in his eyes. "Very well," he sighed. "I must do your bidding." He turned to a communicator. "My dear Mieltrude."

"Yes, Father."

"Go to my private study. At the desk open the drawer marked 'Official No. 4'. Bring me two sheets of parchment, a stylus, and that flask of ink marked 'Official Documentary'. Bring these articles to the library."

"Yes, Father."

A moment later Mieltrude appeared with the articles Nai the Hever had requested. "Thank you, my dear," said Nai the Hever. "Please wait a moment. I want you to witness a document."

Jubal made an instant protest. "She is not only frivolous but undependable. In deference to a father's ears I will not characterize her more accurately. Also, she will never be discreet; our secrets will be the banter of all Wysrod by midnight tonight."

"Calm yourself," said Nai the Hever. "You judge her

too harshly. A witness is a witness. Who else is in the house, daughter?"

"Sune Mircea has been with me, but she is on the point of leaving. Shall I fetch her?"

"Two giddy girls on a matter of such importance?" stormed Jubal. "My suspicions have returned!"

"In that case we will do without Sune," said Nai the Hever. He took parchment, stylus and ink. "First, I write date, place, time. Now the text."

Jubal cried in a voice of desperation. "Really, sir! Not in front of this girl! She is personally concerned. Is this a sensible procedure?"

"Her errors have taught her wisdom," said Nai the Hever. "She has become quite judicious." He turned on the recorder: "Know all men by this document," droned Jubal's voice, "that I, Nai the Hever, in my official capacity..."

Nai the Hever completed the affidavit, signed and sealed it. Mieltrude without comment affixed her signature.

Nai the Hever folded the document, tucked it into an envelope, and handed it to Jubal.

With a wary side-glance at Nai the Hever and Mieltrude, Jubal opened the envelope, drew forth the paper and examined it. "There is a well-known swindler's trick," said Jubal, "called 'foisting the pigeon', in which envelopes are cleverly substituted."

"That is one I do not know," said Nai the Hever. "Are you completely satisfied?"

"Where are my two thousand toldecks?"

"Take them. They are not counterfeit. Be here tomorrow as early as possible. Go to the kitchen and Flanish will give you breakfast."

Jubal ignored the remark. "What time do you wish to conduct the business?"

"At the second gong."

"I will present myself here at the second gong. One final matter: I am now your special agent and an official representative of the state. My salary, at seventeen toldecks a week, reflects poorly upon all of us. A substantial increase would seem appropriate."

Nai the Hever sighed. "Perhaps you are right. I will speak to Eyvant Dasduke. Henceforth you will earn twenty toldecks. Flanish! Show Jubal Droad to the door."

"Sir, in this direction, if you please."

"I will leave as I entered, by the front door."

The time was middle evening; Skay had not yet risen; the sky was dark. Fairy globes, pale white, blue and lavender, illuminated the garden. The driveway curved out to the entry arch, and the Hevers had not troubled to summon a hack for Jubal's convenience.

No matter. Jubal drew the bundle of notes from his pocket: two thousand toldecks, the largest sum he had ever handled. And also in his pocket: the contract between himself and Nai the Hever, a document no less comforting than the notes. He set out along the path toward the main gate.

A hack turned into the driveway. Had the Hevers after all considered the comfort of their visitor?

The front door opened; someone came from the house—a person slender and graceful, wearing a dark green cloak. Jubal recognized Sune Mircea.

She went to the hack; Jubal crossed the driveway and approached her. "May I share your hack into town?"

Sune had not noticed him; she jerked about startled, then became tense and wary. "What are you doing here?"

"I have been discussing business with Nai the Hever. We are, in a sense, associates; were you not aware of this?"

The light of the fairy globes illuminated Sune's face. Jubal studied the fragile bones of her jaw and forehead, the piquant slant of her cheek. What was going on in her mind? Certainly nothing straightforward or simple. In a thoughtful voice Sune said, "Yes, you may ride in the hack; where are you going?"

"Toward the center of town."

"That is on my way." She stepped into the hack; Jubal followed.

"Where do you live?" asked Jubal, for want of a better topic.

"Up on Trembletree Heights. It is the oldest district of Wysrod. The Mirceas are Setrevant caste, which we hold to be more ancient than Istvant and equally honorable, though nowadays Istvants perhaps make more of a flourish."

Jubal sat stiff, erect and cautious. Sune seemed quite relaxed, and spoke on, seemingly without reserve or calculation.

"Aren't you the person who created such a terrible cataclysm at the Parloury?"

"I am Jubal Droad. I am a Glint, as elevated as the best of Wysrod."

Sune laughed, an easy unrestrained laugh. "I had forgotten the notorious Glint pride. Very well then: are you not Jubal Droad the Glint who precipitated Ramus Ymph from high to low?"

"I reported a fact to Nai the Hever. The fact did the

damage. I have no pity for Ramus Ymph; he is a scoundrel."

"Oh come!" Sune protested. "He is hardly that! Ambitious, zestful, gallant, invincible—all of these perhaps.
Even unprincipled—but not a scoundrel."

"Call him what you like; he and that ammoniated
Mieltrude roundly deserve each other."

"Oh, the match is broken now. The Nobilissimus no
longer needed the association. Ramus Ymph was
unconcerned; his feelings were not really engaged."

"Understandably not."

Sune laughed again. "You really misjudge Mieltrude.
She is not as icily statuesque as she likes to pretend. It
is all a game with her. I think that she prefers the world
of imagination to ordinary life. She is not really
gregarious, you know."

"And you, on the other hand?"

"I am at home in all classes of society. It is tiresome
always to be impinging caste."

The hack, now trundling along one of the boulevards,
slowed at an intersection. Noting a small café, Jubal said:
"Perhaps you might wish to alight here and take a cordial
or a goblet of wine?"

Sune observed him sidelong. Somewhat slowly she
said: "I am fond of green wine; I would find a goblet of
Baratra refreshing."

Jubal halted the hack; they alighted and walked back
to the café. Sune selected a table in the shade of a
dendifer vine, and pulled the hood demurely up to
shadow her face.

With reckless extravagance Jubal ordered a flask of
the superb Baratra-Baratra, at the price of a day's pay.
Sune sipped and looked musingly off down the avenue.

At a loss for topics, Jubal said: "So the Lady Mieltrude is no longer to espouse Ramus Ymph. Is she melancholy?"

"One never knows about Mieltrude. She guards her private thoughts with great skill. Sometimes I would think her indifferent toward Ramus Ymph, then other times she exerted herself to be amiable. Perhaps she played at the whole relationship; who is to say? She never fully confided in me, that much is certain."

Jubal refilled her goblet. "Something very strange and frightening happened to me."

"I am surprised to hear a Glint admit to fear."

Jubal heaved a sigh. "Do you remember the occurrence at the Parloury?"

"Of course. How could I forget?"

"The evening after, I was set upon by executives with a warrant for my punitive torment. The warrant was signed by Mieltrude and it was falsely arbitrated. Nai the Hever will not listen to my complaints, and I want to get to the bottom of the matter."

"There is really no mystery whatever. Mieltrude is embarrassed by the circumstances. After his rejection, Ramus Ymph met Mieltrude and myself in the Parloury buffet. Mieltrude explained your role in the occasion and Ramus was furious. He claimed that you had maligned him with absurd lies, and said that you deserved at least ten, or better, twenty, strokes of the birch upon your bare backside. The idea amused Mieltrude and she declared that such treatment might deflate your 'foolish Glint vanity', as she put it. Ramus Ymph said, 'Excellent, we are of a mind. Step just up the stairs to the warrant office and we will elicit a warrant. You must sign it because I would forfeit dignity were I to do so.' Mieltrude was in a flighty mood, and it pleased her to feign feckless irresponsibility. So she merely laughed and tossed her hair, and when Ramus Ymph produced the warrant she scribbled her name on it with utter insouciance. That is the story. You must not blame Mieltrude; she was only playing a game."

"Do you know to what effect? I was to be primed with hyperaesthesic, soaked in herndyche, suffer thirteen breaks in my arms and legs, then abandoned on the beach to live or die."

"And what happened? You are not dead."

"No. I was lucky enough to defeat the executives. No thanks to Ramus Ymph or Mieltrude Hever."

Sune said thoughtfully: "Ramus Ymph is harsh with his enemies. Still, he is more than indulgent with his friends."

"You sound as if you approve of him!"

Sune shrugged. "He is a dynamic and handsome man. But let us talk of other things. You are now employed by the Nobilissimus? In what capacity?"

"I am to undertake a dangerous mission. I would like to discuss it with you but I have been warned to discretion."

"Exciting! So you have become one of D3's secret agents!"

"D3? I work from D3 as an inspector."

"You need not be coy. D3 is the secret intelligence bureau. Don't you work under Eyvant Dasduke? How romantic! You are a lucky man! D3 agents work as they wish, and draw salary in hundred-toldeck packets!"

"I have not quite advanced to that level. I draw my salary in one very slight packet of single-toldeck notes."

"The Nobilissimus is notoriously penurious—both with

public funds and his own. Never reveal that I so informed you!"

"Never. You can trust me—with anything."

Sune drank half the goblet and set it back on the table. "I must go. Please call me a hack."

"I will see you home."

Sune touched his hand with her fingers; nervous vibrations coursed up Jubal's arm. "Remember that I am a Mircea. My father would become excited to see me with a person such as yourself."

"And what of you? Are you embarrassed because I am a Glint?"

Sune thought a moment. "Let me be frank. Here I am not embarrassed. I enjoy your company. I consider you a remarkable man, and it is not your fault that you were born in Glentlin. But, elsewhere, with my family and friends, I am not strong enough to cope with the pressure."

"Then I may see you again?"

"Yes. But we must be discreet."

Jubal leaned forward, took her two hands in his. "Could I dare to hope that you think kindly of me?"

Sune gently disengaged his grasp. "Here is a hack; call it to the curb."

Jubal signaled the hack and with thumping heart helped her into the compartment. She gave him her hand. "Goodnight, Jubal Droad."

"When will I see you again?"

"Telephone at my home. Announce yourself as Aladar Szantho. And tell no one that we are friends or everything will be spoiled."

"I will do as you say."

The hack rolled off up the boulevard. The rear lamp

dwindled and vanished. Jubal turned away and set off along the boulevard toward his own lodgings.

He tossed the packet upon the bed. Two thousand tol-decks. He could now afford a respectable suite, at a decent address. He could dress in garments after the Wysrod style. He could buy Baratra-Baratra and Dravny bonbons; he could escort Sune Mircea where and how she chose, and perhaps she would overlook the fact that she was Setrevant and he was Glint.

Chapter 9

In the morning, precisely upon the appointed hour, Jubal arrived at Hever House. The door slid aside; Flanish stood in the opening. "The orders are definite," said Flanish. "You are requested to use the informal side entrance, which you will find around to the right."

Jubal responded with a curt nod. He wrote upon a slip of paper and handed it to Flanish. "When the Nobilissimus wishes to see me he may call at this address." He turned and strode back toward the street. A minute later a footman came running after him. "The Nobilissimus wishes to see you at this time."

Jubal returned to the house and marched through the front door, where Flanish stood with eyes averted. Nai the Hever waited in the foyer. "Confound it, Jubal Droad, these games must cease! I have neither time nor patience to truckle to your whims. Once and for all, you must accept the realities of life here in Wysrod, and act as etiquette requires you to act."

"Quite the contrary; it is you who must deal with me, a noble Glint, on the basis which my caste makes necessary. Otherwise there will be no dealings."

"Very well," said Nai the Hever coldly. "It shall be as you wish. The matter is really trivial. Come." He took Jubal into the library and gestured him to a seat. "Listen carefully. I will repeat, if necessary, but you must learn to assimilate information instantly.

"You are going to a Gaean world named Eiselbar, across the Hole, in the constellation Quincunx. Our information regarding Eiselbar is scanty. We know little of other worlds; we are ignorant even of Skay. Zangwill Reef is an utter mystery. In due course I propose to amend this lack; this is one of our future programs. For now a unit of the Space Navy will convey you to Frinsse Junction on Bossom's World, and the weekly packet will take you to Kyash on Eiselbar. You will carry ingots of palladium, which are convertible into Gaean currency. Your papers identify you as Neval Tibit, a tourist from the planet Phrist. Eiselbar is accustomed to travelers, and no one will question your identity. Still, you will be briefed regarding Phrist to the best of our information.

"At Kyash you will start your investigations. The Eisels are an idiosyncratic people, with customs quite different from our own. You must adapt to these customs. There can be none of your usual blether about noble lineage; you must, for a change, adapt yourself to local habits. Can you do this?"

"If necessary."

"It is necessary. You must be more than subtle. If Ramus Ymph becomes alarmed, we lose our advantage. Under no circumstances make yourself conspicuous. Abandon a line of inquiry rather than expose yourself. Is this clear?"

"Quite."

"I believe that I spoke to you of certain inexplicable facts, which we find not only mysterious but alarming. We are of course involved in counter-Binadary operations; in fact, last month we lost three of our best inspectors." Nai the Hever showed Jubal a wry smile. "On this account you have been selected for the mission to Eiselbar. I will say no more on the subject, except to indicate that Ramus Ymph may or may not be involved in these odd occurrences, so whatever you may learn will be useful.

"Now, this is what I know of Eiselbar. It is a world somewhat larger than Maske. Tourists come in great numbers; tourism, as an industry, is well developed. The Eisels are gregarious and also strongly egocentric. Candor is neither expected nor is its absence remarked. The society is egalitarian. The Eisels attach enormous importance to a balance of obligations. Everything has a specific price; nothing is free.

"A child born into an Eisel family incurs a birth-debt, which eventually must be paid to his parents. Bastards consider themselves lucky; they owe no birth-debt. The runaway child who claims to be a bastard in order to avoid his birth-debt is commonplace. When mature the child must maintain his parents in case of need. However, if the parents are ailing, senile, or simply too much of a financial burden, the son or daughter may subject them to euthanasia. For this reason, financial security is a prime consideration among all classes of people.

"The economy is based upon tourism, and the export of chemicals. Mobile slimes inhabit the surface sands—in fact, roads and walkways of Eiselbar are elevated above the soil to avoid the slimes, many of which are both poisonous and feral. The slimes use an unorthodox metabolism and synthesize compounds considered impossible by orthodox chemists. Some of these substances act as catalysts of remarkable efficacy, and command very large prices.

"The language is standard Gaean. You will undertake a set of exercises designed to suppress your Thariot accent, though on Eiselbar an accent is given no particular attention. As a tourist you will be treated with great courtesy unless you steal. Theft is considered a heinous crime, property representing as it does a goodly proportion of a man's life-effort: ergo, his vital force. Property is life; on Eiselbar do not steal, Jubal Droad."

"Never in my life have I stolen so much as a splinter!"

"As soon as you fulfill the terms of your mission, return to Frinsse, where a certain signal will summon your homeward transportation."

Jubal said: "I have grasped your requirements. In essence, I am to learn whatever I can of Ramus Ymph's activities without calling attention to myself."

"Exactly." Nai the Hever placed a card upon the table. "Go to this address, where you will be fitted with a wardrobe. I should mention that Eiselbar is a noisy world. Sound is considered an indispensable adjunct to life, and everyone wears a sound-producing instrument, by which he controls his emotional environment. Some Eisels use psychokinetic impulses; others train certain of their muscles, so that the sound, or music, if you will, responds almost unconsciously to their requirements. As a tourist you will project only a set of standard themes, which you will select by hand.

"Sexually, the Eisels are relaxed; escorts for tourists are freely available at convenient prices. The food is said to be excellent, and accommodations are comfortable."

"Eiselbar would seem a sybarite's dream," said Jubal.

"It is also very expensive," said Nai the Hever. "The Eisels expect good return on their investments, and no one works at the cheap. You will use the strictest economies and keep a ledger of your expenses. The Gaean SVU is approximately equal to the toldeck in purchasing value, so you may judge your expenses accordingly. Do you have any questions?"

"At the moment, no."

"Then that is all for now. Other instructions will presently be forthcoming."

Jubal and Sune Mircea took lunch in the shady back garden of a country inn, twenty miles east of Wysrod. Sune wore a pale green gown and a pale green ribbon to bind her dark hair, and Jubal was enchanted by the effect. "You might be Azolais of Cloudland, or a dryad of the Magic Forest!"

"Please don't call me a dryad," said Sune. "I always think of the Waels and their unwholesome habits."

"When I become wealthy I'll buy a beautiful felucca, and we'll sail the Happy Isles and the Violet Sea. We can put into Wellas and learn the truth of the Wael dryads."

"No, I would never go to Wellas. I have heard remarkable tales of the tree-lore and tree-worship. They are said to be more irredemptible than ever."

"But you will sail with me to the Happy Isles?"

Sune smiled. "If I said no, you would sulk. If I said yes, you would recklessly assume a hundred impossibilities. So what shall it be?"

"I will not tolerate the word 'impossible'."

Sune looked off across the garden. "Unfortunately the word exists. You must expect nothing of me. I am rash so much as to meet you here."

"Then why do you do so?"

Sune made an arch grimace. "You should never ask such questions. But still accept the fact: it is all so futile!"

"Where are the difficulties? They exist only in your mind! They can be defeated!"

Sune shook her head, her expression melancholy and wistful. Jubal circled the table and sat close beside her. "Look at me."

Sune obeyed, long lashes shrouding her eyes. Jubal implored in a low earnest voice: "Say that you have at least a quiver of sympathy for me!"

Sune turned away. "You must not make such demands! Have you no feeling for my position?"

"My feelings are for you! I am entranced; I burn with longing!" He put his arm around her shoulders and bent to kiss her. She drew away, then mischievously looked back. Jubal kissed her, which she allowed, but when he attempted a more fervent embrace she withdrew to the end of the bench. "Jubal Droad, you would gladly take us into regions from which we could not return."

"Why should we wish to return?"

"Consider the facts! I am Sune of the Mircea ilk and the ancient Setrevant caste. Here at Wysrod your status is unknown. You are employed as a secret agent, a most precarious life. Even now you leave on a far and dangerous mission. I may never see you again!"

Jubal grunted. "I suppose Mieltrude delineated every detail of my mission?"

"Of course. We are confidantes."

"And you told her that you are seeing me?"

Sune shook her head. "She would never understand. I fear that Mieltrude is a creature of rigid concepts."

"Does she still feel for Ramus Ymph?"

"I doubt if she ever considers him. He has gone to his manse in the Athander Fens. No one has seen him for weeks."

"He is like a voulp in a cave; he sits in his chair, grinding his teeth and planning new abominations."

Sune laughed merrily. "Poor Ramus; you should not abuse him so! At heart he is a zestful boy, surging with romantic dreams."

"He is a zestful boy, overflowing with depraved impulses and infantile cruelties. He and Mieltrude make a fine pair. I can hear them now as they plot in the Parloury." Jubal spoke in an affected falsetto: "'Oh, Ramus, I am desolated by your defeat! The Glint nobleman disclosed certain truths about you!'" Then, in a gruff grumbling voice: "'The irresponsible villain! I will punish him!'

"'Oh, do, Ramus! I dislike his hairstyle! And he cast a lascivious glance at Sune rather than at me. He deserves a good bath in herndyche and twenty broken bones. That will teach him not to offend favored darlings of society like ourselves.'

"'My dear, your fancies are charming! I can propose an elaboration which will amuse you. First we will startle his nerves with hyperas, and he will feel each pang a hundred-fold.'

"'Oh, Ramus, what a delightful idea. Allow me to sign the warrant!'"

Jubal, grinning, looked at Sune. "And that is how matters went. Am I right?"

"Not exactly," said Sune. Jubal could not decide whether she were vexed or amused.

"But close enough?"

Sune shrugged. "The episode is finished and closed."

"You underestimate the length of a Glint's memory."

Sune looked at him in perplexity. "You are as mutable as a flitterfly. One instant you declare your fervor in regard to me, the next you tremble with rage at poor Ramus. It is not really flattering."

"My apologies! I think only of you."

"Still you are anxious to venture far across the Great Hole on a glorious adventure with no thought for those at home."

Mieltrude was remarkably indiscreet, reflected Jubal. "I suppose you know precisely my destination?"

Sune nodded sagely. "I am told that the Eisel are an intemperate people, and that the girls lack all decorum. Do you wonder now at my caution? You will befriend some brassy creature with huge breasts and flaunting buttocks. I will be far from your mind while the creature instructs you in a dozen vulgar exercises."

"Believe me," cried Jubal. "No such intention has entered my head! I am captivated by one person only! Need I mention the person's name?"

"Please do not trouble. I suppose your mission is secret, even from me, but at least I am entitled to know if you will be in danger."

"No, or at least I hope not. I am to gather information only."

"What concerns us on Eiselbar? It lies far across the Great Hole!"

"Well—I am to investigate the activities of certain persons, who may be working to our harm."

"I find this hard to believe. Who would threaten us from Eiselbar, so far away?"

Jubal frowned up toward the sky. "I am not supposed to discuss the matter. Still, since you seem to know most of the facts—" he hesitated.

"I am not interested," said Sune. She slid back along

the bench, and tilted her face up toward Jubal. "You are not obliged to tell me your secrets."

Jubal slowly bent his head. Sune did not draw back, but after a moment broke away from the embrace. She looked across the garden and uttered a startled exclamation. Jubal, following her gaze, saw a party of six folk settling themselves at a table.

"They must not see me!" breathed Sune. "My cape, oh where is my cape?"

Jubal handed her the garment; she threw the hood up over her head. "While they are ordering refreshments we must go," said Sune. "It is the Noble Teviat and the Lady Nanou and the voluble Lady Dimmis; they must not see me here with you...Now! We will go. Quickly; walk between me and that group."

They reached the road without exciting recognition. Jubal rather sullenly escorted Sune to the hack. "Is your incognito really all that important? It discredits no one to be seen with me."

"Yes, I know." Sune's voice was tired. "You are Jubal Droad and a Glint nobleman. The Lady Dimmis however might not make the connection. We must be careful."

Jubal said nothing. They rode back toward Wysrod with silence heavy between them.

Sune at last tried to mend matters. She reached across the seat and took Jubal's hand. "Please don't be annoyed. I simply can't afford to have the world come tumbling around my head."

Jubal heaved a sigh. "No more can I...I must think matters over, very carefully."

Sune tossed her head. "If you are having second thoughts, your remarks clearly were not sincere in the first place."

"That does not follow," said Jubal. "But otherwise I agree with you."

"Which 'otherwise' is this?"

"Since I am on the verge of departure, I should not pay my addresses to you."

"You are absolutely incomprehensible! First you blow hot, then cold!"

The hack turned into Trembletree Avenue and halted near the tall old mansion of the Mirceas. Jubal jumped out and assisted Sune to the ground. Without words she pulled the cape about her and walked quickly off along the avenue. Jubal stood beside the hack watching the slender form retreat. She turned through the portal; Jubal saw the pale gleam of her face as she looked back; then she was gone.

Chapter 10

The Peripheral Line packet *Hizbah* floated in space half a million miles from Eiselbar, awaiting clearance from the Kyash space-port. Jubal Droad walked the promenade, self-conscious in his Eisel garments: flared white trousers with black fidget-ribbons, a yellow jacket tight at the shoulders and belled at the hips, scarlet slippers and a bright green katch.* Overhead hung the yellow giant Bhutra. Photo-selective glass blackened Bhutra's disk and tempered the glare of the corona; plain to see were gigantic prominences: swirling tongues of yellow flame licking out from the surface.

The *Hizbah*, receiving clearance, shifted toward Kyash and presently landed.

The atmosphere had long been adjusted; the passengers filed from the ship, through medical inspection, past the visitor's register, out into the great lobby.

Jubal halted to take stock of his surroundings. The sense of other-worldliness was strong. By the color of the light, by the taste of the air, by a dozen subconscious

---

The masculine Eisel headgear: a rimless hat of pleated cloth, ordinarily worn at a jaunty angle.

sensations he knew that he walked the surface of a strange planet.

He stood under a flat conic dome, formed from alternate segments of green and orange glass*: the lobby vibrated to an energetic light. Men and women of many races transacted business at the counters, arrived, departed, met friends, family or commercial associates, conversed in small groups, or simply sat waiting. They used a great variety of novel postures and attitudes which Jubal found fascinating. The air pulsed with sound: voices shrill and guttural; the shuffle of feet and the rustle of garments; the thump, whine and drone of a thousand superimposed musics from the shoulder sets of every Eisel present.

Ornate red and yellow characters over a portal formed a sign: TOURIST RECEPTION CENTER. Jubal crossed the lobby, passed through the portal and entered a large chamber under a second dome of green and orange glass. Around the periphery a ring of counters displayed decorative goods, garments and souvenirs. From a circular desk at the center a dozen clerks dispensed information.

As Jubal approached the counter a young woman stepped smartly forward to proffer her services. To an amazing degree she resembled that version of Eisel womanhood which Sune Mircea had defined: a tall, large-bosomed creature with great masses of brassy curls

---

*The light of Bhutra being intense, the Eisels live under shades and screens, often glass panels of monochromatic quality. Over the centuries they have developed a sensitivity to combinations—chords, so to speak—of monochromatic light. The discriminating Eisel can perceive visual combinations much as a trained musical ear is sensitive to the components of chords.

pinned with ornaments of carved bloodstone. Her vermilion sateen blouse was trimmed with pink floss; pale yellow pantaloons fitted tight to bursting around her hips. Her 'personal music'* warbled and skirled: a gay feckless melody underlaid by a rasping obligato. She smiled with effusive cordiality, displaying large white teeth. "How may I oblige you, Husler?"†

"Perhaps you would recommend me to a comfortable hotel."

"We may not suggest specific hotels. However—" she produced a pamphlet "—here is a graded list of accommodations, and you may take it for granted that those marked with five golden smiles are of superb quality."

Jubal glanced down the list. "I am seeking a friend who arrived a week or two ago; how might I find him?"

"As to that, Husler, I can't help you. We entertain thousands of visitors and we are at pains not to trouble them in any way, so we can't possibly follow their affairs in detail. Wouldn't that be a great imposition, after all?

---

*A limping and inadequate translation of the term chotz: that music with which an Eisel surrounds himself, to project his mood, or to present an ideal version of his personality. It is interesting to note that the Eisels are uninterested in the composition or rendition of music; they rarely sing or whistle, although occasionally they jerk their fingers or tap their feet in reflex reaction to the rhythm. The ability to play a musical instrument is so rare as to be considered a freakish eccentricity. The 'personal music' is produced by an ingenious mechanism programmed, not by musicians, but by musicologists

†Husler: honorific appellative, applied to all persons. Eisel society lacks formal caste distinctions, status being essentially a function of wealth.

At Kyash everyone pursues the style he fancies most, without stricture or tish-tush."

"All very well," said Jubal, "but I still would like to find my friend."

"Why not inquire of mutual acquaintances, or go to his usual resorts? Sooner or later you will meet him; Kyash is a happy, friendly city. Should you require a congenial escort—" she gave Jubal another pamphlet "—here are photographs of persons available for duty, at a fee of ten SVU per diem."

"Thank you." Jubal turned to leave.

"One moment, Husler! Another most important matter. I take pleasure in presenting you with this musical adjunct. I fix it to your shoulder. This is the selector, which affords you a carefully planned assortment of themes, including *Stately Mien, Joviality, Pensive Dreams, Skylark Song, Receptiveness to Novel Ideas, Proud Assertion, Caprice and Original Whimsy, Quest for Love, Verve and Vivacity, Condolences, The Glory of Beauty,* and others. This toggle adjusts for 'Morning', 'Afternoon', 'Evening', 'Night'; this for 'Solitude', 'Boon Companions', 'Erotic Proximities', and 'Crowds'. If you are interested in theoretical musicology, you may read this little pamphlet."*

While the clerk spoke, her *chotz,* or 'personal music', altered to a tinkling set of chords, spaced at precisely logical intervals, to emphasize the immediacy of her remarks.

Jubal glanced at the musicological pamphlet, then studied the hotel list. "The preferred hotel—this with the seven smiles—appears to be the Gandolfo."

---

*See Glossary #6.

"True. It is absolutely luxurious."

"And expensive."

"Inevitably the qualities are associated."

"I will at least seek my friend there."

"He would seem to be a person of discriminating taste." She touched a button. "A conveyance is at hand, Husler; if you will be so good as to walk to the door."

Under a portico waited a small vehicle, marked by a blazing gold and scarlet sunburst, the emblem of the Hotel Gandolfo. A doorman assisted Jubal within. "What of my baggage?"

"You will find it already at the hotel, Husler Tibit."

The conveyance slid smoothly away, with Jubal somewhat bewildered. If all were so relaxed and unregimented, how had the doorman known his name?

The vehicle drifted along the Avenue of Amplitudes, a dome of photo-selective glass protecting Jubal from the sun-blaze. Umbrella palms, gigantic ruffleworts, pale blue zagazigs, white shag-trees growing beside the road cast a shade which, by optical reaction against yellow Bhutra-glare, seemed almost dark blue. The conveyance turned into the grounds of the Hotel Gandolfo: a structure of five domes and five shdavis,[*] each blazoned with the gold and scarlet Gandolfo emblem.

The conveyance halted under one of the domes. A doorman, hastening forward, assisted Jubal to alight. With a polite smile he switched on Jubal's music-box, deftly twitched knobs and toggles; *Stately Mien*, 'Afternoon', 'Solitude' permeated Jubal's surroundings.

---

[*] *Shdavi: a tower supporting a residential globe high in the air, the construction resembling (and perhaps patterned upon) the stem and spore-pod of the indigenous myrophode.*

"Thank you," said Jubal.

"My pleasure, Husler Tibit! Will you step this way?" He ushered Jubal along a raised glass walkway. On the dry sand below, four of the famous Eisel slimes rippled and scuttled: gaudy creatures of mottled black and yellow.

Jubal paused to watch. "Are these slimes dangerous?"

"Dangerous, Husler? Well, indeed now, they'll give you somewhat of a sting."

"Just a sting? I heard they were deadly poisonous."

"Scare stories, Husler. Tourists should keep to the walkways, unless they're wearing sand-boots, then there's never a problem."

"And what if I walked on the sand without boots?"

"Well, some of the slimes admittedly have a bad reputation. But why worry? Merely stay on the walks!"

"Suppose I fell, and one of the bad slimes stung me, what then?"

"No doubt you'd be a bit uncomfortable. Still, it's not my place to prognosticate, being no medical man, nor a mortician."

"In other words, I'd die?"

"Well, perhaps. That's the morbid rumor; however, we never let it interfere with the pleasure of our guests, who are hardly the sort to attempt some giddy trick, like walking narrow ways while intoxicated."

Jubal entered the reception hall, where he was greeted and congratulated upon his choice of accommodation. "What will you require, sir? The grand suite? An ordinary suite? Possibly a simple bed-chamber with attached bath and garden?"

Recalling the recommendations of Nai the Hever, Jubal requested the simple chamber. Carelessly shifting the pamphlets supplied him by the Tourist Center from hand to hand, he dropped a photograph upon the counter. "It's my friend, Husler Aldo," he told the clerk. "He's staying here I believe? Or has he departed?"

"Husler Aldo is not among our guests, Husler Tibit."

"'Aldo' of course is his personal name," Jubal hastened to say. "He probably uses his clan name here. A most handsome man, don't you agree?"

"Naturally!" The clerk's *chotz* lilted in a fulsome arpeggio. "But I don't recognize the gentleman. Perhaps he selected another hotel."

"To his misfortune."

"Quite so."

Jubal rode a lift to his chamber in the north shdavi, where he instantly switched off the music-box. He bathed; then, after consulting the menu which appeared on the wall-screen with illustrative photographs, he selected a meal, the price of which, converted into tol-decks, represented half of his week's salary at Wysrod.

The meal was served on his garden balcony, under a screen of gray metaphotic glass through which Bhutra appeared as concentric rings of carmine red, pale green, yellow-white, bitter copper-blue. Foliage of black lace framed his view across the city: elevated streets, shdavis standing two hundred feet high, and in the distance the snow-capped Ririjin Mountains shimmering like a mirage.

Jubal dined luxuriously and without guilt: appetizers with a goblet of chilled cloudy-pale wine, tart and tingling on the tongue; a salad of delicate herbs; twists of fragrant paste and slivered pepper-crusted meat; a skewer of small broiled fowl, hot and sputtering on a slab of grain-cake, with a garnish of sour melon-balls; a parfait of five fruit-flavored frosts. Jubal had never before dined so delectably, and the comforts of his lodging would have pleased the most exacting sybarite of Wysrod. Sune's concern in regard to the danger of his mission at the moment seemed farfetched. Well then: what of Ramus Ymph? No facile method of locating him suggested itself. He could hardly go from hotel to hotel displaying the photograph; at the hotel where Ramus Ymph actually resided the clerk would notify Ramus Ymph that a 'friend' wished to see him and the fat would be in the fire. Very well, some induction then. Ramus Ymph had evidently come, not as a tourist, but with a definite purpose in mind. He would not necessarily be found at the tourist resorts, but more likely in company with persons of importance. At Kyash such persons were the wealthy enterprisers.

Or perhaps Eiselbar was no more than a convenient rendezvous, where Ramus Ymph could transact business with persons from any of the far worlds. If such were the case a hotel would be the logical place to look for him.

The most obvious source of information was the Tourist Reception Center. Although the clerk had discouraged his inquiries, no doubt they controlled agencies to discover whatever information might interest them...Jubal looked over brochures and pamphlets celebrating places of touristic interest. He read of the Ririjin Lodge, perched on a twenty-thousand-foot crag, with a view over hundreds of miles of snow, ice, wind-whipped clouds, knife-edge ridges. From Ririjin Lodge a monumental toboggan slide descended by a route twenty miles long to the Openlands Resort at the base of the Ririjin Scarp. The track followed first a trestle to the Mountain God Glacier, down the glacier to the Slew, where the snow became undependable and a trestle with an artificial surface had been constructed; down the chasm of the Ushdikar River and by a series of exciting switchbacks and traverses down the face of Protubular Scarp. The brochure described the three classes of toboggan: the Deluxe, the Special, and the Senior Comfort, which was enclosed, air-conditioned, equipped with a beverage bar, a steward and cinematic entertainment. All classes of toboggans were electronically monitored and controlled, and all provided continuous music of a carefully selected nature to augment the enjoyment of the adventurer.

Another pamphlet described the Priest's Diadem, a system of lakes in the Great Salt Desert two thousand miles west of Kyash. The lakes, in a highly mineralized region, had become saturated with, in the first case, copper salts to tint the water a limpid blue; in the second case, with vanadium and selenium sulfides and complex sulfo-silicates, to produce a crimson solution like diluted blood. The third lake, by the skill of Eisel chemical engineers, had been tinted lime-green, to complete the color cycle. Visitors might inspect the lakes in comfortable glass torpedo-cars which, securely guided by a rail, conveyed the sightseers past banks of giant crystals, through caves illuminated to striking effect, all to the accompaniment of a continuous commentary with musical background. "For a finale," read the brochure, "The Nineteen Naughty Naiads perform their unique and mirth-provoking underwater ballet, to the strains of never-to-be-forgotten Liquid Music (actually transmitted through the water), with enchanting special effects. Refreshments are available in all cars."

Jubal read of the Gardens of Paradise, raised on glass stilts above the desert, where "the amazed tourist while sauntering along safely elevated lanes will behold no less than two hundred thousand botanical and quasi-botanical curiosities, imported from many distant worlds. When pleasantly languid, the tourist will be anxious to take refreshment at the Pavilion of Delight, where superb meals are served by our charming Flowers of Grace, who also perform amusing pantomimes. Through glass panes the visitor may watch on the sand below the antics of the local clown-slimes, as well as the predacious stone-tigers and the sinuous twisters."

Another pamphlet described the slime-processing plants. "Our deserts yield an inexhaustible variety of these strange creatures, toward which we use the general word 'slimes'. Earnest students of the subject are well aware that these slimes exhibit notable differences. What they have in common is their most unusual metabolism, which functions by systems too complicated to be discussed here, and which, in many cases, is not entirely understood.

"Tourists are cheerfully conducted through the processing plant by gracious guides who have evolved a pleasing and unique method of singing their descriptions of the technical process to melodious tunes, which renders the concepts all the more interesting.

"Finally the tourists are treated to a demonstration of the effects of the strange and wonderful chemicals derived from our remarkable indigenes."

Jubal read of the Vertigat Caves through which tourist convoys were transported in 'troglodyte wagons', to a music synthesized especially for the occasion. He learned of the Haruga Tundra and the Inn of Storms far to the north, and the Great Salt Ocean, with its floating islands (propelled by submarine jets to the most scenic locations), with their comfortable air-conditioned 'Buccaneers Lairs'.

Jubal put the brochures aside. Had Ramus Ymph come to Eiselbar to enjoy the range of touristic delights?

If not, why had he come?

Bhutra dropped behind the western horizon. The sky glowed with a sunset effulgently gold and orange. Jubal went into the chamber, and as if by signal a man in a white smock appeared, tinkling with sprightly *chotz*. "Husler Tibit is proposing to go out for an evening promenade? Shall I anoint his head with emollient salve, and curl his hair into the popular 'Dionysian' style? Or may I fit Husler with a proper wig, that he may appear with a bounty of rich ringlets?"

"Thank you," said Jubal. "My present hair is sufficient to my needs."

"Ear-shells? Pastilles for Husler's breath?"

"Thank you, nothing."

The man in the white smock departed; a young woman in pantaloons of glossy yellow silk and a scant criss-cross bodice appeared. "Husler is fatigued; I would suggest a massage to arrange his muscles."

"No, thank you."

"Ah! The room is quiet and dispirited; allow me to bring music to Husler." She went to the bed-stand and the room reverberated with sound.

Jubal called out, "Thank you; however I am just going out!"

"If Husler requires a charming lady escort, he need merely press the white button."

"I see. And what is this black button, and this red button, and this green button?"

"Instructions are contained in the manual yonder."

"I will bear this in mind."

As Jubal departed the hotel the doorman stepped forward. "Husler has forgotten his *chotz*!" He twitched the dial to Jubal's music-box. "For a serene evening such as this, why not *Receptivity?*"

"Why not, indeed?"

"Pleasant hours, Husler Tibit."

Jubal proceeded along the boulevard. Occasionally conveyances drifted past, and as often carryalls loaded with tour groups of precisely forty persons, bound to one or another resort for an evening of pleasure.

With nothing better to do, Jubal kept a careful watch for Ramus Ymph, going so far as to examine customers at sidewalk cafés, mechanical game-rooms, souvenir emporiums and clown gardens. Many of these establishments, he noted, were arranged so as to accommodate groups, or modules, of forty persons, the number of persons in the standard tour group.

In tour group or alone, Ramus Ymph was nowhere to be seen.

Jubal returned to the Gandolfo in a disconsolate mood, his music-box playing *Pensive Dreams*. He rode the lift to his room, switched off the music, undressed and, reclining on the couch, fell asleep.

Chapter 11

Jubal stirred, stretched his legs. A sensor, detecting the motion, switched on the music and the room became bright with diffused sunlight. Jubal showered and ate breakfast. His mind was made up; during sleep he had arrived at a decision.

His single hope of discovering Ramus Ymph resided in a judicious use of the photograph. The logical starting point for an inquiry was the Tourist Reception Center.

Jubal set his music-box to *Skylark Song* and departed the hotel. A conveyance wafted him along the boulevard to the Tourist Center.

Jubal entered the dome. He waited his opportunity, then approached the young woman with whom he had spoken previously. After a brief flicker of uncertainty, she recognized him. "Good day, Husler! You are enjoying your visit?"

"To a certain extent. I am troubled because I can't locate my friend."

"A pity! We certainly don't want dreary faces on the streets of Kyash. You must seek diligently!"

"Yes, that is why I am here." Jubal tossed the photograph to the counter. "If you were to recall advising him..."

The young woman examined the photograph with a

negligent smile. "Even so, Husler, our rules prevent us from imparting information."

"Well, let me ask you this: do you recognize the photograph?"

"Since you ask, I seem to recall such a person approaching this desk. So handsome a man impinges upon the memory."

"Would you be good enough to make inquiries of your colleagues? There is no rule concerning the exchange of information among yourselves."

"That is true. Well, what's the harm? Now, as I recall..." She took the photograph to the clerk next along the counter who examined the photograph first casually, then with interest. She nodded, and gestured across the room toward the display racks, then turned and looked sharply toward Jubal. The two spoke earnestly and finally the young woman returned to Jubal. "My colleague says that I am definitely mistaken and that we are under no conditions allowed to discuss our patrons."

"Very well," said Jubal. "I appreciate your courtesy." He departed the counter, and going to a news-stand pretended to study the periodicals on display.

The second clerk had recognized Ramus Ymph. She was an older woman, with gaunt cheeks and great masses of russet hair: not a person to overstep either the letter or spirit of official regulations.

Jubal sauntered to the wall-cases and became interested in a display of amethyst brooches, each carved with a toboggan and the legend 'Memento of Ririjin'. A case containing glazed ceramic representations of slimes next claimed his attention, then a perfume counter offering attars from the northern deserts. Case by case, counter by counter, Jubal worked his way around the room, finally arriving at that section toward which the woman at the information counter had gestured. With keen interest Jubal examined the contents of the racks; in some manner they concerned Ramus Ymph.

The section appeared devoted to textiles: silks with many-colored lusters of the sort favored by the Eisels; chemises with scenes and mottos; small souvenir wall-hangings, embroidered with views of the Ririjin Mountains; schematic maps of the Jewel Lakes. Perhaps Ramus Ymph had purchased one of these decorated shirts? Nearby hung a pair of rugs, loomed in glowing tones of blue, purple, green and black, in patterns of near-microscopic intricacy. Jubal bent close, felt the nap, examined the knotting. Djan rugs. Of very good, but not the best, quality. Nonetheless, superb rugs, and how did they arrive at Kyash except through the agency of Ramus Ymph?

Jubal strolled on, and feigned fascinated interest in a set of cosmetic cases. In due course, the sales-clerk, observing Jubal's interest, stepped from his office and approached.

"Charming items, are they not, Husler? The material is a beautiful synthetic produced here at Kyash through the instrumentality of our wonderful catalysts. The price is a mere nine SVU."

Jubal made an ambiguous sound. "And these pantaloons—they seem rather striking."

"They will fit you to perfection. The color becomes you, as well."

"Are they made here at Kyash?"

"Yes, most of what we sell is local produce."

"Those two rugs are interesting articles. Are they local?"

"No, as a matter of fact, they are from a world out around the Reach. Meticulous work, but rather dull for our tastes, and perhaps not the best quality."

"You surprise me. I am ignorant in these matters and I assumed them to be made very carefully."

"Carefully made, yes; but our local rugs are better. We use a flat resilient matrix containing entrapped air-bubbles. It is called 'iseflin'. Designs of choice are printed upon this material; the resultant rug is inexpensive, durable and decorative. The two rugs yonder are survivals from the hand-craft days."

"And how did you obtain such odd specimens?"

"They were placed here by a certain Husler Arphenteil who deals in exotic rugs. I warned him that his price was far too high, that they would never sell in competition with our good Eisel floor coverings, but he was insistent."

"I might be interested in one of them as a curio, if the price were right."

"He asks six hundred SVU apiece."

"What! For those small dull scraps?" Jubal made a quick calculation. At Wysrod such rugs would sell for perhaps three hundred toldecks. If an SVU and a toldeck were of equal value, Ramus Ymph was pricing his rugs high. He said in a scornful voice, "In a reckless moment I might pay twenty SVU, but no more."

The clerk shrugged. "Husler Arphenteil envisions no such reduction."

"Perhaps yes, perhaps no, I will consult him. Where is he to be found?"

"I have no idea, Husler. He appears at irregular intervals."

"The rugs will never sell at his price. How long have they been on display?"

"Almost six months. They arouse little interest, and of those who inquire, everyone is appalled by the price."

"I will keep my eyes open for Husler Arphenteil. You don't know his usual hotel? Or anyone through whom he might be reached?"

"I'm afraid not, Husler."

Jubal departed the Center before he aroused the suspicions of the woman at the information counter, who already had been eyeing him sidelong.

At a garden café Jubal seated himself under a sprawling shagwort. Half an hour he sat musing over a decanter of wine punch. At last: traces left by Ramus Ymph! They were no less perplexing than the total absence of clues. The Ymphs were not poverty-stricken; why should Ramus Ymph demean his caste by involving himself in trade?

Jubal called for a Kyash directory. He consulted the section labeled: *Floor coverings: rugs, carpets and iseflin.* If Ramus Ymph had attempted to deal at one rug outlet, he might well try his luck with others.

He summoned a conveyance and coding the first address into the director was wafted away down the boulevard. Jubal sat back and watched the passing scenery. Suddenly surfeited with *Skylark Song,* he switched to *Bold and Daring Enterprise.*

The conveyance halted beside a pavilion under a green-glass dome. A white and orange sign read:

> The Emporium of Total Comfort,
> where furnishings for home, office
> or sport-place may be purchased.

Jubal drew several deep breaths to calm his nerves. Slightly increasing the volume of *Bold and Daring*

Enterprise, he alighted from the conveyance, crossed the walkway with a firm tread and entered the pavilion.

No large selection of goods was on display. In booths around the periphery clerks caused holographic projections to appear before those customers who preferred to make their choices at the display room rather than in their own apartments. A table displayed materials: fabricoid, iseflin, metallite, sklam, in assorted colors and textures, and a rack supported the rugs themselves: sheets of elaborately embellished iseflin and a single small Djan rug.

Jubal looked about the premises and fixed upon a portly little man notable for his great pyramidal mass of auburn ringlets. His *chotz* was both complex and ponderous: a sequence of droning chords, knit together by a fluttering of pipings and warblings. Jubal asked: "You are the manager of this establishment?"

"I am Director Kliffets."

"Yes, that is the name Husler Arphenteil mentioned. He wants to know how many more rugs you will require."

Director Kliffets raised his eyebrows and his pale blue eyes seemed to bulge. "More rugs? I have not yet sold the rug yonder. Everyone is aghast at the price. I told Husler Arphenteil as much myself, not ten days ago. Did he not inform you?"

"He was hoping that affairs might have changed for the better. Also, I am authorized to offer you more favorable prices. I have here a schedule..." Jubal drew some papers from his pocket, and as if by chance came upon the photograph. "Here is our friend now." He displayed the photograph to Director Kliffets. "Or was he wearing his mustache when you saw him?"

Director Kliffets was not interested in photographs.

"No, he was as in the representation. Now, as to the new schedule of prices—"

"I seem to have left it at my hotel. You can inquire of Husler Arphenteil, if you like. I suppose you have his current address?"

"No. He is a man of reserve, and his *chotz* is somewhat self-important. In my opinion Husler Arphenteil's desires exceed his capabilities."

"Indeed? Why do you say that? Not that I disagree with you."

Director Kliffets pointed to an agency across the boulevard. "Only persons of important wealth patronize the Intersol Company. His conduct does not suggest that sort of wealth."

Jubal leaned forward. "I will tell you something in confidence. Husler Arphenteil derives from a family in decayed circumstances. As a child he became accustomed to the best, but now he cannot achieve his goals."

Director Kliffets nodded. "This would accord with my personal observations; I am a keen student of the human personality."

"So much is evident. What price has Husler Arphenteil placed on his rug?"

"Four hundred SVU. Quite unreasonable, when a delightful iseflin carpet may be had for a tenth as much. Who cares that the fibers in Husler Arphenteil's rug have been knotted by hand? That the dyes are vitalized by the magic of shamans? That the fibers must be plucked one at a time, from four different sources? Does a person's foot need to know all this, as it treads the rug? Are the colors brighter for this reason? Quite the reverse! Notice the gayety of yonder iseflin, in contrast to the purple murk of Husler Arphenteil's rug."

"Tastes differ," said Jubal. "Husler Arphenteil mentioned none of his plans?"

"No, he is not confiding, even though, during our interview, he switched *chotz* to *Comrades Together.*"

"He is at times difficult," Jubal agreed. "Allow me to offer you a confidential hint—but you must never reveal it to Husler Arphenteil—in fact you had better not mention that I have been here. Is this agreed?"

"Certainly."

"Then—first I should ask, when do you expect to see him next?"

Director Kliffets thoughtfully puffed out his cheeks. "He was indefinite. In fact, I gather the impression that he has lost interest in his rugs. On our first meeting he was most enthusiastic, but now he seems—not precisely indifferent, but as if his thoughts are elsewhere: perhaps Intersol and its marvellous toys. But what is this confidential hint?"

"It is this. If you demand twenty percent more commission than he now allows you, he will accede. Grudgingly perhaps, but you must be firm."

Director Kliffets nodded glumly. "All very well, but what good is a commission on an unsaleable item? He must price his merchandise competitively; then conceivably he might hope to sell one or two."

"He is as much a mystery to me as he is to you. Did he say nothing which might reveal his future plans?"

"No. He is a man of almost contemptuous reserve."

"I know this all too well. It has been a pleasure talking to you. Remember, you have not seen me!"

"Agreed and understood!"

"Goodby then. I think I'll just look into Intersol myself, and acquaint myself with Husler Arphenteil's latest fad."

Jubal stepped out into the yellow sun-blaze. The walkway cast a blue-black bar of shadow along the sand below; slimes wandered here and there ingesting the myrophode filaments which were their principal sustenance. Smaller parasitic creatures, riding their backs, gnawed at ruffles, drilled holes into the dorsal tissue, implanted sucking tendrils. Jubal watched a moment, marveling at the variegated colors: pale green with black ruffles, brown-purple with white spots, gray stippled with vermilion. He dropped a pebble; those slimes nearby darted with astonishing speed to the pebble, apparently attracted by the vibration of impact. They nudged the pebble, then, finding nothing either to attract or to excite, wandered away.

Jubal became oppressed by Bhutra's glare, so different from the cool clear light of Mora. It surrounded him, dazzled his eyes, started perspiration from his forehead and neck. He crossed the boulevard, followed a walkway through a garden of black cactus, and gratefully stepped into the shade of Intersol's green and white dome. He was instantly aware that he had entered an environment of affluence. Sumptuous yellow plush furniture was arranged around a floor of transparent black glass which glittered with constellations to represent the night sky of Old Earth. A counter supported a dozen space-yacht models, and photoscape panels along the walls depicted famous Gaean cities. At a desk sat the Intersol agent studying a prospectus.

The agent rose to his feet—a middle-aged man wearing a decorous maroon wig, a mustard-ocher jacket belled over maroon trousers; his music was a subdued murmur, without egoistic insistence. "How may I serve you, Husler?"

"A friend recommended that I visit your premises, and I decided to do so."

"I am delighted to hear as much." The sentiments, so the agent's manner suggested, were more formal than heart-felt. With the experience of many years he had gauged the weight of Jubal's purse, and saw no reason for effusive cordiality. "In what precisely are you interested?"

"Perhaps you would inform me as to the range of your products."

"The models yonder represent the scope of our current production, though of course we will always work to special order. This is the top of our line, the Magellanic Wanderer. Notice the forward promenade and the after lounge, both paned with photochrometz. There is accommodation for sixteen, plus a crew of six. The engines are four Furnos dynos, two separately operating Thrussex Intertwists, six Meung gravity-pods. The appointments are excellent, without compromise. Instrumentation includes a pair of separately functioning trans-galactic navigators with dial settings to any world of the Gaean Reach. The price is SVU 327,000."

"Very nice," said Jubal, "but rather beyond my means."

The agent nodded without surprise. "At the other end of the line is this little Teleflo, with accommodation for six and a crew of two. Appointments and fittings are of high quality; technical specifications are quite adequate. The price is SVU 18,500. We are also agents, incidentally, for the Devaunt Cadet Planet-Jumper, at SVU 9,800."

Jubal pretended to ponder, as if calculating his assets. "Of course I can't hope to match my friend Husler Arphenteil's resources...I believe he was interested in the Magellanic Wanderer?"

"Everyone is interested in the Magellanic Wanderer. Husler Arphenteil's friend, however, has influenced him in favor of the Sagittarius—this model here. It is a very luxurious craft with accommodation for twelve and a crew of four."

"Which friend was this?"

"I do not know his name. He is evidently an important merchant." In a slightly warmer tone of voice, the agent inquired: "What are Husler Arphenteil's plans? He was also considering a Bendle Spacemaster, but he will make a great mistake if he decides in that direction. The cost is a trifle less, but Bendles lack the workmanship of our models, and there is a long history of troubles with their Defiance pods, which are merely second-rate imitations of the Meungs."

"I believe he is inclining toward the Sagittarius, although I haven't seen him for a week or more. By any chance do you have his present address?"

"Isn't he still at the Shirbze Palace? I know of no other address."

"Strange. I looked in the other day and they gave me to understand that Husler Arphenteil had moved. Probably a misunderstanding. Incidentally, please don't mention that I have been here, as he might think me presuming beyond my station. Though for a fact, I would willingly own a Teleflo."

"Yes, the possibilities for marvellous discoveries are the same, no matter what the price range. May I offer you one of our brochures?"

"Thank you."

Jubal rode a conveyance to one of the garden cafés along the Boulevard of Mercantic Visions. He was well-pleased with himself. Through skillful investigation, of which even Nai the Hever must approve, he had assembled a substantial amount of information. Ramus Ymph had come to Eiselbar as a rug dealer, a ludicrous idea in itself and one which should amuse Nai the Hever. Ramus Ymph's motives could at least be glimpsed: he coveted a space-yacht, for the purchase of which toldecks were valueless, even were the transaction not flagrantly in violation of Thariot law.

With a satisfying sense of achievement Jubal consumed an expensive lunch. The *chotz* of other guests and the café attendants knit a not unpleasant embroidery of sound. His visit to Eiselbar had been not only productive, but also enjoyable. Spending Nai the Hever's money was a pleasure in itself. What of Sune Mircea's premonitions of danger? Absurd. Kyash was a most orderly city. Ramus Ymph was not to be credited with either scruples or self-restraint, but still he could hardly come up to Jubal's room at the Gandolfo with a cudger gun and do murder.

Or could he?

Of course not! Jubal drained his goblet with a decisive gesture.

He switched his music-box to *Verve and Vivacity*. Now was not the time to rest on his laurels. More information was necessary.

By the time Jubal had finished his lunch he had decided upon an apparently feasible tactic. He returned to the Gandolfo, changed to Eisel afternoon wear: a blue bell-shaped blouse, tight salmon-red pants with black flounces and a black cummerbund. He telephoned the valet for a wig, of a style at the discretion of the valet, and was fitted with a voluminous contrivance which, rising high from his scalp, shrouded his forehead, ears and neck under tufts of liver-colored ringlets.

Jubal inspected himself in the mirror and was satisfied with his appearance. Descending to the boulevard, he walked through the yellow dazzle of afternoon to a public telephone at a nearby café.

Before calling, he noted the somewhat strident quality of *Verve and Vivacity* and changed to *Sincere Integrity*. Then he pressed the 'Call' button. "The Hotel Shirbze Palace."

The screen displayed the smiling face and tumultuous blonde curls of the receptionist. "Hotel Shirbze Palace! At your service, Husler."

"I am Husler Dart, of the Distant Worlds Rug Import Company. Is Husler Arphenteil on the premises?"

"One moment, Husler." She spoke to the side: "Is Husler Arphenteil here?"

She listened to the reply, then returned to Jubal. "Sorry; we no longer enjoy Husler Arphenteil's patronage."

The tension which had stiffened Jubal's nerves relaxed abruptly. He said in a hollow voice: "When did he leave?"

"Six days ago."

"How may I reach him now?"

"Husler Arphenteil left no instructions, I am sorry to say."

Jubal expressed his thanks and terminated contact. He stepped out upon the boulevard and stood glumly looking this way and that, sweat from under the wig trickling down his neck and the music-box suffusing the surroundings with a brave march-time tempo. Jubal, becoming aware of the now irrelevant *chotz*, in irritation switched to *Far Clouds in Stately Formation*.

A conveyance, sensing his presence, halted; Jubal climbed in and gave a terse direction. "The Gandolfo Hotel."

The conveyance moved eastward along the boulevard, with Jubal sitting stiffly on the edge of the seat.

The five splendid shdavis of the Hotel Gandolfo loomed overhead. Jubal made a growling sound in his throat. He would not give up so easily! "Alter course. Take me to the Hotel Shirbze Palace."

The conveyance swung in a semi-circle, returned westward along the boulevard and halted beside a triple-groined dome from which rose three shdavis, the highest chalk-blue, the second dust-beige, the lowest a pale rosy-pink. Two enormous black umbrella trees leaned across the entrance; letters forming the words HOTEL SHIRBZE PALACE floated above, swinging and bobbing on the breeze.

Jubal, alighting from the conveyance, switched back to *Sincere Integrity* and went purposefully into the hotel.

He approached the reception desk, behind which stood a pair of clerks. Both emanated placid afternoon music. "I am Husler Skanet of the Trans-galactic Space-yacht Company. I have important papers which must be delivered to Husler Arphenteil. Shall I leave them in your care?"

The first clerk smiled and shook his head. "You may leave your papers, Husler, but Husler Arphenteil is no longer with us, and we cannot guarantee to deliver them."

"What a nuisance!" exclaimed Jubal in disgust. "He was most insistent! Of course he never left us a new address. He is a vain man who ignores the convenience of others."

The clerk said cautiously, "Quite right, Husler. He simply departed our premises."

"The fault is not mine, for which I am grateful," said Jubal. "Mark me well, someone will suffer over this! But it will not be me, for he will claim that he left the address with you, and he has wealthy* friends." Jubal placed an envelope upon the counter. "Here; give me my receipt and the responsibility is yours."

The clerk threw up his hands and backed away from the counter. "We cannot accept important documents on this understanding."

Jubal with a grim smile pushed the envelope further across the counter. "Husler Arphenteil ordered these papers delivered to him at this hotel. I am pleased to have done my duty. Husler Arphenteil is an impatient man, who lashes out blindly when he is perturbed. You must deliver the papers."

"Impossible! He left no forwarding address! I call upon you to witness my statement!"

"Well then, where can he be found? Did he not come here with friends who might assist you?"

The clerk looked dubiously at his assistant. "Who was that large man in the pale wig who seemed Husler Arphenteil's intimate? You must tell!†"

The word among its cluster of meanings includes power, grandeur, disinclination to receive rebuffs gracefully.

†*An idiom signifying urgency and enjoining the person addressed to accurate disclosure.*

151

The second clerk nodded. "I claim beneficence!* The friend is an important man of great wealth, whom I am proud to recognize. He is Husler Wolmer, who controls the People's Joy Tourist Agency. Husler Arphenteil, so I believe, has gone on a tour."

The first clerk by some subtle means adjusted his music to a serene and confident andante. "You may take advice of Husler Wolmer as to the disposition of your documents. Our responsibility is finally and absolutely ended."

"I will do as you suggest," said Jubal. He departed the hotel.

Once more he stood out in the open, and filaments of fire seemed to stream down from Bhutra to lick along the boulevards of Kyash. A conveyance sidled up beside Jubal; he stepped within. "The People's Joy Tourist Agency."

The conveyance turned down a side-street and crossed a viaduct over a gully, barren except for wild slime-banes and thickets of black cactus.

The street entered a plaza, where a fountain threw jets of nonvolatile liquids, stained different colors, high into the air. A hundred domes of as many enterprises surrounded the plaza, each with a sign floating above. The conveyance stopped by a dome where floating letters read: PEOPLE'S JOY, with below the script: *Pleasure designed to suit the tastes of all.*

Jubal entered the cool interior. At four counters clerks conferred with customers; others waited on benches. A

The responsive idiom, signalizing the service about to be rendered, and including it into the balance of obligations existing between the two.

receptionist spoke to Jubal: "Your name, Husler? I will notify you when your turn has arrived."

"I am Husler Delk. Tell me, which of these gentlemen is Husler Wolmer?"

"None of them. Husler Wolmer is proprietor of the firm."

"Is he here at this moment?"

"No, Husler, he does not normally frequent the premises. You must make an appointment to see him."

"Thank you."

While Jubal waited he watched the photoscape panels which advertised tours of the worlds Dwet and Zalmyre, next out in orbit from Eiselbar. On Dwet safaris of forty persons rode air-conditioned glass vehicles across jungle, swamp and savannah, inspecting strange and awful beasts at close quarters during the day and resting by night at first-class jungle lodges with filtered air, tasteful music, excellent cuisine and gaming casinos. On Zalmyre a three-week tour included a visit to the Black Opal Mountains, a submarine tour of Lake Meya, and a voyage in modern forty-passenger vessels down the mighty Orgobats River, with stops each night at luxurious native-style hostels, where Eisel managers and staff guaranteed full cosmopolitan comfort. Fares were calculated on the basis of the forty-module; larger groups might expect a discount.

Eventually the receptionist approached Jubal. "If you please, Husler Delk, our 'pleasure expert' is anxious to gratify your wishes."

She led Jubal to a counter, behind which sat a blank-faced young man whose bleached white hair enclosed his face in a dandelion-fluff nimbus. He twitched his lips in a welcoming smile, touched a button which by raising his chair, elevated him into a politely erect position. "Good afternoon, Husler Delk. Please be seated." His own chair lowered; he subsided to a sitting position, for the hundredth time that day spared the fatigue of jumping to his feet to greet his clients. "And how may People's Joy serve you? We are known as 'the pleasure experts'; we are anxious to fulfill the promise of our soubriquet."

"I am not sure whether you can help me," said Jubal. "I came to see Husler Wolmer, but apparently this is impossible."

"Yes, Husler Wolmer is a very busy man. Perhaps I can at least assist in meeting your needs?"

"I might wish to bring members of my association to Eiselbar, but first I must investigate your facilities."

"How many in your group, Husler?"

"Approximately seventy-five or eighty."

"Two modules. A convenient number. All of our attractions are designed in terms of modules; we find it far more efficient: all except the Temenk River Resorts and the Happy Valley Lodges which by their very nature must segregate the clientele on a different basis."

"These are the 'therapeutic resorts'?"

"Yes, they are luxurious hostelries where clients are encouraged to explore, define and perhaps resolve their erotic problems. Each of the lodges specializes in one or another facet of this large matter. This pamphlet will provide you explicit details; study it at your leisure."

"Thank you. Incidentally, before we proceed, at the Hotel Shirbze Palace I became acquainted with Husler Arphenteil, an intimate of Husler Wolmer. Where might I have the pleasure of seeing him again?"

"Husler Arphenteil?"

"Yes; this wealthy gentleman." Jubal displayed the photograph.

"I believe that this is the client Husler Wolmer is now personally entertaining. They are currently on Zalmyre."

"Where are they staying?"

"I could not say, Husler. I know nothing of their business. When would your group arrive?"

"In about six months."

"Excellent. We of course are agents for all the spaceship lines and we will arrange the tour from space-port to space-port. Now, as to details—"

"I wish to talk over special arrangements with Husler Wolmer. Maybe I will see him on Zalmyre."

"You wish to visit Zalmyre, Husler?"

"Yes, I think I should do so—in the interests of my group."

"I will fit you into Module A-116, which departs tomorrow."

Chapter 12

The time was dark mauve twilight; Skay, at the full, dominated the east. Jubal Droad half walked, half ran down Sprade Way, in that rather dismal district of Wysrod known as the Basse. He moved with furtive stealth, keeping to the shadows where the narrow-fronted houses blocked out the light of Skay. He halted at a telephone kiosk, looked quickly up and down the street, then slipped inside. He spoke into the mesh: "The House of Hever, on the Cham."

The pane displayed a two-headed flying snake: the emblem of the Hevers. Jubal felt a dour scrutiny, then heard the curt voice of Flanish: "What is your purpose in calling?"

"Connect me instantly to Nai the Hever!" He peered down the street toward a moving shadow.

"The Nobilissimus is engaged for the entire evening. I suggest that you present yourself at the Parloury offices in the morning."

The moving shape slowly approached the kiosk: an anonymous human hulk. Jubal spoke in a tense voice: "Inform Nai the Hever that I am on the telephone; be quick!"

"Your business is urgent?"

"Of course it's urgent! Why else am I calling?"

"I will mention your call to the Nobilissimus."

"Hurry!"

The shape seemed to hesitate, then, passing through a bar of Skay-light, showed a sultry gleam of face and eyes, moved on along the street and away. Jubal bent his head to watch it recede.

A moment went by. Jubal drummed on the shelf with his fingers.

Nai the Hever's image appeared on the pane. "Where are you?"

"At a kiosk in Sprade Way."

"Come up to my house at once."

"Has Ramus Ymph returned to Thaery?"

"Yes; he is at his manse on the Athander Fens."

"I fear that I am being followed."

"Quite possibly. Attack or evade the offending party, as you please, but come at once."

"A hack is coming; I shall hire it."

"Along Sprade Way? At this hour? Odd. Leave the kiosk, run to the corner and conceal yourself before it arrives. Then as quickly as possible, come to my house."

"Do you have my three thousand toldecks on hand?"

"Two thousand was the stipulated sum."

Jubal slipped out of the kiosk, crossed to the deepest shadows and ran light-footed up Sprade Way.

The hack, so he imagined, increased its speed. Jubal ducked around the corner, stepped into an areaway. The hack, emerging from Sprade Way, turned in the opposite direction.

Jubal left his hiding place and proceeded along the street. Presently he encountered another hack; climbing into the gaunt compartment, he spoke the address of Hever House.

Along the tree-shrouded boulevards, up the hillside, around the Cham he rode; down Hever Lane, up to the front entrance.

Flanish slid aside the portal a minimal gap, crooked a finger. Jubal entered, and at Flanish's gesture followed him along a corridor. They passed a drawing room, from which issued voices and laughter; glancing through the doorway Jubal saw a group of young men and women sipping from crystal goblets, discussing those topics which amused them most. Sune Mircea looked up and Jubal thought that perhaps she saw him, though her eyes were unfocused.

Nai the Hever waited for him in the library, a fold of newspaper on the table before him. "Your exploits have preceded you. 'The anonymous hero who with unswerving courage', and so forth."

"My name is not mentioned? My identity is unknown?"

"What difference does it make?"

Jubal had resolved to maintain at all times a mien at least as cool and imperturbable as that of Nai the Hever. "I wonder exactly how and why the event occurred. In short: am I known by name or by description? Or was the affair a mistake? If not a mistake, then who betrayed me?"

"These are interesting questions," said Nai the Hever. "Exactly what occurred?"

"As I approached Wysrod, I fell into a strange mood. My Uncle Vaidro has urged me never to ignore a hunch, and remembering my previous experience I put myself on the alert. Arriving at the depot, I became even more apprehensive: justly so, as it turned out. In the foyer I noticed a small man in a dark blue quat standing at the side. He showed no interest in me, but as I went out he followed. I halted just beyond the door, as if I were awaiting someone. He came after me, walked a few paces to the side, then turned and aimed his gun. I dropped to the ground and his shot struck a man unlucky enough to be walking past. Before he could shoot again I threw my knife and pierced his neck."

"Thoughtless," grumbled Nai the Hever. "You should have overpowered him."

"With his gun poised for a second shot? You are poorly advised in defensive tactics. In any event, since I wished no notoriety, I retrieved my knife, wiped it on the dead man's shirt, for which he had no further use, and departed as quickly as possible."

"There, at least, you demonstrated tact." Nai the Hever touched the paper before him. "The victim was a magnate of high caste, the Noble Cansart of the Waygards. His assassination is a general source of mystification. No one can even speculate as to a motive. Several bystanders extol the courage of—let me see, what is the text?—'a young man apparently not of exalted caste, and of unrecognizable ilk, though certain persons suspect him of being a Glint. This young man demonstrated remarkable resource and seriously disabled the madman, in fact expunging his life. Then, modestly refusing to accept the plaudits of the bystanders, the young man departed without delay. The bereaved Waygard ilk is anxious to express a commendation to the unknown stalwart.'" With a fastidious forefinger, Nai the Hever pushed the paper aside.

"The question remains," said Jubal, "who instigated the attack? And more importantly, how did this person know that I was due to return?"

Nai the Hever compressed his lips. "You must school

yourself against blatantly obvious observations, and also rhetorical questions which only serve to blunt the keen edge of attention."

"Allow me to rephrase the question. Do you know who planned this attack upon me?"

"The natural assumption would be: Ramus Ymph."

"And how did—or I should ask: do you know how Ramus Ymph learned that I was to return to Wysrod on this date?"

"Someone evidently told him."

"Who?"

"I have no certain knowledge. Let us drop the matter. It is essentially a side-issue—"

"Not to me! I emphasize this!"

"Yes. Well, for a moment let us discuss Eiselbar and your findings there. I take it you have something to report?"

"I do indeed. In connection with the second half of my payment, there seems to be some disagreement as to whether the amount was two or three thousand toldecks—"

Nai the Hever interposed an apparently idle question. "How much palladium did you bring home?"

"A trivial side-issue, to use your words."

Nai the Hever wearily brought forth an envelope, which he tossed to Jubal. "Two thousand toldecks."

Jubal flicked through the notes. "No doubt you are recording my remarks?"

Nai the Hever inclined his head.

"Then I must speak deliberately." He paused as Flanish brought a tray of tea and wafers, then quietly departed.

"I arrived at the city of Kyash. It is a remarkable place, quite unlike Wysrod, and the Eisels are no less extraordinary. They ignore both caste and ilk, and gauge a stranger's quality only by the depth of his pocketbook. The system is straightforward, and the folk are congenial, if rather too gregarious. Their music still rings in my ears."

Nai the Hever, gravely sipping tea, offered no comment.

"I took accommodation at the Hotel Gandolfo. Ramus Ymph was not known there. I made further inquiries, without result. Then on a merchandise counter, to my astonishment, I noticed a Djan rug. I discovered that Ramus Ymph, using the name 'Husler Arphenteil', had brought a considerable number of Djan rugs to Kyash, hoping to sell them to the tourists.

"He seems to have met with very little success—perhaps none whatever. The question arises, why should Ramus Ymph, of an important ilk, sell rugs at Kyash? Why should he require Gaean SVU instead of solid toldecks?" Jubal looked inquiringly at Nai the Hever. "Can you guess?"

"No."

"Ramus Ymph has an absolutely grand ambition. He wishes to buy a space-yacht: specifically that type known as the Sagittarius."

"How did you learn this?"

"The idle remark of a rug dealer induced me to visit a space-yacht agency, where I made indirect inquiries."

Nai the Hever made the faint sibilant sound which indicated his approval. "So what then?"

"Eventually I located Ramus Ymph's hotel, only to learn that he had departed. I traced him to the People's Joy Tourist Agency, and once again missed him: he had gone on a tour of the outer planets. I decided to follow and joined a module of forty tourists en route to Zalmyre. This was the only feasible procedure; a single traveler can find no accommodation, as all facilities are calculated for groups of forty.

"The experience was memorable. My thirty-nine fellows were enthusiastic and gay. They were frequently intoxicated and made a great deal of noise. The music was incessant."

"Ramus Ymph submitted himself to this treatment?" asked Nai the Hever in amazement.

"So I am given to understand, though he went in company with a certain Husler Wolmer, who owns the agency. I suspect that he hopes to sell his rugs to the People's Joy Tourist Agency, or otherwise earn the funds he requires for his Sagittarius."

"Did you, then, encounter Ramus Ymph on Zalmyre?"

"By the very nature of the system, I could not do so. The modules move from place to place, one following the other. I could not escape my module in order to join Ramus Ymph's, not even temporarily. I was forced to pick up scraps of information as we moved. These items were meager and essentially meaningless. He was described as an alert and interested tourist, making no complaints, destroying no property, discarding a minimum of litter across the countryside. He was not considered congenial, and certain folk resented his habits of authority. The Eisels are not only gregarious; they are dedicated egalitarians, and what is good enough for one is good enough for all."

Nai the Hever showed a small veiled smile. "So you never met Ramus Ymph?"

Jubal made a gesture, counseling Nai the Hever to patience. "The A-116 Module, or the 'Jolly Wayfarers', as we called ourselves, toured Zalmyre in a glass-domed capsule, stabilized for comfort, air-conditioned, equipped with a refreshment bar, television panes, and individual music suffusers. We drifted down the Orgobats River, each night stopping at a riverside lodge, where we were provided entertainment, gambling facilities, the services of a masseuse or masseur, and souvenir photographs. We visited the Iron-tree Grove, where each of us was allowed to inscribe a leaf. We inspected a Khret-Hurde settlement, which is a society of two disparate indigenous races, interacting to their mutual advantage. They tolerate tourists, but refuse to perform eccentric dances, fertility rites, or shamanistic marvels, and the Jolly Wayfarers thought them somewhat dull. We arrived at Sunset Cape on an ocean whose name I forget, where the group enjoyed a carnival masque with staff escorts and a gala banquet.

"Eventually we returned to the space-port. Ramus Ymph's module, 'the Dauntless Bluebirds', had already arrived and were awaiting the ship. I naturally searched for Ramus Ymph, but he was no longer a member of the group. Somewhere along the route he had detached himself from the tour. I put discreet questions to Husler Wolmer, but found him impenetrable.

"At Kyash I returned to the Gandolfo, to consider my next tactic. I had hardly arrived before two gentlemen came to see me. They identified themselves as officials of the Peace and Tranquility Bureau. I asked them if they were not, in fact, police agents, and they admitted that functionally the roles were similar. They began to question me. Why had I so consistently misrepresented myself? Why had I used so many different names? What was my interest in rugs, not to mention space-yachts and Husler Wolmer?

"I expressed indignation. Was this not Eiselbar, where a visitor could do as he liked, so long as he neither destroyed property nor shoplifted? True, to a degree, they told me, but in order to maintain such an atmosphere of careless irresponsibility, they kept everyone under a quiet but comprehensive surveillance.

"We fell into a philosophical discussion. The egalitarian society, so they explained, is characterized by placidity, order, and the willingness of each individual to restrict himself to his allotted set of perquisites. Such conditions were not automatic, so I was assured, and even many of the tourists confused liberty with license. Since the PTB could not act without knowledge, comprehensive surveillance and detailed records were a necessity.

"In some puzzlement I asked, 'What of the therapeutic sexual resorts, where people go to purge themselves of warps and inhibitions? Surely in this case...?'

"'Every activity is monitored, photographed and recorded,' I was told, 'to the ultimate benefit of the innocent tourist. Troublesome persons, of course, can sharply be brought to heel by any of several means.'

"They returned to my particular case. Were they to understand that I refused to explain my conduct?

"I had already explained it, I told them: the idle caprice of a tourist.

"They replied that I was definitely not the sort of tourist they wanted; they advised me to leave the planet before I tripped while crossing a walkway and fell among the slimes. Such accidents often happened to disruptive persons, especially those who disturbed persons like Husler Wolmer.

"I saw the wisdom of their advice and caught the first ship for Frinsse, and so returned to Wysrod."

Nai the Hever said in a measured voice: "I must say that you have returned with rather more information than I expected. Let us now discuss the matter in full detail."

"Willingly," said Jubal, "but first, if you please, to a subject of direct concern to me. Someone who has access to information regarding my movements is transmitting this information to Ramus Ymph."

"So it would seem," said Nai the Hever thoughtfully.

"Why are you so calm? It is a serious matter! We must identify this person and subject him—or her—to an exacting punishment."

"The suggestion has its value," said Nai the Hever crisply. "Still, I cannot always work as directly as I might wish. The Ymphs are extremely powerful. Delicate equilibriums restrict my options and I cannot simply bring justice to bear, even if I wanted to do so."

"Oh? Why should you not?"

Nai the Hever showed his cold smile. "Because all the mysteries surrounding Ramus Ymph have not yet been illuminated. Those which remain might be most important of all. For instance, how does he transport himself back and forth to Eiselbar? Our reconnaissance on several occasions has observed space-ships putting into Skay, ships never noted on the official register. We are sensitive and anxious in regard to mysterious space-ships. The immediate speculation, that Ramus Ymph is a Binadary, seems absurd. Still, where did he secure the rugs which he attempted to sell on Eiselbar?"

"Why not merely invite Ramus Ymph here for a cup of tea and ask him to explain?"

"The idea has the virtue of simplicity," said Nai the Hever gravely. "I confess that it had not occurred to me. I am always reluctant to pull on strings until I learn where they lead and to what they are attached." He rose to his feet to indicate that the conference was at an end. "Tomorrow we will analyze your report in greater detail. For now—"

"One further matter: I would like to inquire as to my current status and salary."

Nai the Hever tugged at his pale chin. "For a week or so you had better remain inactive, until we learn whether or not your trip has repercussions. D3 cannot afford to employ a person even nominally guilty of crime; our budget is already minimal."

"But I am guilty of no crime!" exclaimed Jubal in amazement.

"True, but someone might make a vindictive assertion that you had engaged in criminal migration and had transgressed the Alien Influence Act."

"In that case your document specifically exculpates me. I acted as an agent of the state."

"Just so. Still, why provoke a useless confrontation? Let us see what develops. If, in due course, no one challenges your presence in Wysrod, then you may resume your previous routine."

"My salary continues, needless to say?"

Nai the Hever hesitated. "It is not the usual practise." He raised his hand as Jubal started to speak. "But in this case I suppose we must sidestep regulations."

"What increment may I expect?"

Nai the Hever spoke with an edge to his voice. "As I have already made clear, you must reconcile yourself to the usual rise through the ranks. Your present salary is quite adequate to a person of your caste and condition. Incidentally, since we are discussing money, where is the surplus palladium?"

"I left it at the depot. Here is my accounting." Jubal passed across a sheet of paper.

Nai the Hever glanced at the entries. "Hm. I see that you did not stint yourself. 'Gandolfo Hotel'—the place must be a shrine of sybaritic luxury."

"It is the best hotel of Kyash."

"Hmf. 'Rent of wig'. I am perplexed. Why need you rent a wig?"

"Disguise."

"And this entry: 'Regalement—five farthings'?" Nai the Hever looked at Jubal with raised eyebrows.

"I observed the Mountain Veil Waterfall on Zalmyre through a pay telescope. It might be argued that I should bear this expense myself."

Nai the Hever put the paper aside. "I will study your accounts when I have more time. For now that is all."

"One more question: what of these attempts on my life?"

"I doubt if they will continue. Still, it might be wise to change your lodgings, or undertake a walking tour of the Glistelamet Dells."

Four days later Nai the Hever summoned Jubal to his office in the Parloury. He wasted no time on preliminaries. "You must truncate your holiday; I am able to employ you in a manner which will not compromise the agency. The matter concerns Ramus Ymph. During the middle of the night he departed Athander by scape. We have traced him to a village named Forloke, in Glentlin."

"That is near the lodge of my Uncle Vaidro!"

"Exactly. He has taken lodging at Dintelsbell Inn, using the name Serje Estope. You are now to visit your uncle. We must assume that Ramus Ymph is acquainted with your appearance; and you must alter yourself, with a clouche,* face pigment, a short black beard."

"And then?"

"I am interested in his activities. Why has he gone to Glentlin, of all places?"

Jubal reflected a moment. "I have never mentioned my first encounter with Ramus Ymph. It may or may not relate to his present movements. He tried to buy Cape Junchion from the Droads."

"When did this occur?"

Jubal described the circumstances. Nai the Hever listened with no more expression than a lizard. "You should have spoken of this before."

"It did not seem noteworthy."

"All facts have meaning." Nai the Hever caused a map of Glentlin to be projected upon the wall-pane. "Show me Droad House and Cape Junchion."

"Here and here. Junchion is both the westernmost and northernmost point of Thaery."

Nai the Hever considered the map. "As you say, the matter may be of no consequence. In any event, my personal scape will fly you to Forloke. You observe Ramus Ymph and inquire into his activities. Remain inconspicuous and avoid personal contact."

Just after sunset, with the sky a welter of purple, cerise, red and blue, Jubal approached Dintelsbell Inn on the

---

*Close-fitting casque or bonnet, of leather or felt, with a pointed crown and earflaps, an article worn by Glint mountaineers

outskirts of Forloke. He entered, requested accommodation and was conveyed to a pleasant chamber under the gables with a view down Wildwater Valley. He dined in a near-empty hall, notable only for the absence of Ramus Ymph. Later, in the tavern, a few idle inquiries revealed that Ramus Ymph had departed the premises earlier the same day, leaving no information as to his future movements, nor had he communicated anything during his stay other than a few terse civilities.

Jubal went to the telephone and called the mountain lodge of his Uncle Vaidro. Vaidro's face appeared on the pane. He stared uncomprehendingly at the dark face with its short dark beard.

"This is Jubal. I have modified my appearance. I am calling from Forloke."

"What are you doing here in Glentlin?" Vaidro's voice was curt.

"I plan to visit your lodge tomorrow morning; I will explain everything then."

"Best that you come tonight. I leave for Droad House early."

"Of course, if you are unable to delay. But would not tomorrow morning be more convenient?"

"You have not heard the news then?"

"Evidently not."

"You remember Cadmus off-Droad and his claim to the Droad succession?"

"Very well."

"He has made his claim good. He brought perrupters to Droad House; he has killed your brother Trewe, and now occupies the premises."

"In that case I will kill him."

"You may be deprived of the privilege. I have notified the kindred. There is to be bloodshed at Droad House."

"I will come at once."

Chapter 13

The era of warfare among the Glint clans had departed but traditions lingered, and blood-feuds spanning generations still persisted. If Cadmus off-Droad thought that the assertion of his claims would excite only a nominal response, the immediate convergence of the Droad kindred upon Droad House must have come as a dampening surprise.

Droad House occupied the center of a meadow, to the side of the River Alys, with steep forested hills surrounding.

For Cadmus off-Droad to arrive during the night with his company of masked* perrupters, to pound on the door, to present his demands to Trewe Droad and then, upon Trewe's defiance, to shoot him dead, was the work of only minutes; the process of quelling Trewe's children and killing the most obstreperous required a further ten minutes; and then, Cadmus off-Droad considered that

---

*The usually mild Djan, when isolated from his fellows, is apt to become a rogue. When solitary Djan are recruited as perrupters, they are required to wear masks, to prevent them from establishing normal social relationships with their fellows, to the detriment of their fighting qualities.

the best part of his work was finished—at, after all, a very small cost.

Cadmus off-Droad, a man obsessed rather than depraved, stood a foot taller than most of his fellow men. The hair clung close to his huge head in yellow-gray knots; his eyes, under lowering brows and shaggy ledges of hair, glimmered dull as the eyes of a dead fish. Enormous hands swung loose as if dangling on chains; his knees bulged forward and he stood with a bent crooked posture. Cadmus had brooded the better part of his life on the trivial technicality which had elevated Trewe to rank and debased Cadmus. He had now righted the wrong and he was confident that the world in due course would accept his point of view.

At noon on the day following his assault upon Droad House, he was summoned to the telephone by the cowed chamberlain. Vaidro Droad's face stared at him. "The entire ilk is gathering. Will you come forth from Droad House unarmed to meet your fate, or will you fight and take innocent men to death with you?"

Cadmus at first failed to gather the import of the words. "I am the Droad; I have taken what is mine. There can be no talk of death."

"You are a murderer, and the ilk will tear you into pieces."

"Let them try," said Cadmus indifferently. "Do you think me helpless? I have weapons—as many as I need. I have perrupters in unlimited numbers; when one falls two others will take his place."

"The kindred are coming down from the mountains," said Vaidro, "by the tens and dozens and scores and hundreds. Tomorrow Droad House will be surrounded."

"Surround away. I hold hostages: Zonne Droad, and the daughters."

"And Bessel Droad?"

"He attacked me and destroyed my scape; I killed him in return. Whoever else troubles me I will kill, and I will burn his house. Do not think me weak and helpless; I have resources of which you are ignorant and I will wipe the mountains clean. I am Cadmus the Droad and Droad House is mine—and you must accept the fact."

The pane went dark.

Vaidro and Jubal stood in the shade of a low stone-oak on the flanks of Broken Mountain. A quarter-mile distant and a hundred yards below was Droad House.

Vaidro said: "He has about fifty perrupters. Cadmus is quite right. We can't attack without losing a hundred men. We can't starve him out because we starve the hostages. But we can wait. And do you know what will happen?"

"Cadmus will become very restless."

"True. He will find that his prize has lost its savor. But also his perrupters will start making squares. This is unavoidable. And then they will be useless."

"So he cannot afford to wait. And therefore he will attack."

"That was his threat. He said he would wipe the mountains clean of the Droad Kinship."

"Not with fifty perrupters."

"Which suggests that he commands more perrupters elsewhere."

"The obvious approach would be down the Aubrey Gulch from Grandmother Pass. This is the nearest route from Djanad to Droad House."

"We should set out scouts and arrange for ambushes."

"If Ramus Ymph has involved himself, as I suspect, he will also bring pressure to bear, from one direction or another: perhaps above."

"Then you must communicate with Nai the Hever. Ramus Ymph lies within his range of interest."

At the nearby Trestle Glen Inn, Jubal made telephone contact with Nai the Hever, and described the events at Droad House.

Nai the Hever seemed abstracted. He listened with only lackluster interest. "This is no concern of D3. The Glints must police their own irruptions."

"Let me restate certain facts," said Jubal. "Cadmus off-Droad arrived in a scape, which was certainly not his property, and which has now been destroyed. He expects reinforcements. I suggest that Ramus Ymph, in return for Cape Junchion, has agreed to provide decisive support."

Nai the Hever made a soft sound of displeasure. "By reinforcements, you presumably mean perrupters...We'll order out a patrol. The reinforcements will not arrive." Nai the Hever reached to break the connection, then, as if by afterthought, said: "If possible, take Cadmus Droad alive."

"Circumstances will decide that matter."

A day passed, a night and a morning. The Droad kindred, as Vaidro had promised, surrounded Droad House, and every hour saw the arrival of fresh contingents from the remote homesteads. From Ballas Harbor had been brought a pair of antique long-rifles, once used to guard the tide-locks. They were battered and corroded, but still capable of projecting a succession of explosive pellets along a line of light. These, mounted on North

Knoll and Pomegranate Knoll, commanded the approach to Droad House.

At noon Cadmus Droad showed his bulk briefly on one of the upper balconies. He peered right, then left from under lowering eyebrows, raised his clenched fist high in a savage awkward gesture, then stepped back into the shadows.

Halfway through the afternoon Jubal again telephoned Nai the Hever and presented a report, brief because there was nothing much to tell. Once again Nai the Hever seemed only marginally interested in the siege. He troubled himself to remark that Ramus Ymph had not yet shown himself either at Ymph House, or at Gais Palace in the Athander Fens. Almost incidentally, he revealed that patrol craft had discovered and destroyed a large force of perrupters in Great Shome Valley, along the route to Droad House.

Vaidro exulted at the news. "Cadmus is caught in a cleft stick. He can neither back up nor go forward. If he attacks he will be slaughtered. If he delays, his troops will set up housekeeping. I will call him again and give him the option of surrender."

Cadmus Droad's face, appearing on the pane, was haggard and drawn, like the skull of a bison a month dead in the desert.

"Your reinforcements will never arrive," said Vaidro. "Did you know this?"

Cadmus merely stared. At last a husky growling sound rose from his throat. "I need no reinforcements. I am resident in my rightful house. Come put me out."

"There is no hurry."

"Do you think to starve us? First to die will be Zonne

Droad and the girl-children. We will eat them and throw their bones from the balcony."

"We do not intend to starve you. But let me issue to you a threat. You are to die now: this is ordained. It is as sure as the black hulk of Skay. But if your hostages are harmed, you will die very slowly. Those are your choices."

Cadmus Droad produced a harsh guffaw. "There are surprises due you! It is I who will be stating conditions!" The pane abruptly went blank.

Vaidro slowly turned away. "He is a madman. But he is not yet beaten. He still reckons resources."

"Which means Ramus Ymph."

"If Ramus Ymph is in fact involved. We have no direct proof."

"The indirect proof is sufficient."

"Perhaps so. In any case, Cadmus will not be reinforced by land. So we must watch the sky."

At sunset clouds swelled up the northern sky; dusk was accompanied by heavy triple- and quadruple-pronged slashes of lightning. Two hours later the clouds had dissipated, and the sky was dark and clear. At midnight a gibbous Skay rose in the east.

High over Droad House appeared a dark shape: at first no more than a blur, then, as it swiftly settled, a solid object.

The object had not gone unnoticed. Vaidro had altered the single functioning range-finder of the two long-rifles to contrive a crude sensor; before the shape had taken on optical substance, Vaidro had watched the dull pink mark descending the range-finder scale.

Vaidro shook Jubal awake from his dozing. "Look up yonder."

The object settled with a kind of deliberate stealth. From the top of Plum Tree Knoll came the beam of a searchlight; the object was revealed as a large scape, paneled with an improvised armor of detervan shields. From the long-rifles issued two more beams of syrupy green-yellow light to touch the scape. Along each beam, like bubbles in a glass tube, sped a succession of luminous pellets. The scape became an instant incandescent flourish of falling fragments.

"Cadmus Droad's expectations have diminished," said Jubal. "There went his reinforcements."

"More likely his vehicle of escape," said Vaidro. "Now he will attempt a sortie; he no longer has other options. I predict that within one half hour he will try his destiny."

"And I predict that he will make his thrust through the back garden. He will burst through the garvet hedge and strike for the Low Woods."

"I believe that you are right, and we will prepare for his coming."

A half hour passed, each minute quivering with an almost audible vibration. Nervous flickering lights showed from Droad House, where ordinarily there were none. Among the knolls and under the trees shapes shifted position, muttered together, looked to their weapons.

In the garvet hedge a gap quietly folded aside to leave a stubble of cut stumps. Through the gap ran the perrupters, holding shields before them. Behind lumbered Cadmus off-Droad, a four-foot cutlass in one hand, a six-pound cudger gun in the other. To his right loomed another man, clad like the perrupters in black, with a black war-mask concealing his face, a black grandee's hat pulled low over his forehead.

Searchlights from right and left illuminated the meadow. Cudger guns snapped and stuttered. The perrupters, shifting their shields to protect themselves, doggedly drove for the Low Woods. Gun-fire found chinks between the shields; perrupters fell, opening new gaps; suddenly the firm ranks became a welter of struggling bodies. Cadmus bawled frantic curses, to see his plans go awry. The kindred advanced from cover. Vaidro yelled: "Stay back! Stay back! They still have their weapons!"

Cadmus halted, then turned to retreat to Droad House. The kindred, abandoning caution, rushed forward to block his line of retreat, firing cudger guns as they came. Vaidro cried: "Take Cadmus alive! Don't kill the brute! Take him alive!"

The perrupters, dazzled by the searchlights, turned away from the Low Woods to attack their tormentors, but were almost immediately destroyed.

Cadmus threw down his shield. Swinging his cutlass and brandishing his gun, he strode over the corpses, hacking at the kindred, shooting, shouting.

"Take him alive!" screamed Vaidro. "Don't kill the beast!"

"Take me alive if you can!" bawled Cadmus. "Approach, you Droad dog-spit! Taste my steel!"

"I am here," said Jubal.

Cadmus pointed the six-pound cudger gun. "Now you shall be nowhere."

Jubal threw his knife. The blade glimmered instantly in the searchlight, plunged into Cadmus' wrist. The gun dropped from shocked fingers. Cadmus stooped to grope.

Droads swarmed upon him. Cadmus toppled, fell with a grunt, then heaved himself erect, shaking off his enemies. Once more he held the gun. He aimed at Jubal; Vaidro sadly shot him through the forehead. Cadmus stalked backward on stiff legs, then toppled.

"A pity," said Vaidro. "It could not be avoided."

Jubal recovered his knife, then turned to search the field. The man in the black hat had retreated into Droad House. The kindred stood panting, staring numbly down at the dead.

Into the glare of the searchlight stepped the man in the black mask. By her ankles he held aloft a wailing girl six years old: Sanket Droad. In the other hand he held a knife, the point pressed against the child's face. Behind came three other men, each clasping a hostage: Zonne Droad and two girls of eight and ten, Merliew and Theodel.

The masked man stood full in the beam of the searchlight. An awed hush stilled the kindred.

The man called in a trumpet voice: "Detain me, no one! I intend to walk from here, and all must stand aside. Else these four females feel the knife!"

Jubal slowly came forward. He halted ten feet from the masked man. "Do you know me?"

"I do not care to know you. Stand aside!"

"I am Jubal Droad. Put down the girl and fight me with your knife. If you live, you will go free, I swear it."

"I will go free regardless." The masked man's voice rang sharp and clear, as if he were singing. He stepped forward. Jubal stood in his way. The man, slinging the girl over his shoulder, clasped her so that the point of the blade touched her eye.

Something flickered bright in the searchlight—a thrown

knife hurtling in from the side, across Jubal's shoulder, toward the masked man's throat, only to clatter and glance from the gorget of his mask. He cried out in rage, his muscles tensed. The knife in his hands jerked and the girl screamed, her eyeball pierced.

Jubal lunged forward, but a pair of hands seized him and held him back. From over his shoulder came Vaidro's voice. "Let him go! He will kill her!"

"He has blinded her!"

"She has one eye left. Bide your time. Thaery is not all so large."

The man stepped past Jubal; picking his way stiff-legged across the corpses, he entered the shade of Low Woods and disappeared. No one went after.

Flames roared high from Droad House. Jubal watched for a moment or two, then turned and walked away.

At noon of the following day, Jubal called Nai the Hever from the telephone at the Trestle Glen Inn.

"Cadmus off-Droad is dead. Ramus Ymph escaped."

"You identified Ramus Ymph?"

"I am certain it was he."

"You are certain? Or do you merely entertain a suspicion?"

"My suspicions are very strong indeed, even though he wore a mask."

"Then you cannot absolutely identify him."

"No."

After a moment Nai the Hever said: "Are you not now the Droad chieftain, or sachem, whatever you call your notables? Why are you so glum?"

Jubal stared into the still white face. "You expect me

to rejoice at my brother's death and the burning of my ancestral home?"

"It is sensible to enjoy the gains arising from any situation."

"I have no gains to enjoy. Only losses."

"You must be the judge of this. What, precisely, were the circumstances?"

"Ramus Ymph brought Cadmus off-Droad to Droad House in his scape. They murdered my brother, but my brother's son destroyed the scape. Its wreckage rests on the meadow. My kindred at once surrounded Droad House and Ramus Ymph became a prisoner, along with Cadmus off-Droad. He ordered in a relief force from Djanad; it was intercepted by your patrol. In desperation he called for an armored scape in hopes of escaping. We destroyed this scape and killed Cadmus. Ramus Ymph found himself in most unhappy circumstances. He used my brother's widow and her three daughters as hostages to free himself."

"What then? Assuming that this man was indeed Ramus Ymph."

"He traveled down the Flant River to Arrasp; under the cliffs he abandoned his hostages and went aboard a National felucca. He put to sea and I traced him no further."

"You have fulfilled the essential requirements of your mission," said Nai the Hever. "We now suspect the nature of Ramus Ymph's activities. But his motives still elude us. Why, for instance, is Ramus Ymph anxious to acquire Cape Junchion? From your base in Glentlin you will now explore his movements in detail and try to explicate these motives."

"Ramus Ymph has departed Glentlin, taking his

motives with him," said Jubal. "There is nothing more to be learned here. I am anxious to discuss my suspicions with Ramus Ymph face to face."

Nai the Hever sighed. "Your Glint instincts are most inconvenient. This confrontation you envision is not presently useful; in fact your presence in Wysrod now becomes an actual embarrassment."

Jubal stared into the pale face. He carefully controlled the timbre of his own voice. "Why an embarrassment?"

"Events have occurred; perspectives have shifted. Specifically, the Ymphs have learned that you are a returned emigrant, and wish to deal with you on this basis. I prefer you to remain in Glentlin."

"How did they learn of this?"

"We can only speculate."

"Exactly. I speculate that only two persons knew of my mission to Kyash: yourself and your daughter."

"There were others," said Nai the Hever airily. "Certain officers of the Space Navy, for instance."

"They did not know my name."

"These affairs inevitably excite comment."

"Still, if Ramus Ymph is a returned emigrant, they can scarcely insist upon prosecuting me, especially since I am under your protection."

Nai the Hever smiled faintly. "All is not so simple. You have made yourself obnoxious to the Ymphs, who are the first ilk of Wysrod. It is always reckless to challenge powerful men, unless you can bring to bear a compensating power. This is simple reality."

"The murder of my brother and the burning of my home: is this not also real?"

"The past is never real," said Nai the Hever. "The flux

of events is the present; unless you are able to enforce a pattern upon this flux, it is wiser not to try."

Jubal said slowly: "All this is undoubtedly correct."

Nai the Hever prepared to break contact, then said: "It is barely possible that you may be approached—either by Ramus Ymph or through an intermediary—in regard to Cape Junchion. If this occurs, communicate with me at once."

"I will certainly do so."

Chapter 14

R agged clouds hurried across the night sky,
alternately obscuring and revealing the bright
half-face of Skay. The air carried dampness and
the Hever House gardens smelled fresh of wet foliage
and damp soil.

An ancient hack entered the grounds; a dark-haired
man alighted, wearing splendid garments of pale purple
and white. A black quat with a dangling amethyst
covered his head; a short black cape hung down his back.
He ordered the driver to wait, then walked with long
elastic strides to the front entrance.

A footman slid aside the tall doors; Flanish advanced
even more sedately than usual. He peered uncertainly at
the newcomer. "Good evening, Your Honor?" The rising
intonation conveyed the absence of recognition.

"Please inform the Nobilissimus that I have arrived,
and wish to consult with him on an urgent matter."

"Certainly, sir; what name shall I announce?"

"Merely mention a connection with the name 'Ramus
Ymph'."

Flanish departed. The dark-haired man waited in the
foyer, where first he inspected his reflection in a mirror,

then went to a carved satin-wood table, idly to turn the pages of a journal.

He heard steps and looked up to see Mieltrude descending the sweeping stairs. She was dressed for a party, in white, with a dark blue jacket. Clasping her pale hair was a circlet of enormous sapphires, the color and luminosity of her eyes. She paused to look at the visitor, at first artlessly, with only casual attention, then with increasing perplexity.

The visitor made a polite salute. "Good evening, Lady Mieltrude."

"Good evening...I'm sure that I know you—but I can't recall your name."

"Our acquaintance has been only casual."

"Yes, but I am puzzled. I feel..." She studied his face, then gave a sudden incredulous laugh. "The Glint!" She laughed again. "Now I remember your name. Jubal Droad!" She crossed the hall, paused to look back over her shoulder.

Nai the Hever appeared in the doorway. He inspected Jubal with an expression of mild inquiry. Mieltrude murmured something to him with a choking bubbling laugh, and Nai the Hever's expression changed to grim amusement. He spoke to Jubal. "Your regalia is most splendid, but why are you here?"

"As for the regalia," said Jubal, "the last time I came to Wysrod I was met at the airport. Now I come secretly and disguised as one of your local jackanapes."

"But did I not clearly intimate that you were to remain in Glentlin?"

Jubal said: "I came to Wysrod for three reasons: to report to you, to collect my salary, and in accordance with your advice."

"I advised you to come to Wysrod?"

"Indirectly, yes. You told me to explore Ramus Ymph's movements in detail and to discover his motives."

"I specified that you confine your researches to Glentlin."

"No. You instructed me to conduct the inquiry from my base in Glentlin. I did so. The trail led here to Wysrod."

"The instructions perhaps were ambiguous. I suggest that you leave at once. As for your salary, it is nonexistent; you are no longer employed by D3."

"For what reason?"

"Because the Ymphs have you under proscription, and I can tolerate no embarrassment at this moment."

"Does it mean nothing that Ramus Ymph murdered my brother, burned my home and blinded my brother's daughter?"

Nai the Hever made a skeptical sound. "Derson Ymph informs me that Ramus has been resting at Sarpentine Lodge for over three weeks. I am forced to accept his word."

"In the face of proof to the contrary?"

"What sort of proof?"

"I told you that he had taken ship at Arrasp. I arrived at Wysrod a week ago, and I have made inquiries and gained some very interesting information. First I located the felucca in which Ramus Ymph sailed; I have obtained an identification from the master of the vessel, and in the presence of witnesses I have lifted the fingerprints of Ramus Ymph from the cabin of the ship. This is definite proof that Ramus Ymph participated in the assault upon Droad House."

Nai the Hever made a sour sound. "The information

is futile and irrelevant. I want placid relations with the Ymphs until certain patterns reveal themselves. That time is not now." He touched his chin with a forefinger, on which glowed a milk-opal. "From sheerest curiosity, what else have you learned?"

"Am I definitely employed by D3 or not?"

Nai the Hever looked at him blankly. "Definitely not! Have I not explained my position?"

"Then I will reserve the information and act as I see fit."

Nai the Hever gave an almost petulant shrug. "If you bring yourself to the attention of the Ymphs, they will prosecute you as a renegade emigrant."

"What of that? You will assert the official nature of my business."

"And reveal the extent of my knowledge? By no means. You will be forced to pay the penalty, I warn you."

"But you cannot disavow our signed and witnessed contract."

"Of course I can, and I will."

"Your signature is quite clear."

"Indeed? Have you examined the contract lately?"

"Why should I? I recall the terminology."

"Please do so now."

"If you wish." Jubal brought forth a sheaf of papers, from which he selected an envelope. "This is the document."

"Open the envelope."

Jubal turned Nai the Hever a questioning glance, then broke the seal, lifted the flap, withdrew the paper and unfolded it—to reveal a virgin blankness. Jubal dubiously studied the empty sheet.

Nai the Hever said: "The ink has evaporated, and with it your privileged capacity. You should know that I could never give such a document currency. I would be compromising myself."

"I thought along these same lines," said Jubal. "On that same night I made several notarized and certified copies of the original." He selected another paper. "Here is one of them. It is a legal document."

Nai the Hever inspected the paper, the corners of his mouth drooping. "This places a different light on the matter. You are an unscrupulous man. I must consider a moment."

Mieltrude made a flippant gesture. "I am already late; I must go. Flanish! Call my hack!"

"Not just yet, if you please," said Nai the Hever. "I want a word with you, on tactics which perhaps must be revised. You will see our messenger tonight?"

"Yes."

Nai the Hever looked at Jubal with a speculative expression. "You are at your old address?"

"Why do you ask?"

"It is not important. Call me tomorrow; we will formulate a policy. I can tell you no more now."

"What of my salary?"

"It continues, of course."

"In view of past services, I request an increase to, let us say, forty-five toldecks a week."

"This may well turn out to be possible," said Nai the Hever mildly. "Goodnight."

Jubal departed the house unescorted by footman or major-domo. Clouds still wandered across the vast bright half-face of Skay; Skay-light waxed and waned, and perhaps infected Jubal with its influence. He thought of

Mieltrude descending the stairs, of her amusement and her over-the-shoulder glance as she started from the foyer; of Nai the Hever's bland duplicities and Mieltrude's careless connivance. He stared up at Skay, and became charged with an emotion to which no name could be attached, one which he had never felt before: sad-sweet longing mingled with passion and reckless resolve. What use was his one, single life if he did not use it bravely? Instead of departing Hever House and proceeding about his affairs, he went to his hack and called the driver down from his seat. "I have decided to play a joke upon my friends. Here is ten toldecks; I will drive the hack; you go to the Hexagram Café, near Travan Square and wait there for me."

The driver looked from Jubal to the ten toldecks and back to Jubal. "How shall I convey myself to the Hexagram Café?"

"Walk, run, ride a hack; however you like."

"But you may wreck the hack!"

"I am a careful man. Your hack will be safe."

"Ten toldecks is truly not enough."

"Here: five more. Now off with you."

With backward glances the driver departed on foot. Jubal took the hack to the entrance portal and waited.

Silence across the Cham, which presently refined to near-silence, as near-imperceptible sounds impinged on the ear: the creak of gyjits in the damp mold; the sibilant murmur of a garden fountain; a similar sound, even fainter, generated by the city Wysrod itself.

Ten minutes passed. Down the lane came a hack. Jubal stepped into the driveway and waved it to a halt. "The call was a mistake," he told the driver. "Another hack had already been summoned." He gave the driver a tol-deck. "This is for your pains."

"Very well, sir, and thank you." The hackman turned his vehicle and drove away.

Jubal turned up the collar of his cape and pulled the quat down over his forehead. He drove the hack up to Hever House and halted in the shadow of the portal.

The door slid aside, Mieltrude came out. She ran to the hack, jumped in, settled herself. "Take me to Bazenant House, up around Mathis Mount."

Jubal drove the hack up the lane and out upon Cham Way. He turned down the Baunder, toward the Marine Parade, rather than continuing through the hills. Mieltrude, lost in meditation, failed to notice for several minutes, then cried out: "You're going the wrong way! I want to go to Bazenant House, on Mathis Mount!"

Jubal stopped the hack and turned to face Mieltrude. "There is no mistake."

"Jubal Droad the Glint!"

"Yes; please don't protest." He selected another of his documents. "This is the warrant I took out against you, for your illegal attempt to have me murdered. It has not been challenged, contested nor voided. It is valid, and it stipulates two years penal servitude, at the discretion of the plaintiff, together with two blows of the rat-whisk daily. I now serve this warrant upon you. For the next two years, you will be at my orders. I am sorry that you will miss your party but tonight—not ten minutes ago—I decided to take you into custody. It is a convenient time, especially since your father was planning to have me killed tomorrow. Possibly with your connivance. He must now reconsider."

Mieltrude said in a hushed voice: "How do you know all this?"

Jubal chuckled. "He agreed to a raise in my salary."

"You happen to be wrong. He knew that the Ymphs would kill you. Why should he exert himself?"

"It amounts to the same thing," said Jubal. "His plans include my corpse. My plans do not. Therefore, I choose this time to serve the warrant. The punishment, incidentally, is well-deserved."

"Do you really intend to inflict this upon me?"

"Of course. It is the force of the law."

"I need hardly point out that you will ultimately be the loser."

"What have I to lose?"

"Your life."

"Death comes to everyone: Droad, Ymph and Hever alike. Meanwhile you will gain useful experience, for which you may eventually thank me."

Mieltrude said nothing.

"Now be so good as to sit upon the floor, so that I may spare you the indignity of gag, blindfold and bonds."

Mieltrude tried to leap from the hack. Jubal seized her and bore her to the floor. For a moment they wrestled and then she lay subdued, her face inches from Jubal's, both panting, her hair disarranged, her tart flower fragrance tingling in his nostrils.

He slowly drew back. She lay quiet, and did not move when he started the hack. Looking up and out the window she could see only foliage brushing across the half-face of Skay, the occasional glimmer of street-lighting.

The hack turned cautiously into a shadowed lane, halted. Mieltrude could hear the whisper of Duskerl Bay's modest surf.

Jubal opened the door. "Out with you."

Mieltrude, drawing herself into a sitting position, eased out of the hack. She recognized the area: the beach near Sea-Wrack Inn. Behind her glowed the lights of Wysrod; the bay sparkled with Skay-light; across loomed the long bulk of the Cham.

"This way."

Mieltrude looked over her shoulder. If she screamed someone might well hear and, at the very least, summon the security patrol. But the Glint, standing by her elbow, would allow no such signal. He took her arm; she cringed from the contact.

They walked down the beach. Jubal picked up a line and drew it in, hand over hand, while Mieltrude stood hunched and shivering. A dinghy grated stern-first up on the beach. Jubal motioned. Mieltrude gingerly climbed aboard; Jubal pushed off through the surf, jumped upon the stern, then, clambering to the bow, heaved on another line. The dinghy presently drifted alongside an anchored vessel.

At Jubal's signal, Mieltrude climbed aboard, gloomy and apprehensive, at last fully aware of her plight.

She suddenly ran to the rail and heedless of grinder-fish tried to dive overboard; Jubal caught her around the waist and hauled her back. "You are attempting an illegal act. The warrant stipulates two daily strokes of the rat-whisk. If you want it applied smartly upon your bare person, continue along these lines."

Mieltrude found the concept so outrageous that she stood quivering, at a loss for words.

"This boat is under my command," said Jubal expansively. "It is named *Clanche*. You will undergo at least a period of your servitude aboard this boat."

Mieltrude, now more than half-confused, stammered: "I thought you were a Glint; how can you be a National?"

"I have chartered this boat with toldecks paid me by your father. I am still a Glint, and the Droad of Droad House."

"You are a despicable scoundrel!" cried Mieltrude bitterly, "and you shall be punished."

"You dare to call me a scoundrel? You performed the crime, not I!"

Mieltrude, recovering her composure, became stonily silent.

"I will reassure you to this extent," said Jubal. "You need not fear a violation of your person. Unlike yourself, your father and your friend Ramus Ymph, I have scruples. For the foreseeable future you will serve aboard the *Clanche* as cook and stewardess."

"Show me your warrant."

"Step aft into the cabin."

By the glow of the night-light Mieltrude inspected the warrant. Then she went to sit in the armchair of carved Dohobay skaneel. "How much money do you want?"

In a precise voice Jubal asked: "How much are you prepared to pay?"

She reckoned a moment. "For three thousand toldecks you can hire two stewards."

"True. But is this justice?"

Mieltrude made an impatient gesture. "Let us talk of reality."

"I was hoping you would get around to doing so. Look around this cabin. This table, these chairs, the berth yonder, the rug on the deck: this is reality. Even your father would concede this. This warrant derives from your insolent disregard of my life and comfort. The warrant is reality. If you continue your insolence you will feel the rat-whisk. That too is reality."

Mieltrude listened without expression. She said in an almost idle voice: "I am not afraid of your rat-whisk. It means nothing to me. I will do as I see fit. I will not become your servant."

"In that case," said Jubal graciously, "you will remain in my custody until you decide to begin your penal servitude. Please notify me when the moment arrives; we will reckon two years from that instant."

Mieltrude sat brooding. She was younger than he had supposed, thought Jubal, and certainly younger than Sune Mircea, whose charms, in retrospect, seemed somewhat obvious. To rollick Sune around a bed no doubt would be a rewarding experience for nerve, gland and body. To stand by the taffrail of the *Clanche* with Mieltrude, shoulders touching, watching the night sky and the monstrous rising of Skay, would be an exhilaration of the soul, to linger a lifetime. Talk of rat-whisks was simply preposterous.

Mieltrude finally spoke. "I assume that you are putting to sea?"

"Very likely."

"So now you run away," sneered Mieltrude, "Glint that you are, who breathed such fine fire against Ramus Ymph!"

Jubal managed a bitter laugh. "Yes, I run away, or rather sail away. Wysrod is too hot for me, thanks to you and your father."

"These are matters beyond your comprehension."

"I doubt that. Still, I have not forgotten Ramus Ymph; far from it."

"What do you propose to do?"

"I don't know yet. I won't know until my mate comes aboard."

"And who is your mate?"

"The owner of the *Clanche*. He should be aboard by dawn. And now, observe this locker. It is commodious, dark and not too uncomfortable. It is ventilated and it has a stout lock on the door. Inside, please. I must go ashore, to return the hack, and to arrange that a message be delivered to your father. He will be relieved to learn that you are in good hands. In with you! I will be no more than an hour; don't be frightened."

An hour later Jubal returned. He opened the door to the locker; Mieltrude, huddled in a corner, looked at him with the dilated gaze of a wild creature.

"Come," said Jubal gruffly. He took her hand and lifted her erect. "Tonight you can sleep on the couch yonder."

Mieltrude wordlessly went to the berth. She sat down and watched as Jubal drew a chair in front of the door and after dimming the lamp settled himself.

Mieltrude turned and half sitting, half kneeling, looked miserably through the porthole out across the Skay-lit bay. The Cham interposed its dark long hulk between bay and sky. Mieltrude thought she could see the lights of Hever House, and tears welled into her eyes. She half turned her head toward Jubal, then resolutely controlled her emotion. She was Mieltrude Hever of Hever House and she would never plead with a Glint. Especially not with Jubal Droad.

Skay crossed the sky, settled past the stern casements and down behind the Cham. The wind shifted; the *Clanche* swung about its mooring and the casements faced eastward.

The night passed. A silver-purple luster formed on the eastern sky and became a dull magenta glow. Mora rose into the sky. Something thudded against the hull and from the deck came the scrape of footsteps.

Mieltrude sat up on the berth, aroused by sudden hope. Could this be succor? Jubal no longer occupied the chair. She ran to the door; it refused to open. She peered through a porthole across the midship deck.

A tall harsh-faced man clambered aboard and went to sit beside Jubal on the hatch. He wore loose gray breeches and a faded blue singlet. Mieltrude knew him for a National.

Shrack spoke to Jubal. "I sat with Torquasso at the Chambros Inn and tried to match him cup for cup. I failed. He is a vast man. He has been cautioned to hold his tongue, but he despises Ramus Ymph and regaled me with all he knows. His charter extends for two months; this you know. He has provisioned the *Farwerl;* it is ready to sail. At midnight he was delivered a message. Torquasso is a perverse man. All evening he deplored his fate: hanging on the anchor at the whim of Ramus Ymph. The message distressed him no less. He is notified to be ready for immediate departure and suddenly Torquasso discovers that he has not yet drunk dry the taverns of Wysrod. When I left, he was hard at work."

"Did the message mention a destination?"

"No." Noticing a flicker of motion at the porthole, Shrack remarked, "I see that you have shipped a passenger."

Already Jubal had begun to wonder at his Skay-madness of the night before. He felt defensive and a trifle foolish. "I served my warrant and took the person into custody."

"It is your affair," said Shrack.

"I'm not sure that the act was really sensible, but what's done is done. And," said Jubal shortly, "now I must take care of her."

"Nai the Hever will be annoyed, but evidently you do not care."

The observation in some small degree vitalized Jubal's morale.

"I am annoyed with Nai the Hever."

"Well, we shall see whose annoyance proves the more pungent. Incidentally, a dinghy is leaving the dock. It might be bound for the *Farwerl*, and that hulk in the stern is surely Torquasso...No, Torquasso is aboard the *Farwerl*; his dinghy is at the stern."

The two men climbed to the quarterdeck. Shrack took up a macroscope and studied the dinghy. He handed the instrument to Jubal.

"It is Ramus Ymph," said Jubal.

"He is taking pains not to be recognized."

"I know him by the way he sits...By the emanation which leaves his body."

"So—what now?"

Jubal watched the dinghy sliding across the bay. "Theoretically I am still in the employ of D3. Nai the Hever would certainly instruct me to follow and investigate. We shall do so."

Shrack put the macroscope back in the locker. "If you want to follow the *Farwerl* we should put out to sea now, then we won't be quite so obvious."

Jubal ran forward and cast off the mooring cable. The *Clanche* swung in a lazy half-circle and powered to the tidal lock. Twenty minutes later the vessel heaved to the surges of the Long Ocean. The kites went aloft, the wake bubbled astern, and Mieltrude's hopes either of rescue or Jubal coming to his senses were finally dashed.

Chapter 15

The dawn wind had died; the Long Ocean heaved to the slow swells which moved forever around the world. The surface showed glossy, viscous as waterglass. The black hills and pale violet sky reflected in wavering liquid distortions, and Mora was a dancing puddle of molten purple-white.

Shrack, barefoot at the control pedestal, had warped the kites to those few breaths of air which disturbed the calm. Already Shrack had put aside his shore garments and wore only a cocked black cap and baggy black breeches cut short above the knee. Jubal also had shed his blouse; beside Shrack's oak-brown torso his skin appeared pale.

The *Clanche* drifted to the north, making barely perceptible headway. "When the *Farwerl* leaves the locks," said Shrack, "we'll have the wind on her, what wind there is, and we can follow any course without obtruding upon Torquasso's attention. Here he comes now."

The tide-locks opened; the *Farwerl* moved out into the ocean. Up went the great kites, pink and pale blue; coincidentally the air began to stir and the *Farwerl* moved sedately forward.

Shrack watched through the macroscope. "He's sailing a free reach. Maybe a point or two on the wind."

"Where will that take him?"

Shrack indicated the chart. "See for yourself."

Jubal studied the chart. "They'll make the Dohobay coast east of Wellas, unless they're bound for the Sea of Storms."

"They're not, or Torquasso would be on power, with kites folded, to make easting during this calm. I guess Wellas."

"What would Ramus Ymph want in Wellas?"

"What would he want in Dohobay or in the Sea of Storms?"

"True." Jubal swung down the companion-way to the main deck and slid back the door to the great cabin. Mieltrude sat in the carved skaneel armchair. Jubal stared at her from the doorway, fighting qualms of guilt and shame. How pitiful this resplendent airy creature of silver and gold, miserably caught in a trap. Jubal angrily marshaled before his conscience her bill of offenses and steeled himself to obduracy. He entered the cabin and seated himself on the settee. "Why does Ramus Ymph sail to Wellas?"

Mieltrude's reply was indifferent and almost flippant. "The Nationals won't allow him to fly."

"What reasons could he have?"

"I haven't the slightest idea."

"You can't even guess?"

Mieltrude ignored the question. "What are your intentions regarding me?"

"I've already explained."

"I want to communicate with my father."

Jubal shook his head. "Impractical, from my point of view."

Mieltrude's mouth drooped. "If I were to explain all the circumstances, would you take me back to Wysrod?"

Jubal leaned back on the settee. "You can justify your conduct?"

"If necessary."

"I'll listen, but I promise nothing in return."

"Listen then. My father as you know commands the operations of D3. He carries a great responsibility and he must act accordingly. For several years he has known of strange and secret influences, which he is unable to comprehend.

"Meanwhile Ramus Ymph has been acting most peculiarly, and my father wondered if the mysteries were connected. In order to learn, he has been studying Ramus Ymph in a most careful manner. He dares ask no questions; he cannot threaten or molest; he can only apply cautious stimulation, such as barring Ramus Ymph from the Servantry."

"And you participate in this stimulation."

Mieltrude said evenly, "I fail to understand you."

"You became betrothed to him. The match was either one of affection, convenience—or stimulation."

"'Stimulation' is not an appropriate word."

"But it applies, in the present sense?"

"Yes."

"And you contrived an illegal warrant against me to make the 'stimulation' more convincing?"

"I contrived nothing. I did not sign the warrant."

"Your signature is there."

"Do you believe I would deliberately sign such a document against a stranger, no matter how crass? The warrant carried my signature only because someone had signed my name."

"I have heard otherwise."

"From whom?"

"Someone who was on the scene."

"That would be Sune Mircea," said Mieltrude without emphasis. "She is Ramus Ymph's mistress, and utterly unprincipled. She signed my name to the warrant herself; she has a talent for such tricks."

"I thought her to be your dear friend."

"I find it hard to tolerate her. My father insists that we seem intimate so that he may transfer apparently secret information to Ramus Ymph. I am supposed to prattle secrets indiscreetly, and Sune takes them to Ramus Ymph."

"Such as the fact of my return from Eiselbar so that I might be murdered?"

"That information came through Ymphs in the Space Force. But you had not yet been connected either with D3 or with the affair at the Parloury. Since my father could tolerate no conflict with the Ymphs, you must be rusticated to Glentlin, and by unhappy chance you ran afoul of Ramus Ymph in connection with Cape Junchion."

"And what does he want with Cape Junchion?"

"That is one of the mysteries."

"Come with me." He took her up to the quarterdeck. Five miles to the northwest sailed the *Farwerl*, pink and blue kites leaning over the horizon. Shrack stood at the pedestal holding his own green and blue kites low and slack, but gradually easing the helm in order to follow the *Farwerl*.

Jubal spoke to Shrack. "They hold the same course?"

"They're directly for Erdstone Pool: two weeks voyage." He jerked his thumb toward Mieltrude, at the taffrail, looking wistfully back along the wake toward Thaery. "What of her?"

"She claims to be innocent. She says the warrant was forged with her name."

"Anyone would say the same."

"I believe her."

Shrack laughed. "Why didn't she tell you so before?"

"Simple arrogance, I suppose."

"So we turn back?"

"Never. She is secondary to Ramus Ymph." He went aft to the taffrail. The wind ruffled Mieltrude's pale hair, revealing dark gold glints and shades. "Come look at the chart," said Jubal.

She glanced at the display board. "Well?"

"There is Glentlin, terminating in Cape Junchion. Here is Wellas. What do you notice?"

Mieltrude shrugged. "They are almost opposite each other. Each extends into the Narrows, Cape Junchion from the south, Wellas from the north. There is nothing else to notice."

"Except this. Ramus Ymph tried to sequester Cape Junchion. He is now in the boat yonder, bound for Wellas."

Mieltrude examined the far kites of the *Farwerl.* "You should return to Wysrod and notify my father."

"I don't trust your father."

Mieltrude curled her lip. "Why didn't you follow his instructions? From the first time you swaggered into our house you have behaved as if you and not he were the Servant. He has been most patient with you! Do you wonder that you are out of sympathy? Now you kidnap me, and even after I have explained the situation you refuse to release me."

"I served my warrant in good faith. Perhaps, for a fact, you are guiltless; if so you should have appealed the warrant."

"It was beyond conception that you would dare serve it."

"Then you have brought the inconvenience upon yourself."

Mieltrude made no reply.

Jubal pointed to the northeast. "There sails Ramus Ymph, on another of his mysterious missions. If your father knew, he would increase my salary and order me to give chase, without regard for your convenience."

"Possibly, possibly not."

"For a fact, our goals are different. He wants me to observe Ramus Ymph and learn his secrets. I want to tow him back to Wysrod at the end of a rope."

Finding words inadequate, Mieltrude went to lean on the taffrail, to look broodingly back down the wake.

Mora rose high; the wind freshened. Swells approaching from the east lifted the *Clanche*, passed below and onward on their course around the world. The *Farwerl* had all but disappeared over the horizon. Skay rose in the east like a pale white mountain and swelled prodigiously up into the sky. Shrack overhauled the anchor winch. Mieltrude had gone to the cabin. Jubal sat on the quarterdeck, leaning back against the taffrail. Mieltrude emerged from the cabin and climbed to the quarterdeck. She gave Jubal only a cursory glance, then stood gazing at a great bank of cumulus clouds which, rearing high, eclipsed the lower limb of Skay. She still wore her party frock and pale blue slippers: an incongruous costume which somehow she managed to invest with dignity.

Jubal thought of Sune: treacherous, deceitful Sune,

beguiling him in order to aid her lover. How foolish she must have thought him! Thoughtfully he studied Mieltrude's graceful proportions. Could such a semblance also conceal duplicity?

Quite definitely yes. Already she had played falsely with Ramus Ymph, if her own statements were to be believed.

Mieltrude seemed to feel the pressure of Jubal's attention. She turned to face him. "I am curious as to my present status."

Jubal gave the question consideration, though the same question had preoccupied him during the morning. "The question becomes: do I believe your explanation?"

"I am not accustomed to having my word doubted."

"Before you're home at Wysrod you'll be accustomed to all manner of things."

Mieltrude's voice became even more frigid. "Then I must still consider myself a prisoner?"

"No," said Jubal. "Not really."

"Then you are rescinding the warrant."

"Not altogether. In fact, no."

"You should not detain me if your complaint is invalid."

"Your father has even less right to victimize me. It is, in a sense, a balance of inequity."

"And I am the scapegoat!"

"'Fulcrum' is a better word."

"So in plain words, I am still a captive."

"I took you into custody; I brought you aboard this ship; it is my responsibility to see you safely home."

"Then turn this boat around and take me home now."

"And lose Ramus Ymph? Your father would be viciously annoyed."

Mieltrude turned angrily away.

The afternoon passed; Mora sank into the west. An hour before sunset a shoal of fortress-fish approached from the west. Shrack brought the ship's gun to bear.

One of the creatures drifted to within a hundred feet of the *Clanche*, its dorsal turrets, each equipped with an eye and harpoon, rearing six feet above the boat's gunwales.

The creature swung past, each eye in turn inspecting the boat and its occupants, then veered to join its fellows.

Mieltrude watched from the quarterdeck. For the first time Jubal saw animation in her face: interest, awe, a grimace of relief when the creature cruised away. She asked Shrack: "Do they ever attack?"

"Often enough. Seventy feet is the range of its harpoons. Any closer and I would have sunk it."

Mieltrude looked around the sea with something like solemnity. "Do you often encounter danger?"

"If I remain alert I am seldom in danger. Except perhaps along the Dohobay coast where danger sometimes comes looking."

"Why visit the Dohobay coast then?"

Shrack shrugged. "It lies on the world-route. The trade is profitable, if one avoids reefs, rocks, ship-breakers, pirates."

Again Mieltrude studied the sea. "Don't you become bored with the solitude?"

Shrack shook his head. "Malaise[*] is more troublesome. The ocean is changeless. Sometimes a boat is found

---

[*]*A loose rendering of the word ankhe: futility, depression, discouragement.*

sailing by itself, with no one aboard. Malaise is always suspected."

"And do you ever feel malaise?"

"I'll feel none on this voyage."

Mieltrude glanced toward Jubal, but made no comment. Presently she said: "The *Farwerl* has disappeared. How can you follow it?"

"The *Farwerl* is steering toward Erdstone Pool. That is also our course."

"Will we see Waels at Erdstone Pool?"

"Not many. They keep to themselves."

"I am told that their irredemptibility has led them in strange directions, that they keep to themselves, worship trees, and that their Great God is a single tree, ancient as time."

"There may be truth in what you say. Every Wael tends a grove of jin trees and devotes his life to them. Just as in Thaery, there is overpopulation. Not too many Waels, but too many jin trees. They grow everywhere and there is room for little else, which makes life difficult for the Waels."

"Do you believe that they are a mixed race, of Gaean and Djan?"

"I don't know. They might even be a race mixed of men and trees. I heard of a National who raped a Wael girl. Soon after he became covered with a green moss which sprouted black flowers, and then he died."

"And did the flowers bear fruit, or seeds?"

"No one knows; he was sunk in mid-ocean."

"What is at Erdstone Pool?"

"A town of sorts, with warehouses for trade goods and boatyards along the beach. And of course Tanglefoot Tavern."

"Is this where *Farwerl* is bound?"

"So it seems."

"What could Ramus Ymph want on Wellas?"

"Maybe he wants to buy a boat."

"Unlikely."

"There's nothing else there, and they won't allow him away from the village."

"It is all very strange...Sometimes I feel as if I were dreaming."

The afternoon passed; sunset approached. Mora set in a glory of royal reds, cerise, dark blue, and finally a flush the color of the shachane flower, from which the Djan derived their purple dye.

Shrack, understanding that Jubal was too stubborn to cook for Mieltrude and that Mieltrude would starve before she troubled to feed herself, much less serve himself and Jubal, philosophically took himself to the galley and prepared a stew of meat and herbs. The three dined by lantern light on the midship deck, with a jug of soft green wine.

The wind died; the *Clanche* moved through the water on the impulse of its jectrolets. At the line of the horizon the glimmer of the *Farwerl*'s masthead-light appeared. Shrack disconnected the power and the *Clanche* ghosted by Skay-light. Jubal somewhat grudgingly cleared the galley; when he emerged Mieltrude sat on the taffrail bench with a goblet of wine while Shrack leaned against the binnacle. Jubal poured himself a mug of wine and sprawled out on the deck.

Shrack spoke of the sea-trader's life. "It is at least expansive, and a man becomes accustomed to the horizons. Routine is less insistent than one might think; in fact, I would say variety is the more typical situation, sometimes to an unnerving degree. No two places could be more disparate than, say, Jorgoso on the Sea of Chills and Ling on Great Mork, or either from Wysrod. By the time the ship puts through the Throtto, one looks forward to a placid sojourn on Duskerl Bay. It is dampening to discover that horrid affairs occur at Wysrod no less than at Lakhargo under Cape Navlus. Not long ago I discovered two insensate thugs about to murder Jubal Droad upon the authority of an illicit warrant."

Mieltrude made a fretful motion but said nothing. Shrack continued. "Two months at Wysrod is enough. It is impossible for an outsider to know the pleasures of Wysrod. The Waels are outgoing by comparison. I begin to think of the wide seas and the clouds and the eery midnights to the light of Skay and the Happy Isles lifting over the horizon. Even the Dohobay saloons have their appeal. Once more I push out through the tide-locks and set out to the west. The way around the world is long; I sail the Long Ocean. There are familiar places to visit, old friends to meet. On each occasion the friends are older and the places have changed. Or perhaps only I have changed. But when the wind is fresh and the kites are charged and the boat surges down the swells—then one forgets the Skay-lit midnights, and Jorgoso on the Sea of Chills."

Mieltrude gave her shoulders a petulant jerk. "You make your own choices. I never would have ventured on the ocean of my own volition."

"You should be grateful to Jubal Droad," Shrack told her with a grin. "Through his judgment and enterprise you are enjoying a novel experience."

"Through his intolerable presumption! He lacks all sense of proportion."

Chapter 16

Days passed: sunrises, noons, sunsets, nights lit by the phases of Skay, or dark with Zangwill Reef a pale curtain across the sky. The *Farwerl* disappeared over the horizon and was seen no more. Shrack displayed no concern, and Jubal had no choice but to accept his opinion that Erdstone Pool was the port of destination. Mieltrude gracelessly accepted a pair of short breeches and a singlet from Shrack and walked barefoot. She had no words for Jubal but conversed with Shrack when the mood came upon her.

Each day at noon Shrack marked a point on the track between Wysrod and Erdstone Pool; daily the ratio between the distance ahead and the course astern lessened, and early one morning a dark shadow appeared across the north: the coast of Wellas.

As the day advanced the wooded hills rose sharp on the sky. The sea was empty of boats and the only sign of habitation was a feather of gray smoke trailing across the sky. Shrack indicated a pair of headlands and a line of rocky islets across the water between. "Erdstone Pool. The channel is called 'the Ballows'. There is no mole, and ships can enter only at the turning of the tide. We'll go in at the end of the neap."

"I thought there was a town," said Mieltrude.

"The village is around the shore, beside the boatyards. The smoke rises from the fire under the glue cauldron; it never goes out."

"I don't see the *Farwerl*."

"She'll be inside the pool, at moorings."

"Suppose Ramus Ymph changed his mind and sailed elsewhere?"

"We'll know in about an hour."

The *Clanche* approached the Ballows. The incoming tide had flooded the harbor, but currents still swirled and snaked among the rocky islets. Shrack folded the kites and steered slowly through the sentinel rocks, into a circular bay of now placid water, ranging in color from dark blue to green. Erdstone Town flanked the beach; beyond were the boatyards and a dozen hulls in various stages of completion. A long floating pier thrust out into the pool; two ships swung to anchor; another lay alongside the pier. Shrack indicated the third ship. "The *Farwerl*."

Jubal studied the boat through the macroscope. "I see no one aboard."

"Torquasso will be at the Tanglefoot Inn, yonder along the beach. Ramus Ymph might be there as well, depending upon the urgency of his business."

"What business could Ramus Ymph have here?" muttered Mieltrude. "I suspect that you've made a foolish mistake."

"What business could Ramus Ymph have at Cape Junchion?" Jubal demanded. "Or at Kyash on Eiselbar? In any event, please keep out of sight so that he won't recognize you."

Mieltrude gracelessly moved back, into the shadows under the quarterdeck.

The *Clanche* approached the pier, a construction of timbers and buoyant tanks lashed together with cables.

Shrack eased the *Clanche* alongside; Jubal jumped ashore and made fast the mooring lines. Waels working on the beach, mending nets and turning sea-weed on drying-racks, gave him only a few incurious glances. They were lithe pale brown men with soft blunt features, of no great girth or stature, with a suggestion of the curious Djan metal-green luster playing along their skins. They wore their black hair in short loose shocks; panels of colored cloth were tied around their hips, leaving feet and torso bare.

Mieltrude became bored with the shadows under the quarterdeck. She started to climb the companion-way, but Jubal halted her. "One moment."

From the stern cabin he brought out a red and blue kerchief which he tied around Mieltrude's hair and forehead. Grinning, he looked her over, from bare feet, torn breeches and singlet to red and blue head-covering. "I doubt if you will be readily recognized."

Mieltrude asked coldly: "Am I such an amusing spectacle?"

"Enough so that Ramus Ymph won't recognize you if he walked across the deck."

Mieltrude made a scornful sound. "You had better be careful that he doesn't recognize you."

"I doubt if he'd know me if he saw me. Still, I won't run risks." He went back into the stern cabin. Mieltrude turned to Shrack. "Are you involving yourself in this business?"

"Strictly speaking, it is none of my affair," said Shrack. "Still, if one of us must lose his charter fee, I prefer that it be Torquasso."

"So now you're going ashore?"

"Seamen customarily visit Tanglefoot Tavern. We shall find Torquasso there, and perhaps Ramus Ymph."

Jubal came out upon the deck wearing baggy gray breeches, a faded pink vest, a gray stocking-cap pulled low over his forehead, to seem an earnest young lout of uncertain parentage. Shrack inspected him without comment and jumped across to the dock; Jubal followed. Shrack looked around the Pool, then called down to Mieltrude: "Keep an eye on the lines when the tide shifts. If they go taut, give them scope."

Mieltrude turned away in vexation. So now she must perform menial tasks about the vessel! What did they take her for? She watched sullenly as the two men sauntered up the dock. Then she climbed to the quarter-deck, where she commanded a wider view of the shore. Jubal and Shrack proceeded along the waterfront to a long low structure behind a leafy arbor. They paused a moment to confer, and looked back toward the *Clanche*. Mieltrude turned away and gazed off across the Pool; when she looked back, Jubal and Shrack were entering the Tanglefoot Tavern.

Mieltrude scowled and went to sit on the taffrail bench. Circumstances pleased her even less than usual. Her docility had been taken for granted. She was free to do as she liked. No one had troubled to warn her, or extract promises; she had agreed to nothing. She could walk ashore and demand sanctuary of the Wael factors. She could search out Ramus Ymph, or even throw off the moorings and sail back across the ocean to Thaery.

She considered the range of her options, but none appealed to her, and she only slouched angrily back against the taffrail in a posture which two weeks before she would never have permitted herself. Raffish clothes and raffish companions made for raffish conduct, grumbled Mieltrude to herself.

From the corner of her eye she watched Tanglefoot Tavern. Jubal Droad's mission was none of her affair. She hoped no one would be hurt. She liked Shrack well enough; after a casual fashion he respected her dignity. She had even come to regard Jubal with a grudging tolerance. She wanted neither killed or even injured; the idea gave her a queer pang. Nonetheless, the possibilities for violence were now very real. Ramus Ymph she knew to be both ruthless and reckless: a man who never forgot an injury. He would expunge Jubal Droad with vindictive delight...Thinking of Ramus Ymph, she gave her shoulders a jerk of distaste. Her father's schemes were sometimes over-intricate and often cynical. The betrothal had been more elaborate and cynical than most. Ramus Ymph, no less devious, had diligently tried to exploit the situation—all the while carrying on his affair with the unspeakable Sune. Pulled this way and that, forced to feign and dissemble, was it so strange that many of her friends thought her eccentric? What if they could see her now? The idea brought with it a flicker of sour amusement.

Time passed. The tide began to ebb; the pier settled with a groaning of wet wood. The mooring lines needed no attention, since the *Clanche* settled as well, but Mieltrude from sheer boredom slackened them anyway. There was really no reason why she could not have accompanied Jubal and Shrack to the Tanglefoot Tavern. Admittedly her makeshift disguise might not deceive Ramus Ymph. Though, of all the persons on Maske, that whom he would least likely expect at Tanglefoot Tavern would be herself.

Jubal and Shrack finally emerged from the tavern. They walked slowly to the head of the dock and paused to converse. Clearly they were not in accord. Jubal persisted in his views and Shrack reluctantly submitted. They separated, Jubal continuing along the beach, Shrack coming down the pier. Arriving at the *Clanche*, he inspected the lines and jumped down to the deck.

Mieltrude could not restrain her curiosity. She called down from the quarterdeck: "Did you find Ramus Ymph?"

"Not exactly."

"Where did Jubal Droad go?"

"Off on a madman's mission."

"That is his special talent. What is it this time?"

"Let me find a bite of food to settle my stomach; the Tanglefoot toddy has a life of its own."

Shrack brought bread and sausage from the galley. He sat down upon the hatch. "We went to the tavern and entered with caution, but we found only Torquasso. Ramus Ymph was not on the premises. We joined Torquasso and exchanged talk. Torquasso is wholly disgruntled; Ramus Ymph has been an exasperating passenger. He chartered the *Farwerl* at a minimal fee, then brought aboard stores of fine victual and drink for his exclusive use. During the morning his moods were surly but later, after a flask or two, he would become expansive, and urge Torquasso to zeal and loyalty, by which he might earn the command of a whole flotilla of boats, of a sort to amaze the Nation. Torquasso consistently declared himself content with the *Farwerl*, a preference which Ramus Ymph derided.

"When they arrived at Erdstone Pool, Ramus Ymph

arranged that the Erdstone Factor meet him at Tanglefoot Tavern.

"Torquasso, arriving at the tavern, intent upon his own business, found them secluded in a booth. Ramus Ymph first proposed, then argued, then cajoled, then took a rather stern line. The factor finally made some sort of concession, which Ramus Ymph accepted without gratitude. He summoned Torquasso. 'I cannot finalize my business here,' said Ramus Ymph. 'The factor lacks authority. I must travel to a place called Durruree. I will return in four days; be ready to sail on the tide.' He immediately departed with the factor, and Torquasso sits now at Tanglefoot Tavern, drinking toddy and renewing his friendship with the house-girls."

"What of Jubal Droad?"

"He has gone to make inquiries of the factor."

"And what then?"

"We await Ramus Ymph's return, so I expect."

"Four days? With nothing to do except stare across Erdstone Pool? Already I am bored!"

"Erdstone is not totally dull," said Shrack. "Up the lane yonder is the market, where you can deal for amethyst, sachet and magic shoes. If you wander out of town you will surely find someone dancing in his grove; by Skaylight the sight is entrancing. You can inspect the boatyards, where every plank is shaped by hand, to imaginary plans. They cut the wood into strips and then weld them to the hull with *mais*—'the stuff of life', which they keep in bottles of black glass. What is *mais*? No one knows but the Waels. If they curse a ship, the *mais* loosens in mid-ocean and the ship becomes a tangle of sticks."

"They seem a captious race. I have heard of their superstitions."

"The Waels are like no one else of Maske. Ask them about *mais*. You will hear frank and solemn remarks but learn nothing. They will pet you and comb your hair and oblige you as you like. If you hurt them they sing a strange music, and you are perplexed. But ask a Wael for truth and you are asking water to flow backward."

Mieltrude looked off to the tree-covered hills behind Erdstone Town. "How can Ramus Ymph expect to transact business with folk so capricious?"

"I can't say, knowing nothing of Ramus Ymph's business. The Waels lack food; they plant their sacred jin trees in all the good soil, and Waels say that this is how it must be. Yet, hungry men have little energy for dancing, and if Ramus Ymph can provide food to their taste, no doubt they will listen."

Mieltrude gave an irritated shrug. "I am not anxious to confront Ramus Ymph; what else but humiliation for us both? Jubal Droad does not consider my feelings; he is naïve and tiresome."

Shrack went to look along the dock. Jubal was nowhere to be seen.

Mieltrude demanded: "So now what must we do?"

"Wait."

The afternoon passed. Mora sank behind the hills into a sky the color of persimmons and plums. The tide drained Erdstone Pool, then came rushing back through the Ballows.

Shrack became uneasy. He told Mieltrude: "If Jubal Droad intends to absorb all the toddy at Tanglefoot and console all the wenches, why should he work alone? It is only fitting that I join him."

Mieltrude cried out: "Again you leave me here, at the

mercy of every skulker! I am bored sitting alone on this boat!"

Shrack considered her sidelong. "There are no skulkers at Erdstone Pool, except perhaps Torquasso. Still, come along if you're of a mind; the vessel will tend itself. Hurry; the light is fading."

"I am ready."

As they jumped from the boat to the dock they were met by a Wael youth clad only in a two-tufted red head-cloth and a white kirtle about his hips. "I carry a message for Shrack of the vessel *Clunche*."

Shrack took the message and held it up to the glow of the sky. He read, then passed the paper to Mieltrude, who glanced along the script with studied unconcern. The note read:

> *I have divined Ramus Ymph's plans. He is more wicked than you can conceive. I am going to Durruree, to thwart him before he can gain the safety of Wellas.*

Shrack spoke to the messenger: "When did you take the message?"

"During the day."

"Why did you not bring it before?"

The messenger began to move away, respectful but distrait, his mind full of the twilight. "The needful was done."

"Where is the man who gave you the message?"

"He has gone to the place we call Durruree."

"Where is this place?"

"Over the hills and through the Werwood."

"Can you take me there?"

"It is too far to go." The messenger, smiling over his

223

shoulder, went off down the dock. Presently, as if impelled by uncontrollable exuberance, he broke into a long spring-legged run and disappeared into the dusk.

Shrack muttered: "We'll still go to the Tanglefoot."

Chapter 17

J ubal rode a scape of a style out of memory. The scape, guided by some unseen system, moved in profound silence barely ten feet above the forest floor. Foliage overhead alternately obscured and revealed the great half-face of Skay. Occasionally Jubal saw wavering lights to right or left; once a lonely dancer glided away through the forest.

Jubal settled back into the cushions. He dozed, waking to wonder at the tree-tops moving above him. Skay slid across the sky. Jubal slept again. He awoke to find a gray rime in the east. A man in a three-tufted white head-cloth sat cross-legged at the end of the scape. Jubal lifted up on his elbow. The man spoke in a soft voice. "This is an important matter."

"Yes," said Jubal. "I agree to this."

"Aren't you afraid?"

"Afraid of what?"

"Of concerning yourself in affairs so important?"

Jubal blinked his eyes and wondered if he were dreaming. "I suppose so, to some extent."

"There will be a judgment, you know."

"A judgment of whom?"

"Of you."

Jubal sat up and rubbed his forehead. "I haven't done anything wrong."

"Don't be too confident. At Durruree you must never bluster."

"I'll try not to," said Jubal shortly. "When do we arrive at Durruree?"

"Later in the day. There is to be a conclave. We do not take this matter lightly."

"Why should you? It's very serious."

"What do you know of seriousness?" The Wael spoke in mild derision. "An outsider is pain to us all. Look how the leaves curl as we pass; see the branches draw aside. Your mind sends out flaming thoughts; you come through our forest like a raging comet."

Jubal peered at the man, wondering if he were mad. From below the three-tufted head-cloth round eyes dull as pebbles in a round wrinkled face looked placidly back. "Even while I sleep?" asked Jubal.

"Asleep or awake; you must learn control, so that you will not blaze through our sacred jin."

Jubal decided that polite acquiescence might most effectively soothe his eccentric companion. "I'd undertake to do so, of course, but I'll probably never again visit Durruree."

"If you bring deceit in your heart, you will never leave."

Jubal rearranged his position and looked off toward the rising sun. "I plan no deceit."

Silence. Jubal looked around; the man had disappeared. Jubal rose to his knees and peered over the side. The scape rode twenty feet above the forest floor. Horizontal beams of pale violet-tinged sunlight filtered through the trunks. Jubal saw no one, below or aloft...Puzzling. Had he been tricked by his imagination? Jubal returned to his seat. Such incidents were not to his taste, especially at this hour of the morning.

Mora rose into the sky. Jubal ate from the parcel of dried fruit which had been provided him, and drank thin sweet wine from a gourd. The scape drifted north, along the turnings and bends of the forest tunnel. These were jin trees, growing to no perceptible pattern. Jubal noticed an occasional marker or carved stake. From time to time Waels moved among the trees, posturing, ordering the ground, laving the trees with liquid from porcelain bowls.

The scape moved across a glade. Jubal turned to find the man with the three-tufted head-cloth again sitting in the bow of the scape. "I wish I knew how you do that," said Jubal.

"You would gain nothing. Every instant a million events occur one iota past the edge of your awareness. Do you believe that?"

"How can I dispute you?" Jubal answered sourly. "I know only what I can know. What I can't know, I don't know."

"Do you wish to learn?"

"Learn what?"

"That is the wrong question. 'What' is constructed by each person for himself and in spite of himself. You can only learn 'how' and sometimes an inkling of 'why'. The 'what' is merely the quality which distinguishes you from Ramus Ymph."

"I really don't understand you in the slightest degree. I suspect that I am going insane."

The man made a gesture of unconcern. "I will set your mind at ease. The cosmos is various; many environments occupy the same area. The 'whats' and 'hows' and 'whys'

227

are different each from each. All you could learn in Wellas are our local insights. Our realities are our neighbors' superstitions."

"The Waels are considered extraordinary folk; this is true enough."

"And now you endorse this opinion?"

"I feel that you are amusing yourself at my expense with tricks and riddles."

"You are not offended?"

"I am puzzled. For instance, why dance among the trees?"

"For exuberance, and joy, and solemnity. To reassure the souls who live in the trees. To assert Now, and work it into the same substance as Then."

"Still, to dance one must eat, and if the forests grow across all the fields the dancing must stop."

"The halcyon days are gone," intoned the man. "Change is in the air. Ramus Ymph rides through the Werwood, and you follow, bursting with rage, and tonight you will know your fate."

Jubal scowled. "Who are you?"

"I am the Minie."

"Why are you riding with me?"

The man made no answer and Jubal turned away in annoyance.

After a moment he glanced toward the bow, and as he had expected, the man was gone.

Through the forest, across glades and still ponds, into a land of standing rocks, up a shadowed valley, out upon a moor. Clouds drifted across the sky, almost scraping a cluster of crags, the remnants of an ancient volcanic neck.

The scape slid across the moor; crags loomed above; the scape settled to the turf beside a grove of sprawling thick-trunked trees which Jubal thought might be a variety of jin. From a low stone building came a man wearing a white three-tufted head-cloth. With a dreamer's stolid acceptance of the marvellous, Jubal saw him to be the Minie.

Jubal stepped to the ground and the Minie signaled him into the structure. "Come; refresh yourself."

Jubal entered the structure, blinking through the dimness. The Minie conducted him to a rough wooden table and indicated a bowl of porridge. "Eat."

Jubal slowly drew back the stool and seated himself. "Where is Ramus Ymph?"

"He is yonder at the place we call Zul Erdour."

Jubal tensed himself to rise but the Minie spoke in a stern voice: "Eat! Make peace with yourself; order your thoughts. The Sen will not be moved by malice."

"What is Ramus Ymph doing now?"

"He is explaining his business."

Jubal pushed the bowl aside. "How can I refute what I do not know? I want to hear the words from his own tongue." He rose to his feet. "Give me a Wael garment and a head-cloth, so that he does not recognize me; otherwise he will not state his case."

"On the peg hangs a head-cloth and a cloak."

Jubal donned the cloak and head-cloth; still dissatisfied, he dipped his hands in mud and soot and rubbed his cheeks, neck and forehead to darken his skin. The Minie beckoned him. "Follow me."

They walked up a path which led between a pair of crags and into a central glade. A dozen great trees grew to the side. Mist drifted down across the crags to swirl through the high foliage. Jubal stopped in his tracks. These were like no trees he had seen before. Each seemed an entity in itself: a massive creature of incalculable sentience, grim and domineering. In the shadows stood a dozen Waels, all watching something beyond Jubal's range of vision.

"There are the Sen," murmured the Minie. Jubal was not able to determine whether he referred to the trees or the Waels, or perhaps both. "You have arrived at the Zul Erdour," the Minie continued. "Before you leave there will be a judgment."

"I did not come here to be judged," said Jubal. "My business is with Ramus Ymph."

The Minie signed him to proceed along the path, into the shade of the trees. A bed of age-polished serpentine, as dense as jade, rose a few inches above the turf: here stood Ramus Ymph, beside a tree with a massive knotted trunk eight feet in diameter.

Ramus Ymph wore a black suit and a loose cap of dark green and red, with a black panache. He stood straight; his face glowed with fervor; his voice rang with a confident lilt.

"The scope of the plan is now before you," declared Ramus Ymph. "At specified areas along the Wellas shoreline and at several locations elsewhere, depots, or, let us say, commercial enclaves of appropriate size, are to be established, never—so it is stipulated—upon arable land. Within these places the Association undertakes to erect suitable warehouses, technical shops if necessary, and likewise housing, to whatever extent necessary, for employees, commercial agents and casual transients. At these places your goods and services will be exchanged for the commodities useful to you. In the past Wellas has carefully isolated itself from alien contact, that the unique institutions of Wellas might be preserved. I respect this ambition! Nothing will be required from the Waels except passive cooperation. We assist each other in trust and good-fellowship, to mutual advantage. There is nothing more to be said; please now give me the endorsement or the rejection of my proposal." With a polite salute to those persons present, Ramus Ymph moved to the side of the stone platform, and waited. Jubal marveled at his composure; could he not feel the stillness and awe of Zul Erdour?

The Minie stood beside Ramus Ymph, close to the Old Tree. Jubal's jaw dropped in amazement. A moment before the Minie had stood at his side. The Minie spoke in a dry voice. "We have heard your proposals with hope, since our needs are great. We would undertake such a compact without guile; as a weak and timid people, we lack flexibility. By the same token, when we reckon vice and virtue, our judgments are stark. We react with the merciless finality of the weak and timid. You are competent and strong; from you we expect candour: especially here at Zul Erdour, in the shadow of the Sen."

"Just so," said Ramus Ymph, smiling and equable. He looked past the Minie to the great tree. His eyes moved up the trunk to a great gnarl twenty feet above the ground. His face became momentarily puzzled. Jubal, following his gaze, discovered the suggestion of a human countenance in the contorted pattern of the bark. Odd.

Ramus Ymph addressed the Minie in a voice of genial reason. "Why such portentous language? I utter no perorations; I undertake no miracles; I simply place my terms before you for endorsement."

"Words spoken twice are not doubled in meaning,"

said the Minie. "Is the nature of this contract clear to all?" His gaze wandered about the glade.

With a harsh effort Jubal Droad found his voice. "I wish to ask a few questions."

The Minie inquired of Ramus Ymph: "Will you reply in all candour?"

"Willingly! Ask away!"

The Minie stared toward Jubal, who, drawn by the gaze, moved slowly forward to the base of the stone floor. Ramus Ymph watched him approach without emotion. "Ask all the questions you like."

"You have asked permission to commence commercial operations on Wellas?"

"Quite true."

"Where?"

"At various sites along the coast, perhaps in the interior, such sites not to exceed ten acres of area. I undertake neither to pre-empt arable land nor to encroach upon the sacred groves of jin. In return I am to be accorded a patent of free development."

"And what does this mean?"

"That I am to manage the enterprises without hindrance or interference."

"What kind of commercial operations do you plan?"

"Ordinary trade, to begin with. Wellas requires cereals, oils, tools and instruments, fabrics and fibers. At the new depots these will be exchanged for Wael products and services, to our mutual profit."

"Your business then is trading, pure and simple?"

"I trade, I merchandise, I perform services, I represent—but only within the precincts of my rigidly delineated enclaves. The Wael way of life need not be affected, and all construction will accord exquisitely with the landscape: such is my intent."

"How much construction do you propose?"

Ramus Ymph made an off-hand gesture. "Whatever is needed. Warehouses, transfer facilities, adequate accommodation."

"Will not even minimal construction mar the scenic grandeur of Wellas?"

"This is inevitable," said Ramus Ymph. "I would be the last to deny it. The operative word is 'minimal'. I intend only needful construction."

"What of your personnel?"

"I will employ Waels, if possible. If Waels are unable to provide the necessary services, I must naturally look elsewhere."

"You mentioned 'adequate accommodation'—what would this mean?"

Ramus Ymph gazed thoughtfully across the Zul Erdour, then darted a quick sidelong glance toward Jubal. "The term is self-explanatory."

"Agreed. But what is adequate for me might not be adequate for you. Do you intend to live in a tent behind your warehouse?"

Ramus Ymph laughed. "Something better than that. I would hope to provide decent shelter for those who need it."

"Transients? Casual passers-by? Visitors to Wellas?"

"Certainly."

"Accommodation free of charge? That is a hospitable attitude."

Ramus Ymph laughed again and shook his head. "I am hospitable to a point, but not to the extent you suggest. I intend to collect a reasonable fee for any services I provide."

"In essence then, at each of your trade depots you would be operating an inn."

"The word applies, in its broadest sense. I think we have exhausted the subject. Are there questions from anyone else? If not, I would wish to—"

"But I am not finished," said Jubal. "I am curious in regard to these 'inns'."

"There is not much more I can tell you," said Ramus Ymph. "The Association's plans are not yet detailed."

"I am trying to understand the scope of your operation. How many persons will you employ at each trading depot?"

"I can't make even an estimate."

"Your Wael employees would live in their own domiciles?"

"So I would presume."

"Each 'inn', then, would house administrative personnel: perhaps six or eight persons. Are these figures reasonable?"

Ramus Ymph shrugged. "I haven't calculated quite so closely."

"The 'inns' would accommodate, at most, a dozen persons?"

"More or less."

"Certainly not as many as eighteen?"

"I have fixed upon no formal designs. Certainly it is better to plan large than small."

"You would agree that eighteen is an upper limit?"

"Not necessarily," said Ramus Ymph testily. "I would prefer to retain flexibility."

"You might conceivably wish to accommodate more than eighteen?"

"Conceivably."

"As many as fifty."

Ramus Ymph smiled. "Now you are simply plucking figures out of the air."

"I am interested in the extent of your plans. The terms of your proposal allow a great deal of latitude."

Ramus Ymph considered a moment. "I can tell you this. I am an indefatigable optimist and I think in generous terms."

"Still, you do not intend to construct needlessly."

"Of course not. But sometimes an expansive vision is wisest in the end."

"In any event, your inns will house a maximum of how many?"

"I can't specify an exact figure."

"As many as fifty?"

"Perhaps."

"A hundred? Two hundred?"

"These are large numbers," said Ramus Ymph cautiously. "My prime concern is to create the basic fact of the depots."

"But you do not rule out 'inns' housing as many as two hundred visitors?"

"I repeat: I am an optimist and a visionary. I rule out nothing."

"But consider: not three travelers a month visit Wellas. How can even an optimist plan to erect a chain of six or eight large hotels where no need exists?"

"Travelers are unpredictable; they go anywhere if suitable accommodations and scenic attractions beckon

them. And never forget: travelers exude a golden efflu-
ent!"

"Where would they originate? Certainly not Dohobay,
nor Djanad, nor even Thaery."

Ramus Ymph's patience was wearing thin. "Are we
not straying far from our topic?"

"It must be a matter to which you have given careful
consideration. If you prefer to withhold this information—"

"This is not the case. I prefer not to waste time with
irrelevances."

"We have ample time; no one here is impatient, and
all of us are interested in the details of your scheme. For
instance, how will so many travelers arrive and depart?
By National feluccas?"

Ramus Ymph smiled wearily. "Since we are speculating—obviously not."

"Since we are speculating—who then would perform
this service?"

"Why not a fleet of luxurious modern vessels specifically designed for such a service?"

"Why not?" replied Jubal. "But what of the Nationals?
Surely they would forbid the use of their ocean?"

Ramus Ymph smiled scornfully. "It is quite preposterous that a handful of backward mariners should control
the world's ocean. The Association would not allow it."

"You have organized the Association?"

"True. I have powerful friends."

"They are interested in your planned developments?"

"Very much so. They will provide all necessary
capital."

"Who are the other members of this syndicate?"

"Their names would mean nothing to you." Ramus

Ymph, either uneasy or self-conscious, tugged at his mustache. "We comprise an earnest and energetic group. I give you my assurance of this!"

"I would like to learn more about your syndicate. It is based at Wysrod?"

"This is really confidential information!"

Jubal smilingly shook his head. "Under the circumstances no pertinent information can be considered confidential."

From the Minie's still face came an utterance: "You must disclose all information."

Ramus Ymph recovered his poise. "I have nothing to hide. My associates are based at Kyash, on the planet Eiselbar; they are competent and highly experienced; you need have no fears on this score. Every year millions of tourists visit Eiselbar, where they are efficiently housed, transported and entertained."

"This information provides a new perspective upon your proposal," said Jubal.

"Not really," said Ramus Ymph. "We are interested in profit. The Eisel techniques are demonstrably profitable."

"Evidently you will not confine your operations to Wellas?"

"Quite correct. Dohobay is an interesting region, and the Happy Isles are well adapted to our program."

"Despite the opposition of the Nationals, and doubtless the Thariots?"

Ramus Ymph gave a disinterested shrug. "What can they do? With modern weaponry, we can coerce the Nationals and intimidate the Thariots."

"By 'we' do you mean your Association, or the Pan-Djan, or—perhaps—someone else?"

Ramus Ymph stared at Jubal in consternation.

Jubal asked: "What are the motives of your allies? Do you know?"

Ramus Ymph blurted: "You are no Wael! Where have I met you before?"

"On the High Trail. In the Parloury chambers. At Droad House."

The Minie, standing almost against the trunk of the Old Tree, said, "The discussion need proceed no further." He faced Jubal, who involuntarily drew back. "Return to Erdstone Pool; go back to Thaery and do what you must do there."

Jubal indicated Ramus Ymph. "What of him?"

"It is essential that he leaves Wellas. He may not grow here. You must in no way impede his going."

Jubal turned away and walked heavy-footed across the glade. Where the trail passed through the crags he turned to look back. The Minie stood beside the Old Tree, contemplating Ramus Ymph, who moved his lips in speech without producing sound, like a man under water; and again the sensation of unreality came to bemuse Jubal's brain. True fact or hallucination? The dozen somber folk who had stood watching from the shade: where were they? Nowhere to be seen... Below the Old Tree stood the Minie. Jubal looked from the high gnarled bulge which somehow resembled a human countenance down to the face of the Minie. Slowly Jubal turned away and without clear perception found his way down the path...He stopped short. What was that? A hoarse exclamation... Jubal listened. The sound was not repeated.

Chapter 18

A band of pre-dawn violet circled the horizon. Skay was a huge black disk on the foreglow, like the negative image of a sun. The scape slid down a dark valley, fragrant with dew and damp leaves, and arrived at Erdstone Pool just as Mora lifted into the sky.

Folk were up and about at Tanglefoot Tavern. Jubal walked stiffly into the common-room and was served hot pepper-broth in a tall bowl. Through the windows he noted that Erdstone Pool was at low tide. Water trickled across the mud-flats and only a languid current passed through the Ballows. The *Clanche* idled at her moorings. The *Farwerl* was nowhere to be seen.

Jubal tilted up the bowl and finished the broth. Departing the tavern, he walked down the dock to the *Clanche* and jumped aboard.

He went directly to the galley, brewed tea and heated a dish of stew, which he took out on deck and devoured with great appetite. Shrack came aft from the forecastle. He poured himself a mug of tea and joined Jubal on the hatch. "So you're back."

"Where's Torquasso?"

"He left yesterday."

"That's bad news," said Jubal in a dismal voice. "When can we sail?"

"The tide is just starting. Not until noon, at the earliest."

Mieltrude appeared from the great cabin, sleepy and
disheveled. She studied Jubal a moment. "Where is Ramus
Ymph?"

"Over the hills."

Mieltrude came to sit on the hatch.

"What happened?"

"It's a long story. And it's not over yet." Jubal poured
himself another mug of tea and told of events at
Durruree.

In a hushed voice Mieltrude asked: "What will they
do to him?"

"Nothing nice, I suspect."

The three sat silent.

"I want to leave here," said Mieltrude. "This is a
frightening place."

"I want to leave too," said Jubal. "Before anything else
happens."

"What could happen?"

"I don't know."

"At noon when the tide turns we'll sail," said Shrack.
For a period the three sat watching the water surge
through the Ballows. The pier, groaning and creaking,
rose to the flood; the *Clanche* tugged against the mooring
lines.

Jubal, looking toward the shore, gave a croak of frus-
tration. "Noon is too late."

Four men walked slowly from Erdstone Town: the
Erdstone Factor, Ramus Ymph and a pair of somber
Waels. They turned out along the pier. Ramus Ymph,
dazed and uncertain, walked on limp legs.

The four men halted beside the *Clanche*. Jubal ran to

the rail, waving his arms in remonstration. "He is not our passenger! Stand back!"

"He is Thariot and you are Thariot. Take him to Wysrod." The Waels thrust Ramus Ymph across to the deck of the *Clanche*, where he stood glaring blankly first in one direction then another.

"He is not our responsibility!" declared Jubal. "Take him back!"

"He must not grow on Wellas."

"We did not bring him here; we don't want him aboard!"

The Factor studied Jubal a moment, then appraised the *Clanche*. "Your vessel was built here at Erdstone, and fixed with our good *mais*."

"True," said Shrack, suddenly glum.

"Do you wish it to convey you safely across the ocean?"

"Yes indeed; no question about that."

"Then you will take Ramus Ymph to Wysrod."

"We will be happy to oblige you," said Shrack.

"Bind him well and constrict his motion. When he buds, he will become excitable."

The Waels returned to Erdstone Town. Ramus Ymph stood as before, glaring at no one in particular. Shrack finally stirred himself. From the forepeak he brought a pliable metal cable which he shackled in a double bond around Ramus Ymph's neck and waist, then secured the other end to the mast.

At noon the tide reached its height. The *Clanche* sailed out the Ballows and southward across the Long Ocean.

On the second day awareness returned to Ramus Ymph. In dead silence he took stock of his surroundings, noting his constriction with puzzlement and dismay. He looked at Jubal in slow recognition which became a flush of rage; when Mieltrude emerged from the aft cabin he watched in slack-jawed amazement as she climbed to the quarterdeck. But he made no statement, uttered no words, as if he had become quite dumb. He tested his bonds, carefully studied the wrap of the cable around the mast, then looked bleakly off across the ocean. Shrack brought him food and drink, which he consumed without words. Overcome by revulsion, Jubal remained on the quarterdeck. Mieltrude, ignoring everyone, sat glooming on the taffrail bench.

On the morning of the sixth day Ramus Ymph became restive. He walked stiff-legged back and forth across the hatch to the extent of his tether, pausing from time to time to rub his legs and chest. On the eighth day he had torn away his shirt, in order to examine the stipple of dark spots which had appeared on his skin.

The *Clanche* drove south, the great driver-kites taut to the thrust of the trade wind. Mieltrude secluded herself in the after cabin or huddled on the taffrail bench. She spoke as little as possible to Shrack and not at all to Jubal. Only when descending the companion-way, when she could not do otherwise, did she turn her eyes upon Ramus Ymph. Jubal kept her under inconspicuous observation. He had never been able to divine her moods, now even less than ever.

On the tenth day Ramus Ymph became excitable. He swung his arms, beat his fists against his bare stomach, clawed at his legs, where the black spots had become nodules, like dark wens. Shrack dissolved analgesic tablets in wine and served the potion to Ramus Ymph with his midday meal, and for a few hours Ramus Ymph became relatively calm. However, at the midnight rising of Skay he began to hiss through his teeth; looking down from the quarterdeck, Jubal and Shrack saw him brandishing his arms toward the monstrous globe in a frenzy of supplication.

On the day following, he tore away all of his garments. Nodules thronged upon his skin, showing a gunmetal-green luster. Shrack tried to administer another dose of analgesic but Ramus Ymph ignored both food and drink, and stood naked on the hatch. The hot sunlight played on his skin and he became rigid, eyes staring glassily, without apparent focus.

His calmness persisted throughout the night, but at dawn he set up a baleful rasping of the throat.

Mora rose into the sky. Mieltrude came out upon deck. Ramus Ymph lunged like a ferocious animal. The cable jerked him backward and threw him to the deck. He bounded erect, apparently without hurt or pain. Mieltrude scurried up the companion-way, then forced herself to look back at Ramus Ymph. He had become a disturbing sight. The hair was falling from his scalp; his skin had dulled to an ashen green-gray color; the nodules were like black-green acorns. Mieltrude's composure collapsed. Her mouth sagged; tears ran down her cheeks. She turned and ran to the taffrail, where she sat with her hands gripping her hair and her eyes squeezed shut.

Jubal and Shrack muttered together in undertones. Jubal said: "It is no more than an act of mercy to drop him over the side."

"For him, but not for us. Did not the Factor say 'Take him to Wysrod'?"

"The Factor is far away."

243

"What of the Minie and your journey by night?"

"How could they dissolve your glue from so great a distance?"

"If I knew," said Shrack, "I would rule the Nation."

Jubal said heavily, "Wysrod it is. How long?"

"Two more days and two more nights."

They looked from the corners of their eyes toward Ramus Ymph. Jubal asked hollowly: "Do you believe it?"

"Oh yes," said Shrack. "I make no trouble of that."

On the following morning Ramus Ymph stood stiff on the hatch. His hair was totally gone; his bald pate showed a coarse and wrinkled texture. Other changes were evident. His nose had splayed and flattened; his eyes had retreated behind wads of coarse tissue. Some of the nodules had broken, to show fibrous green cores.

The day passed. Mora settled into the sea between a sad procession of clouds; purple evening became night. Ramus Ymph's stertorous gasps began to produce odd secondary sounds: squeaks and a throttled fluting tone.

Mieltrude suddenly burst from the cabin and ran wide-eyed up to the quarterdeck, where Jubal and Shrack sat together. The stern-light shone into her face, accentuating hollow cheeks and strained mouth. She cried out: "You must not let him suffer so! It is horrible! The sounds madden me!"

"Control yourself a few hours more," growled Shrack. "Tomorrow we arrive at Wysrod."

"What effect is this? He is no longer Ramus Ymph; he is a creature in torment! No one deserves so much!"

Jubal asked in a dreary voice: "What can we do except kill him?"

"Give him drugs to ease the pain!"

"I have dosed both his food and drink," said Shrack. "He takes neither."

"Then—kill him!"

Jubal shook his head. "We agreed to take him to Wysrod. I am afraid of the Minie."

"You are afraid when the Minie is so far?"

"Yes, very much so."

"What can he do at such a distance?"

"I don't care to learn."

"This is really incredible!"

"Not so," said Shrack. "If he chooses, he can dissolve the glue." He indicated the dark sea. "And all of us would be floundering out there in the wet, kicking at grinders and slaverfish. The Minie must be obeyed."

"True." A plangent vibration at the edge of audibility. The three looked startled at each other: who had spoken? A stay thrummed in the wind; perhaps here had been the source of the sound.

After a pause Mieltrude spoke in a subdued voice: "And when we reach Wysrod, then what?"

"That is for your father to decide," said Jubal. "I have telephoned Wysrod. He will be on hand when we arrive."

"Does he know I am returning?"

"I expect so. I did not think to inform him."

Mieltrude scowled through the dark. "Am I so negligible, of such trifling concern to everyone, that no one troubles to mention my name?"

"You are in my custody; he knows you are safe."

"I do not intend to heed this ridiculous formality!"

"Do as you like," said Jubal gloomily. "I am bored with it myself. I don't want your custody any longer."

Mieltrude struggled for words, and finding none, sat silent. For some paradoxical reason a pulse of warm emotion came over her: sympathy, affection, gratitude; she was urged to touch Jubal and made a sudden uncharacteristic move, which, equally abruptly, she restrained. Turning away, she sat wondering at the secret currents of her subconscious.

The sounds from the main deck, muffled by wind and the flow of water, were barely perceptible. Mieltrude hunched her shoulders. "What time will we arrive?"

"Middle morning."

Mieltrude sat a few indecisive moments, then went below to the cabin, averting her eyes from the stiff shape on the hatch.

Dawn illuminated the sky. Across the southern horizon extended a dark smudge: Thaery; by the presence of land the emptiness of sea and sky was emphasized. Mora rose, and the shore was revealed in detail. Due south the Cham reached a tree-shadowed arm around Duskerl Bay; beyond spread the gray texture of Wysrod. The *Clanche*, with all kites drawing, drove onward with ponderous and fateful motion. On the afterdeck Jubal, Shrack, and Mieltrude gazed shoreward, each in greater or lesser degree oppressed and silent. As for the half-vegetative entity on the hatch, his eyes were already glazed over with a dim green crust. He had lost the flexible use of his muscles; he no longer uttered sounds. Small green sheafs protruded from the nodes; these, stimulated by the sunlight, began to burgeon.

The *Clanche* passed through the tide-locks into Duskerl Bay, and presently, with folded kites, drew alongside the main jetty, where stood Nai the Hever with Eyvant Dasduke and a number of other folk. Jubal threw ashore mooring lines; the *Clanche* came to rest. Mieltrude jumped ashore and ran to her father. With a trembling finger she pointed to Ramus Ymph, now completely shrouded under blue-green leaves.

Jubal spoke to the stiff shape. "Ramus Ymph! Do you hear me?"

The figure evinced no comprehension. The eyes, dull as cusps of green marble, were barely visible behind the leaves. Shrack stepped up on the hatch, loosed the shackle and threw off the cable.

Ramus Ymph jerked his legs. On swift small steps he tottered to the gap in the rail, leaves rustling as he moved. He lurched ashore in desperate haste; onlookers drew aside. He stumbled to the park beside the esplanade, stepped into a bed of loose soil, twisted his feet until they were covered with moist dirt to the ankles. With an agonized effort he raised his arms on high, groaning and creaking, contorting his body, and in this position he became immobile. The leaves, fully extended to the sunlight, covered his face.

Someone exhaled: a shuddering suspiration. Eyvant Dasduke muttered a soft curse. Nai the Hever turned his head toward Jubal, and the pale eyes, sometimes so mild-seeming, showed the luster of steel. "No doubt that you have a great deal to tell me," said Nai the Hever.

"I have no reason to tell you anything."

"If you please," said Nai the Hever, "let us avoid a tiresome dispute, which can only cause an inconvenience and delay."

"Just as you like," said Jubal. "But if you recall—"

"Yes, yes! Your status, your precious stipend." Nai the Hever spoke in an even voice, without acerbity. He glanced toward the blue-green tree. "I suggest that we conduct our business elsewhere. The Ymphs will shortly be arriving in force. At the very least they will be impelled to extravagant rhetoric. Let us continue the discussion at Hever House where we will not be disturbed."

"Am I then to understand—"

"Yes, yes; whatever you like! At Hever House!"

Jubal gave a grim nod. "Very well. I need five minutes to make arrangements with my friend Shrack and I will meet you there."

Chapter 19

N ai the Hever awaited Jubal in the foyer, standing erect and still, and showing only a trace of that ironic urbanity which Jubal had come to expect. "The morning-room is pleasant at this hour," said Nai the Hever. "Shall we conduct our business there?"

"Wherever you like." Jubal had determined to match Nai the Hever's ease of manner with his own.

"This way then."

By a white-paneled hall, across a succession of three-life Djan rugs, woven of stained cobweb, they came to a chamber beside an antique garden. Nai the Hever indicated a chair of carved white faiole. "Will you take refreshment? Perhaps a gill of this excellent Brown-bottle? Or spirits of larch?"

"Larch, if you please."

Nai the Hever poured tincture into goblets, then, sitting back, he watched Jubal through half-closed eyes. "You are comfortable?" He pushed forward a tray. "These pastilles are delicious; they are imported from Bazan. Or perhaps another gill of spirits?"

"If you please; I am emotionally and physically exhausted; I feel a pleasant relaxation. My mind, however, functions quite clearly."

"This is often the case. And I am glad to find you in such evident health. May I ask as to your future plans?"

Jubal pulled thoughtfully at his chin. "On this topic I would welcome your advice. Do you feel that I can make a satisfactory career at D3?"

Nai the Hever gave the matter consideration. "I can at least say this: your old post has not yet been filled."

"I was never discharged," said Jubal. "In fact—before I forget—I must collect my back pay, which was fixed at forty-five toldecks a week."

"Some such figure was mentioned. Still—"

"In fact, if I am to continue at D3, I would hope for an increment."

"Really, your desires exceed reality! Forty-five toldecks is more than adequate compensation, for the present at least!"

"Very well. I am not a man to wrangle over a few toldecks. Perhaps you will write me out a contract. Please use my stylus and this paper which I have brought for the purpose."

Nai the Hever allowed himself to chuckle. "For once you must trust my good faith. Shall we now discuss Ramus Ymph?"

Jubal came to the end of his account, and for several moments there was silence in the room, as Nai the Hever, standing beside the windows, mulled the matter over. Then he returned to his chair and fixed his quicksilver eyes upon Jubal. "What conclusions do you draw from these events?"

Jubal deliberated a moment or two. "The Waels are not to be trifled with: I am convinced of this. They are a most peculiar people, with urgent problems, but their religious convictions—if this is the proper term—impel them to aggravate these problems."

"Then you consider their convictions impractical?"

Jubal shrugged. "I don't see the need for so many jin trees—but then, I am not a Wael. Perhaps they know their own needs best; for a fact they think different thoughts than I do. I am still bewildered by what I have seen. I suppose that I might have been confused by mentalistic tricks, but if not, what then? It gives one pause to wonder."

"Quite so," said Nai the Hever. "In addition to these metaphysical mysteries, several practical matters call for explanation, and these may be the most significant aspects of the entire episode. For instance, how could Ramus Ymph hope to nullify the hostility of the Nationals, even in concert with the People's Joy Tourist Agency? How could he coerce us, the Thariots? Who would supply such forceful persuasion?"

"The Pan-Djan?" suggested Jubal without conviction.

"They would hardly want to introduce new foreigners to Maske," said Nai the Hever.

"A pity that we can't put a question or two to Ramus Ymph," said Jubal. "Perhaps Husler Wolmer might yield the information."

Nai the Hever nodded. "I am considering such an inquiry. In fact—"

Jubal raised his hand in quick remonstrance. "Please do not ask me to return to Eiselbar; the music still rings in my ears. This time send Eyvant Dasduke."

"Eyvant Dasduke? I cannot spare him, and I am beginning to appreciate your objectivity, blunt though it may be. In fact, I already have in mind another mission for you. But enough for today. You are exhausted and in no mood to learn of new tasks."

"True. But I must discuss another matter. By fault of Ramus Ymph, Droad House is in ruins! Since Ramus Ymph is now no more than a garden ornament, without financial resources—"

Nai the Hever showed a crooked smile. "Do not deceive yourself! He is far more than you suppose! The Ymph ilk will make the most of him!"

"Then I must demand a settlement from the Ymphs!"

Nai the Hever stared in speechless wonder. Finally he asked: "Do you value your life?"

"Certainly."

"If you put such a demand to the Ymphs in their present frame of mind, you will be dead almost immediately, and your blood will be used to fertilize the soil around Ramus Ymph."

Jubal started to protest, but Nai the Hever would not listen. "Think no further along these lines. Tomorrow report to Eyvant Dasduke, and he will instruct you."

"And my back pay?"

"Render an account to Eyvant Dasduke."

Jubal departed Hever House. Nai the Hever returned to his study, where he was presently joined by Mieltrude, and the two spoke at length.

"What of Jubal Droad now?" asked Nai the Hever. "Do you still find him so odious?"

Mieltrude gave her shoulders a flippant jerk. "He is obstinate, forthright and sometimes acts the swashbuckler...Still, for a Glint he is tolerable enough. He is actually a rather pleasant young man."

"I was wondering if you had noticed," said Nai the Hever drily.

Chapter 20

J ubal waited at the Jiraldra, a fashionable pavilion beside the Marine Parade. The time was sunset; the sky glowed with melancholy colors. A russet-red spark showed under a far ledge of cloud; it guttered and vanished; Mora was gone. In the east Skay at the full pivoted upon the Cham, its rotundity emphasized by a gradation of colors: frosty yellow over the upper limb, gold at the circumference, melting peach-rose below.

Jubal glanced at his watch and rose to his feet; Vaidro was known for his punctuality. And there he came, along the Marine Parade, his figure silhouetted against the face of Skay.

The men exchanged a two-fingered tap on the shoulder: the ordinary Glint salute. Vaidro said: "You have been busy since our last meeting."

"I have had an interesting voyage and to some degree I have adjusted our score against Ramus Ymph."

"An exact balance between offense and retribution is hard to attain," said Vaidro judiciously. "You feel that a deficiency still exists?"

"Droad House is a ruin. The heirlooms and trophies are gone; the family documents are ashes. I can only rebuild the house, and maybe after three hundred years, it will regain something of its character."

"This is an ambitious goal in itself," said Vaidro. "Where will you find the money? I have certain funds, but not a fraction of what would be required."

Jubal pointed across Duskerl Bay, toward the Cham. "Just under that high ridge Gawel the Ymph maintains his palace. It is he and the other wealthy Ymphs who should repair the damage, but Nai the Hever tells me that such a hope is self-delusion."

"If anything, he understates the case," said Vaidro. "The Ymphs have suffered a vicious humiliation; they would resent your request."

"Probably so," said Jubal. "You have seen the tree?"

"Only casually; the fence keeps passers-by at a distance."

The two men set off along the Marine Parade, the vast orb of Skay looming over them.

"There seem to be plans to erect a monument or shrine near the tree," Vaidro remarked.

Jubal grunted. "The Ymphs would like to portray Ramus as an heroic martyr, whose worst fault was his adventurous spirit. This is possible because the facts are not widely known."

"And what are these facts? I confess to curiosity myself."

"I can only give you my own version, and my speculations, but I hardly think I am wrong. Ramus Ymph was a man of energy and ambition: vain, proud and undoubtedly brave—in fact, all these qualities seem to have been overdeveloped in Ramus Ymph. I am sure that he felt dissatisfied, even stifled, by the circumstances of his life, so he exerted himself to alter these circumstances, without regard for the consequences. Specifically, he wanted a space-yacht; he wanted to travel at his ease among the far worlds. Such a project is expensive, but Ramus Ymph thought he knew how to gain sufficient money. The Waels, however, resented his irresponsibility, and punished him accordingly."

"The tree, of course, is a handsome sight," said Vaidro. "Ramus Ymph can at least be grateful in this regard."

"Always supposing that his intelligence still inhabits the tree, which is an unsettling thought. Consider! A man dedicated to freedom and far-ranging adventure who now must stand immobile!"

"You are suggesting then that his motives were not inglorious?"

Jubal shrugged. "I myself would like to own a Sagittarius or, even better, a Magellanic Wanderer. I might even try to sell Djan rugs. Ramus Ymph went farther: he tried to sell the planet Maske to the People's Joy Tourist Agency and uncounted modules of tourists. Think of it! With the largest hotel of all on Cape Junchion!"

The two men turned aside and walked through the twilight to an iron fence, and there joined a dozen other men and women who had come to see the tree which had been Ramus Ymph. A light shone upon a massive box of white alabaster and a sign:

> ON THIS SITE SHALL BE ERECTED A SHRINE BEFITTING THE MEMORY OF THAT INDOMITABLE VISIONARY: RAMUS YMPH! ALWAYS WILL HE STAND IN OUR PRESENCE; HIS SOUL SURVEYS YOU NOW!
>
> HIS FRIENDS AND KINSHIP, WITH ALL THEIR CONNECTIONS AND CADETS, AND ALL OTHER FOLK WHO REVERE THE MEMORY OF RAMUS YMPH: LET THEM PLACE A PORTION OF THEIR WEALTH WITHIN THIS

BOX, TO THE LIMIT OF THEIR CAPABILITIES, THAT A
FITTING MEMORIAL TO RAMUS YMPH MAY BE
ERECTED!

"So Ramus Ymph's exploits are to be distorted and
glorified," mused Vaidro. "I suppose that for the Ymphs
it is the easiest way out of their dilemma, even though
everyone loses dignity in the process."

"No one seems embarrassed," said Jubal. "Notice that
portly old man; he has just dropped ten toldecks into the
slot."

"It is an absurd and complicated business. Ramus
Ymph becomes a popular hero, despite his crimes."

A slender figure in a dark cloak came walking on quick
uncertain steps through the twilight; under a hood the
face of a young woman glimmered in the Skay-light.
She went to the fence and for several long moments
stared at the tree, her shoulders drooping. Then, uttering
a soft moan she turned away and with shaking hands
dropped toldeck after toldeck into the alabaster box. She
noticed Jubal and stopped short. "It is you," she cried
fiercely, in a husky almost sibilant voice. "I could have
expected as much! You have taken your revenge and
now you come to gloat!"

"Not at all!" said Jubal politely. "You quite misinterpret
my motives."

"Then why are you here?"

"For very important but private reasons."

"I believe none of this! You have come to take your
vindictive pleasures."

"I assure you to the contrary." To Vaidro Jubal said:
"Allow me to present the Lady Sune Mircea, who at one
time was friendly with Ramus Ymph."

"Friendly?" Sune's voice rose in pitch. "How drab and trivial a word; how well suited to your torpid temperament!"

"I beg your pardon," said Jubal. "I never understood the relationship."

"Naturally not; we were incomparables! How could you know of our passion, our pinnacles of joy, the miracles we performed together? I do not expect it of you. And now I know why you are here! To see me in my misery! Well then, look as you please!" Sune threw back her hood. "Extract your gratification and I despise you for it!"

"Lady Sune," said Jubal, "you are quite mistaken; I have no feelings for you other than pity. I would suggest that you stay away from this place if it disturbs you so."

"Never! I will come every day of my life, and when the shrine is built, I will be the first to trace my sign upon the fane!" She faced the tree: "Ramus, can you hear me? Give me a sign; surely it is possible!"

All three fell silent and looked at the tree. A minute passed. The tree remained motionless. Sune gave a soft moan, then turned and ran away on swift stumbling steps.

"A rather theatrical young woman," Vaidro remarked. "Still, her feelings seem genuine."

"Yes. She ratified them with toldecks, as you must have noticed. Ah well, I feel sorry for her, even though she's played me a bad trick or two." He looked around the enclosure. The folk who had come to inspect the tree had departed; the area except for themselves was vacant. Jubal reached in his pocket and brought forth a stout cloth bag. He went to the alabaster box, produced a key, unlocked the bronze door at the side, and raked the accumulated money into his bag.

Vaidro quizzically watched the proceedings. "I must say that this is an unexpected development."

Jubal locked the bronze door and hefted the bag. "A good day's take—several hundred toldecks at the very least."

"You have become bursar for the Ymphs?"

"The Ymphs are really not involved," said Jubal with a grin, "except to put their toldecks into the slot. They are paying to rebuild Droad House despite themselves."

"You wrote the sign then?"

"Yes, with great care. You will notice the words 'a shrine befitting the memory of Ramus Ymph'. Not 'a magnificent shrine', nor 'a shrine of marble and gold'. I can erect a suitable shrine to Ramus Ymph in half an hour; perhaps a pile of shore-stones, or even a public rest-station."

Vaidro re-read the sign. "You have been scrupulous in the choice of your words; it is a trait I appreciate."

"After all, we cannot know Ramus Ymph's mind. Perhaps he feels remorse and endorses my efforts. Ramus! You in the tree! Do you hear me? What is your opinion? How should I spend this money?"

The tree gave back no perceptible signal, though the two men waited a long minute. But the night was quiet and windless, and the leaves moved by not so much as a quiver.

Jubal hefted the bag and shook it to hear the jingle. "In due course, I'll remove the sign and box, but for now, let the Ymphs pay! I enjoy every toldeck! Are you ready for a glass of wine?"

"Quite ready."

"Then let's visit the Jiraldra, where we can discuss Wellas and Nai the Hever and what lies beyond Zangwill Reef, and I'll describe the music of Eiselbar."

"An idea of great merit! While we are alive we should sit among colored lights and taste good wines, and discuss our adventures in far places; when we are dead, the opportunity is past."

The two men walked out to the Marine Parade and were gone, and the tree remained alone in the light of Skay.

Glossary

1. Yallow: a time of freedom and carelessness, marking the transition between youth and maturity. When their time arrives, the young men and women of Thaery and Glentlin become wayfarers and wander the thirteen counties. They travel by footpath and take shelter at wayside inns, or camp in the meadows. As they go they maintain the landscape: planting trees, repairing trails, clearing thickets of dead bramble, quelling spider-grass, the odious hariah and thorn. If anyone shirks, he becomes notorious, and the epithet *chraus* ('languid', 'small-souled', 'dishonorable') is apt to persist for the rest of his life.

Never is love more poignant or friends more dear. Memories last forever: laughing faces; red wine by lantern light; the music of mandolin and flute; nights on green hilltops, when voices are low and Zangwill Reef hangs like a glowing curtain across the south, or awesome Skay trundles down the sky. All too soon Yallow ends and youth is gone.

2. The Saidanese of Skay and the Djan of Maske comprise the species *homo mora*, which cannot fruitfully interbreed with *homo gaea*—though the Waels of Wellas and certain Dohobay tribes are reputedly hybrid races. Saidanese and Djan manifest a typically human physiognomy, with gracile proportions, small features, black hair, pallid olive complexions, often overlaid with a faint metallic sheen.

Djan eyes range from dark green to black, with elliptical pupils. On Skay a unique set of social imperatives—the so-called First Principle—has stabilized the type. On Maske, the coming of the Thariots created a convulsion, and the type has become somewhat more differentiated.

Both Djan and Saidanese are dedicated to the maintenance of an exact social order. Every possible activity is performed in concert with others, according to a standard method. The minimum Djan social unit is a group of four persons, most often two males and two females, who set up what is in effect a housekeeping cooperative. Each is 'married' to a person from a different household, though a kind of indiscriminate affection or habit of mutual fondling and grooming, which may include sexual contact, permeates Djan and Saidanese society. In effect each household is linked to four others; by widening circles every household connects with every other household of Djanad.

Djan behavior varies as to the size of the immediate group. Four is the smallest group in which a Djan can feel relaxed. Three Djan presently become uneasy, their voices rise; they become restless and over-active. Two Djan, if alone together for any extended period, stimulate each other either to affection or antagonism. The solitary Djan, lacking social restraints, becomes disoriented, unstable, and often dangerous.

Thariots employ Djan workers in large numbers, guided by the following schedule:

One Djan performs aimlessly unless supervised.

Two Djan become intense; they either quarrel or fondle each other. Work suffers.

Three Djan create a disequilibrium; they work with agitation and resentful energy.

Four Djan form a stable system. They respond equably to orders but exert themselves only moderately and indulge themselves in comfort.

Five Djan form an unstable and dangerous combination. Four will presently form a group; the fifth, ejected, becomes resentful and bitter. He may go 'solitary'.

Six Djan yield one stable set and a pair of defiant lovers.

Seven Djan create an unpredictable flux of shifting conditions and a turmoil of emotions.

Eight Djan, after considerable shifting, conniving, testing, plotting, back-biting, yield two stable groups.

The moods of the Djan are a mystery to the most earnest students of the race. The Institute of Djan Studies at Wysrod has prepared the following summation, applying specifically to Thariots traveling in Djanad:

A lone Djan (a rare situation in itself) coming upon a lone Thariot, will seldom (4%) commit an overtly hostile act, but not infrequently (40%) will commit a covert act ranging from mischief to murder. Two Djan coming upon a lone Thariot will more often than not (65%) first harass and eventually attack him, after a peculiar and embarrassing set of psychological accommodations between the three participants. Two Djan will never (0%) attack two Thariots; the four become at least temporarily an uneasy replica of the Djan social atom. Three Djan will rarely (15%) attack a lone Thariot, almost never (2%) a pair of Thariots, and never (0%) three Thariots. Four Djan will almost never (1%) attack a lone Thariot, but are slightly more liable (2%) to attack two Thariots. They will never (0%) attack parties of three or four Thariots.

The above conditions apply most rigorously when Skay is gone from the sky. With Skay visible, the Djan become mercurial, and react to influences beyond Thariot comprehension.

In passing, it may be noted that, while in Djanad thievery is unknown, the Djan in Thaery is a constant, confirmed and unregenerate pilferer. Similarly, the Djan in Djanad is modest and sexually restrained, whereas in Thaery, Thariot men casually copulate with Djan girls, although Djan men never copulate with Thariot women, both through mutual repulsion and physical disconformities.

3. The feluccas of the Long Ocean are manned by the Sea Nationals, who assert sovereignty across the entire extent of the Long Ocean, and control all trade and transit routes. Aerial overflights are absolutely proscribed, and each felucca is armed with a punchern-gun, an automatic finder, and tangs.

The Nationals, numbering scarcely twenty thousand, could hardly enforce their claims without the tacit support of the Thariots, from whom most of the Nationals derive; in fact the Sea Nationals are often regarded as a special Thariot caste.

The feluccas are boats of great intrinsic beauty, crafted by the Waels of Wellas at Erdstone Pool. They range in length from thirty to seventy feet and are powered principally by wind. The trade winds blow always westerly; the Sea National typically sails his felucca downwind, from sea to sea, and port to port, forever and ever around the world.

4. The Parloury at Wysrod consists of three agencies, with their various bureaus: the Landmoote, representing the middle and lower castes; the Convention of Ilks; and the Five Servants. The grand structure on Travan Square is also known as 'The Parloury'.

5. The penal system of Thaery proceeds by an archaic and highly complicated system. The injured, or first party, states his case before a magistrate, sometimes but not necessarily against the defence of the offending, or second, party. If the magistrate considers the case reasonable, a warrant is issued, and the first party may inflict the retribution in person; or he may hire one of several agencies to the same end. The first party specifies the exact act he is penalizing and stipulates such punishment as he chooses. If the second party considers the punishment too severe, he takes the case before an arbitrator. If the arbitrator finds for the first party, the punishment may be increased or punitive costs levied. If he finds for the second party, an official agent visits the exact penalty upon the first party. Reasonable retributions are, therefore, encouraged. The second party may try to evade the penal officials, but he is forbidden to resist with violence,

unless the penalty is death. For this reason penal officials never inflict death—although sometimes the effect is much the same.

6. For the information of tourists: Eisel Musicology.

That our tourists may maximally enjoy their visit to Eiselbar, we are pleased briefly to analyze the subject of music.

Let us begin with an attack upon the basic mystery: how can a succession of noises, no matter how pure the vibrations or how exact the harmonies, evoke emotional reactions within the soul of men? Noise, after all, has no intrinsic meaning.

We consider, then, two aspects of music: corporeal and natural analogues, and symbology. We notice immediately that musical tempi correspond to the range of bodily rhythms, most especially the heart-pulse. Musics progressing at tempi much faster or much slower than bodily rhythms are immediately felt to be unnatural and strained. Only on extraordinary occasions will very slow or very fast tempi accord with a human tempo. The dirge is a sublimation of slow moans of grief; the jig keeps pace with vigorous kicking and stamping of the feet.

Similarly, those musical timbres which have been proved to be most appealing and evocative are those reminiscent of organic processes: the human voice, bird songs, the lowing of cattle. By the same token, musical augmentations of tension and their release, as well as the resolution of chord progressions, find analogues in corporeal stresses and their relief, i.e. the weight of a toilsome load and its easing; constipation and discharge; dread of punishment and reprieve; thirst and the slaking of thirst; hunger and satiation; erotic yearning and fulfillment; flatulence and the relief of flatulence; hot discomfort and a plunge into cool water. Eisel musicologists have made exhaustive analyses in these directions, and are absolutely competent at producing the most effective timbres, crescendos and diminuendos upon their synthesizers. Eisel music is universal! And one need not be a witch doctor or a mad poet in order to derive the meanings. All persons, rich and poor, slow or quick, enjoy the same corporeal sensations.

Musical symbology is a more complex matter, involving cerebral and mnemonic processes.

The perception of musical symbols begins when an infant hears the tones of its mother's lullaby.

Each culture is typified by its peculiar set of musical symbols; when you hear some person claim to understand or appreciate the music of a very alien culture, you may politely regard that person as either a dunce or a diddler.

However, when a general culture, such as that of the Gaean Reach, suffuses a local culture, there will be a mingling of symbologies, so that an ear of World A may to a limited degree interpret certain musics of World B. Eisel musicologists adeptly employ the Gaean symbology with a judicious enrichment of specifically local symbols. They have available a great battery of scales, chords, note sequences, and harmonic patterns, carefully filed, annotated and cross-indexed. With the principles cited above as theoretical foundation, they are able to elicit from their computative synthesizers the remarkable and useful range of Eisel music.

JACK VANCE

In ancient times (and even today in musically backward regions) folk blew into, or beat upon devices of wood, metal and fiber to elicit sounds of irregular and non-uniform quality. The music thus produced was (and is) necessarily impure and inexact, and never the same twice in succession, and therefore unsusceptible to rationalization, no matter how scholarly and experienced the analyst. Such practitioners were (and are) no more than posturing narcissists! They think of themselves as musical autocrats! Such ambitions have no place in an egalitarian society. Eisel musicologists are sternly schooled in theoretical principles. With their mighty computers, their versatile and responsive synthesizers, they formulate for the use of all people the range and scope of Eisel music.